ALL U Can Eat

All U Can Eat

Emma Holly

ⓑ

BERKLEY SENSATION, NEW YORK

THE BERKLEY PUBLISHING GROUP
Published by the Penguin Group
Penguin Group (USA) Inc.
375 Hudson Street, New York, New York 10014, USA
Penguin Group (Canada), 90 Eglinton Avenue East, Suite 700, Toronto, Ontario M4P 2Y3, Canada
(a division of Pearson Penguin Canada Inc.)
Penguin Books Ltd., 80 Strand, London WC2R 0RL, England
Penguin Group (Ireland), 25 St. Stephen's Green, Dublin 2, Ireland (a division of Penguin Books Ltd.)
Penguin Group (Australia), 250 Camberwell Road, Camberwell, Victoria 3124, Australia
(a division of Pearson Australia Group Pty. Ltd.)
Penguin Books India Pvt. Ltd., 11 Community Centre, Panchsheel Park, New Delhi—110 017, India
Penguin Group (NZ), Cnr. Airborne and Rosedale Roads, Albany, Auckland 1310, New Zealand
(a division of Pearson New Zealand Ltd.)
Penguin Books (South Africa) (Pty.) Ltd., 24 Sturdee Avenue, Rosebank, Johannesburg 2196,
South Africa

Penguin Books Ltd., Registered Offices: 80 Strand, London WC2R 0RL, England

This book is an original publication of The Berkley Publishing Group.

Copyright © 2006 by Emma Holly.
Cover art by Franco Accornero.
Cover design by George Long.
Text design by Kristin del Rosario.

ISBN:0-7394-6795-6
ISBN:978-0-7394-6795-4

PRINTED IN THE UNITED STATES OF AMERICA

Acknowledgments

I'd like to express my appreciation to the Orange County chapter of RWA for your warm welcome. Your invitation was too tempting to resist, and you gave me a chance to visit an area not so very different from my fictional Six Palms—minus my fictional shenanigans, of course!

Special thanks to Jen Crooks, Susan and Dennis Johnson, and Leiha Mann for being great company and guides.

Muchas gracias to Deb Dixon for the book trade. *When You're the Only Cop in Town* definitely got this story started.

Roberta Brown, I'm always happy you're my agent, but I'm especially thankful you were able to work your mojo for this book.

Cindy Hwang, thank you for inviting me to play on your team. Here's wishing us many happy collaborations.

Finally, thank you, readers! Many of you have followed me from way back. I am honored, grateful, and very happy about that!

Chapter 1

On nights like this, diner owner Frankie Smith loved her life.

She lay on her side in her big, firm bed in her pretty house hanging on the hill in the southern California beach town of Six Palms. The cantilevered structure was a gift from her gambler dad, its design a reminder that the West Coast was cutting edge. No matter what complaints she had against her mostly absent father, Frankie loved every inch of this house—especially the eyrie that was her room.

Above her hung her prized possession, an outrigger canoe oar her mother had raced with as a teen. Out on her balcony, a potted banana tree whispered a lullaby to the sea-scented summer breeze. Frankie was young, relatively blond, and perfectly healthy. She'd put in a long day serving tourists and had brought in a decent take. Now she was ready to enjoy the good night's rest every hardworking stiff deserved.

That is, unless the hardworking stiff slipping in behind her had other plans.

Frankie's long-time boyfriend, Troy, must have thought she was asleep. She could tell he was trying not to disturb her as he eased beneath the freshly laundered sheets. He was hours later than he'd promised, no doubt kept chained in the office by his overly ambitious boss.

A former model, Troy was as laid back as they came, more at home in flip-flops than a suit. His trademark hollow cheekbones had earned him a small fortune, and she still couldn't believe he'd been talked into switching to real estate. But Troy had always been at the mercy of more forceful personalities. For all her good points, his boss, Karen Ellis, was definitely that. Troy was doing well, at least, and Frankie knew he was proud.

Troy's parents, on the other hand, thought he should have stuck to playing polo and mooching off friends whose families hadn't run through their fortunes yet. Laid back or not, Troy's blood was a very American shade of blue.

It always gave Frankie a private kick that he'd ended up with her instead of some debutante.

She grinned into the darkness as he achieved his favorite snuggling spot. His head was tucked over hers, and his arm draped her ribs with his hand coming up to cup. Troy was a breast man, and hers were just full enough to get him going. His sigh of pleasure was as involuntary as it was relieved. Naturally, he was naked; Troy was too gorgeous and too vain to wear a stitch to bed. He must have showered in the downstairs bathroom, because he smelled as good as he felt—six lean feet of gym-sculpted muscle and polished skin.

Frankie wore cotton panties and a strappy T-shirt, but the places he was warmest were impossible to mistake. His chest was as board-hard as it had been when he was twenty, and his lower body curved around her ass like it was born to fit. Always easy to rouse, his cock stirred against her bottom as if it, too, were wondering whether sleep was what it wanted most.

His body's reaction heated her deep inside, making up for his lateness, making up for all the familiar guy faults he had in abundance. Troy could be an idiot, but he was hers.

Frankie decided the moment was too nice to ruin with a scold. Instead, she wriggled her fanny backward and bit her lip as he hardened more.

This time, he hummed instead of sighed, though he seemed not to realize she was awake and teasing him. His arm tightened around her as his hips pressed forward. In seconds, his erection had reached full length. He was a good-sized man, with a healthy appetite for release. Since Frankie liked sex as much as he did, this had never been one of their problems. Twice a night wasn't too much for either of them, and only rarely had she turned him down. He was good in bed: straightforward but not selfish, and always appreciative. She knew a girl could do worse.

He moaned low in his throat. One of his more endearing traits as a lover was an inability to prevent himself from making noise. A rush of sultry moisture slid from her sex.

Then Frankie's eyebrows rose. The hand that had cupped her breast had moved to the strip of belly skin her T-shirt bared, preparing—she was certain—to slip into her panties and coax her clit awake. Troy's usual mode of rousing her for a quickie was to nudge her shoulder and say her name. This slightly daring change of pace delighted her, but to her surprise, he'd barely brushed her pubic curls when he hesitated, pulled back his hand, and rolled away.

Oh, for goodness sake, she thought, wondering at his scruples. Did he honestly think she'd be mad? It wasn't like she'd sleep through the whole thing.

She was about to let him know she was conscious when she realized what he was doing with his back to her.

His breathing had changed, and his arm moved in a rhythm as

distinct as it was personal. He was jacking off, the slightly wet, clicking sound of his fist pushing his cock skin just audible above the rustling sheets. She could tell how much he wanted a release because, as always, he couldn't stay silent. He was swallowing back little grunts of need. Heat flushed through her like the sun blazing through a window on a summer day. Despite her annoyance that he'd rolled away from her, she knew it was the sexiest thing she'd ever heard.

If she hadn't been so aroused, she'd have listened to it to the end.

"Hey," she said softly, rolling to fit her front to his lightly sweating back. "Want some help with that?"

He stiffened in surprise, then moaned with flattering loudness as she slid her fingers down the taut cords of his forearm. When she reached his fist and the rigid pole it held, she stroked between his knuckles suggestively.

"Frankie," he breathed. "I didn't want to bother you."

He might have been considerate enough not to wake her, but not so considerate that he didn't shift her hand under his. Now his hot, pulsing bounty was in her palm. Clearly, this made him happy. He gripped her tightly, pushing her hold up and down his shaft.

Frankie laughed against his shoulder. "No bother, big guy. I was awake the whole time."

"Jesus," he said, the knowledge making him twitch and surge. When she reached the flare of his penis, the pressure of his hand increased. Knowing he liked the stimulation, she turned her grip back and forth as if his cockhead were the lid to an especially sensitive and stubborn jar.

His groan of pleasure had her slinging her leg over his. The muscles of his narrow buttock were hard enough to get off on.

"So," she said, rocking her groin against him until he couldn't miss how wet she was. "You want to finish like this, or would you rather come inside me?"

He rolled her onto her back so quickly she lost her breath.

More excited noises caught in his throat as he switched on her reading lamp. He looked down at her shaking, sharp-nippled breasts, wagging his head as if he didn't know how he'd got so lucky. Frankie felt pretty much the same. Troy sure was something to stare at. His chest hair glistened gold in the light, and his cock was standing up and thrumming as if she'd tied a string to its rim. A tiny drop welled from its slit. She couldn't resist reaching out to touch, and once she'd touched, she couldn't resist rubbing the wetness around. When his knob was suitably shined up, she brought her fingertip to her mouth.

Watching her suck it was too much for Troy.

"Oh, babe," he groaned, making quick, almost desperate work of her panties. "You're too good for me."

As soon as the cotton was dragged down her legs, he was over her, his knees pushing her thighs wide enough to feel the stretch. Troy was taller than she was, and he liked room. He planted one hand beside her shoulder and used the other to steer his cock to its goal.

"Hey!" she said as the broad, curved tip of him split her labia. He was hot as fire, and she was definitely good to go, but even so she hadn't lost her mind. "Protection?"

"Shit," he said and fumbled for the bedside drawer.

He was quick to cover himself, his graceful model's fingers making him a treat to watch. His jaw was ticking with impatience, his straight streaked-blond hair falling forward as he looked down. Admiring his concentration—not to mention the extreme state of his arousal—as soon as he was done, she smoothed the latex to his root. His shudder of response was worth the delay.

"I'm going to fuck you like you've never been fucked," he warned, swinging into position again on both arms. "You're never going to forget Troy Wilcox took you tonight."

He looked deadly serious, so she bit her lip against her laugh. He might not have had anyone to compete with for the last five years, and he would very likely be taking her tomorrow, too, but she knew it was sometimes better to allow men their vanities.

"Do it then," she said, letting a wisp of smoke color the words. "Put that big, thick cock in me and ride me hard."

He knew her well enough to read the twinkle in her eye. "I will," he said, grinning a bit himself. "You had fucking better hold on."

He wasn't kidding. She gasped and reached for the headboard as he nearly took her with a single shove. She was lucky it didn't hurt because, grunting, he set his knees and shoved again. When this brought him to his limit, he cursed in thanks. She knew exactly why that was. They couldn't usually do this so fast. She was always wet for him, but she was built tight and getting him in completely could take time. Happy to have him inside her without waiting, she hugged him close with her arms and knees.

He leaned down to nip her ear. "You want me bad tonight."

"Maybe you're shrinking."

He laughed. "Bitch."

"Weenie-man."

He nudged his hips back and forth to let her register just how not-weenie he was. His teeth were bared in a wolfish grin. "You want me because you heard me beating off. Face it, Frankie, you're a pervert."

"Want to hear *me* beat off?"

He did. His face flushed dark even before she worked her hand between them. But she really got him when he felt it move.

"Oh, God," he said, his eyes squeezing shut as he swelled inside her. "Oh, God let me see."

He pushed up again, and she let him, aroused by his unexpected intensity. They'd been together so long they did sometimes make love on automatic pilot. Not tonight, though. As she caressed herself—only a bit self-conscious—he began to thrust in slow, deep strokes that didn't interfere with her show. Her fingers bumped him as he pushed in and out. He was really hot tonight. Frankie's breath came faster, but not as fast as his. His diaphragm was lurching with every gasp, his hands clenched white-knuckled in the sheets. She'd never seen him so caught up, so heedless of how desire was twisting his handsome features out of shape. This was different from anything they'd done before, and his reaction rubbed off on her. She was swollen like he was, hard as a little almond under her finger's pad, nearly drowning in her own juices.

His gaze rose and burned into hers. "Tell me, Frankie, does what you're doing feel good to you?"

"I'm too slippery."

Her voice was husky, and he had to swallow before he spoke. He looked down again to watch her hand. "Dry your fingers on my stomach."

She was embarrassed but she did it, loving the way his six pack jerked as he sucked a breath. The friction on her clit was better then—perfect—especially when he added the tug and slide of his own hardness. He must have known she was climbing fast. The muscles of her sheath gripped him greedily.

"Oh, boy," he sighed as if this were his idea of heaven. "Don't come yet. Make it last until I go."

There's a switch, she thought but couldn't say because she was moaning. She wasn't actually sure she could wait for him.

"Not yet," he insisted, leaning down, his lips brushing soft across her collar bone. "Not fucking yet."

He lasted longer than she'd ever known him to, lasted until she was dripping sweat and trembling and literally hanging on by her fingernails. Every thrust drove her closer, and she'd given up on stroking herself. All she wanted now was to help him get as deep as he could. His back was going to have scratches, but he didn't complain and or even gloat. As she rode the edge, something new swam into his eyes, into the perfect muscles of his perfect face. His irises were as blue as a summer sky.

"What?" she asked, touching the groove his ready smiles had etched by his mouth.

He gave her a harder thrust. "I love you," he said. "You're the best friend I've ever had."

His sweetness stung behind her eyes, but his cock was hitting her precisely how she liked it, high and fast and strong. She went over before she could say a word, the orgasm throwing back her head the same as if he'd shaken her. The climax was groaning good, and the sound of her pleasure sent him over, too.

His shout of ejaculation was louder than usual.

When his hips finished shaking against hers, he sank down on top of her. He was heavy, but being covered by a man was a sensation she had always liked. His hand went to her hair, stroking it gently out over the pillow.

"Phew," she said. "That was good."

He grunted—possibly in agreement—half-landed a kiss on her mouth, and pushed off her enough to sit up. The condom was easily disposed of, after which he raked his fingers through his golden locks and tossed his head, a habit he'd hung onto from his days of photo shoots.

"Pretty boy," she teased, but he only patted her thigh absently.

"I need a shower," he said, his gaze on the drapes swelling in and out of her balcony's sliding doors. Frankie trailed her hand down his spine.

"Want me to scrub your back?"

"I'm leaving," he said.

She rubbed her nose. "You have a house to show out of town?"

He looked at her. "I'm leaving. I was going to tell you tomorrow morning. After you'd had coffee. This isn't working for me anymore."

"It isn't *working for you*?"

Understanding now, and hot and cold with it by turns, Frankie sat up. She tugged her clinging T-shirt down to her waist. "Exactly which part of it isn't working? The great sex? The hot meals? Me picking up your socks? Or maybe the part where you tell me you love me and I'm your best friend?"

"I knew you'd be like this."

"Fuck, Troy, a ten-year-old could tell you I'd be like this! We've been together five years. I put up with a lot from you—"

"I know you have."

"You're damn right I have, and now out of the blue, after you *make love to me*, you tell me this?"

He was standing now, his face as red and surly as a teenager. "Making love was your idea." He grimaced at her gasp of outrage, but he didn't take it back. "I was trying not to. That's why I was jacking off. You know I can't lie down with you and not want to . . . Anyway, it isn't out of the blue for me."

"Who is she?"

"It's not about anyone else."

"The hell it isn't! We both know you've cheated on me before."

"You don't respect me," he said. She opened her mouth to lash out again, but the glitter of tears in his eyes stopped her cold.

"Of course I respect you," she said, her urge to yell fading. "I'm incredibly proud of everything you've achieved."

"You say that like you would to a slightly dim-witted kid who got an honorable mention at a science fair. I love you, Frankie, I do, but I want a partner who'll look up to me."

Frankie folded her arms. "I know you, Troy. You wouldn't be leaving if you hadn't already found my replacement."

Even if what she said was true, she hated how shrewish she sounded then, hated the way her scorn made his tears spill down. He wiped them angrily away.

"My leaving isn't about anyone but you and me. I hope—" He gritted his teeth, maybe so he wouldn't cry again. "I hope you'll realize that when you cool off."

"When I cool off," she repeated, shaking her head in disbelief. Did he think five years down the drain was something any woman could "cool off" from? Hell, knowing Troy and his general cluelessness, he probably thought she'd be "best friends" with his new girl, too.

Forgetting the shower he claimed to have needed, he retrieved the starched tan chinos he'd dropped to the floor. She watched him pull on each leg with a sense of unreality. For five occasionally tumultuous years, she'd seen this stunning body strip and dress. In some ways, she knew everything about it, down to the way he'd cup himself before he zipped because he rarely wore underwear. His shirt was next, an off-the-shelf Perry Ellis that looked as good on him as if it were tailored. Just like always, he buttoned it up from the tails.

She told herself he was leaving, trying to get the fact to register in her mind. He'd reach the collar, and she'd never see him do this again.

His head was lowered when finally he spoke. If he had the courage to meet her eyes, she couldn't see it through his fallen bangs. "I'll come by later to pick up my things."

"Forget it." Frankie reached for the cheapest victory. "I'd be delighted to pack up everything you own."

She didn't cry herself until he'd shut the door.

Chapter 2

Broken hearts—or furious ones—didn't stop people from wanting food. Frankie spent the weekend alternately fuming and crying at home. Then, when the surf came up in San Clemente, and her beach boy cook skipped out, she bowed to the inevitable and returned to work.

Naturally, everyone knew she and Troy had split. Six Palms was a small town, and Frankie's All U Can Eat diner was its social hub. Most of city hall ate breakfast there, as did the chief of police. Her insistence on good, plain food even drew local rich folk tired of nouvelle cuisine. Frankie usually worked the register or served, but she still remembered how to flip a burger. For the next six days, she was grateful to hide in the kitchen annex. At least there she missed the bulk of the "poor-Frankie" talk.

On the seventh morning, she woke feeling almost normal. Troy was gone, life went on, and if her customers' pity annoyed her, at least it was well meant.

The day that greeted her was equally kind. Marine gray, of

course—Coastal mornings were prone to that—but the air was cool and refreshing, the ocean indigo with bright whitecaps. Her beloved queen palms waved above her as she enjoyed the mile-and-a-quarter walk down the road to town. Two doors past her diner, Main Street Burritos was already open, but not the post office across the park. Though she'd only been wallowing a week, Frankie felt as if she hadn't seen the world in months. Her diner gleamed with bands of stainless steel and pink porcelain enamel, as fifties-perfect as if Elvis had swivelled his hips in front of it yesterday. Sweet yellow plumeria bloomed beneath the streamlined windows. The thrill of ownership warmed her like a blessing she'd forgot she had.

Jean Yi, her chain-smoking, sixty-year-old Chinese waitress, ground out her stub in the grass by the still-locked door.

"'Bout time," she said in her gravelly, porn star voice. Her arms were crossed in disapproval across her pink uniform.

Frankie looked at the cloudy sky. "Am I late?"

"No, honey. I mean, it's about time I saw that smile on your face again."

Frankie hugged the woman's wiry shoulders and unlocked the door for them both. Jean was part friend, part bossy surrogate mother. Frankie had gone through a tough time when her real mother died three years before. Her mother had been her touchstone, the one person who believed in her without question, whose warm, tight hug could make a bad day good. Troy had tried to help, but it was Jean's tart sympathy that pulled her out of her grief. Without it, Frankie wasn't sure she would have survived.

"I feel lucky today," Frankie said. "Maybe I'll try my hand at that new Mexican omelet."

But as it turned out, she wasn't lucky. Her backup cook showed up an hour into breakfast, and Frankie very stupidly decided to work the front.

The place was packed, every stool and booth occupied. The

scent of syrup and bacon was homier than her home, but the atmosphere was misleading. Despite the crowd, her gaze zeroed in on what it least wished to find. Troy and his boss, Karen Ellis, sat at the very last of the twelve red booths. Frankie's stomach clenched. She could tell they hadn't ordered yet. They were leaning toward each other across their menus.

Karen Ellis was the consummate businesswoman, her outfits always put together, her dark hair perfectly waved and bobbed. This morning she looked uncustomarily soft in a flowered sundress— uncustomarily pretty, too. Her cheeks glowed with a wash of pink that damn well looked natural. A pair of Louis Vuitton sunglasses were perched fetchingly on her head. Even as Frankie stood there frozen, Karen reached across the table to tenderly take Troy's hand.

The gesture said everything Frankie hadn't wanted to know. This wasn't an employer and employee sharing a friendly meal, and Troy hadn't been working late just to get ahead.

Shit, Frankie thought. She's *who he left me for*? She's *the woman he thinks will look up to him*?

Obviously, Troy was further out his mind than she'd imagined. Women like Karen Ellis didn't look up to anyone but themselves.

Frankie couldn't move, though she knew people were staring. This was better than dinner theater for the gossip junkies in Six Palms. From the corner of her awareness she saw heads turn: regulars, the counterboy, even the perpetually laconic chief of police. Her face was hot and her fingers cold. She barely had strength to blink when Jean came up to rub her arm.

"I'll take those two fools, honey. You serve that nice Chief West."

Frankie shook her head. "It's all right. I'll have to face them sometime. Might as well let the folks have their show."

Somehow, her feet took her down the old-fashioned tilework

floor to the new lovebirds. She couldn't bring herself to look at Troy, but Karen was laughing softly when she came up. Frankie gripped her order pad more tightly in the hope that it wouldn't shake.

"Hey," she said just as Karen turned to her and smiled.

It was the same genuinely friendly expression that had made Ellis Real Estate a success. It said Karen was bright and honest and would do everything in her power to get you a deal. While Frankie respected the smile, and Karen had always been nice to her, she knew she had no chance in hell of returning it.

For the first time, she noticed how attractive Karen was. She wasn't like Troy, whose beauty you couldn't miss from a mile away, but her cheekbones were strong and her skin nice and smooth. Her mouth was great, even if it probably wasn't the one she'd been born with. Her nose was bland—too small, Frankie thought—but her eyes more than made up for it. They were a mix of gray and gold: big, dark-lashed orbs that looked as intelligent as they were warm.

Grudgingly, and with no particular pleasure, Frankie admitted she could see why Troy might want to wake up to them.

"Frankie," her replacement said with a slightly embarrassed moue to acknowledge that this was awkward. "We were hoping to see you today."

"Uh-huh," said Frankie, because she really wasn't good at faking things. "Are you ready to order now?"

"I think so," Karen said and picked up the menu again.

That was when Frankie saw it: a rock the size of a freaking planet on the fourth finger of Karen's left hand. Little rainbows shot out of the thing, the stone so clear it rivaled the water sparkling in her glass. Frankie's mind stuttered to a halt. For a moment, she was impressed that Troy could afford it. Then she was simply sick with a depth of humiliation she hadn't known she could feel.

Troy didn't believe in marriage. He'd made sure he told her that the first night they shared a bed.

She couldn't help herself. She looked at him. She could tell he knew what she was thinking. His face was flushed, his eyes pleading. Her own expression must have been pretty stormy, because he hung his head and wagged it at the tabletop.

You little shit, she thought a second before her pencil snapped.

"Oh," Karen said, never slow to figure things out. "I'm sorry, Frankie. I guess I shouldn't have worn this here."

"Forget it." Frankie waved a hand in dismissal. "If I owned a rock like that, I expect I'd never take it off."

Her voice was as tight as a widow's corset, which—come to think of it—was how she felt. She ignored the sound of Troy murmuring her name.

"Well," said Karen. "I guess I'll, um, have the Frankie's Special with whole-wheat toast."

Frankie gritted her teeth at the obvious response to this. From the looks of it, Karen had been having "Frankie's special" for quite some time. "Coffee?"

Karen hesitated. "Not today. Maybe just a glass of milk."

"And you?" said Frankie, turning to Troy. She hadn't thought he could get any redder, but blotches of embarrassment stained the flush already on his cheeks. Even that couldn't make him ugly. He was still the best-looking man she'd ever met.

"Plain scrambled eggs and bacon," he said in a slightly strangled tone. "Black coffee. No toast."

They both knew he didn't have to tell her what he wanted. For the last five years he'd only ever ordered this. She even understood why he was back in here so soon. She *was* his best friend, or she had been. The warmth of this place had been a big part of their good times. She doubted Troy had the imagination to think where else he should go.

Their gazes held, reluctantly stuck together by history. Christ, she wished she could hate him. It would have made her anger so much cleaner.

This being as hopeless as her ever wearing that galactic ring, she turned on her heel. "Your order will be out soon," she said over her shoulder, going to hand it in.

Her arm was raised to stick the order in the clip above the kitchen pass-through when Karen's selection caught her eye again. Karen was a committed coffee junkie: the stronger the brew, the better she liked it. Today she'd ordered a glass of milk.

"Fuck," Frankie whispered, wondering if there was any way to doubt the conclusion she was jumping to.

She didn't think there was. In fact, if Troy was about to become a daddy, everything that had just happened made a lot more sense.

Chief of Police Jack West was nobody's pretty boy. His nose had been broken (twice), his left knee (which had been shot) had more scars than the San Andreas Fault, and the best that could be said about his face was that it was rugged.

The scars he kept inside him weren't any better. He'd been a cop with the LAPD for sixteen years—a good cop, with plenty of important collars—but he'd seen things that had left him a less-than-fit companion for civilians. Coupled with the seriously dysfunctional upbringing he'd had, it was no wonder he was divorced, more or less inept at flirting, and hadn't been laid in so many years he'd probably forgotten how.

On the plus side, knee or no knee, he could run a mile in less than eight minutes, didn't smoke, barely drank, and believed in opening doors for women. He'd been told his shaved head was sexy, though he mostly kept it that way because his hairline was creeping back. He was tall enough to date a supermodel (not that he wanted to), willing to dance with the right partner, and rarely lied unless it helped catch bad guys. He also spoke fluent Spanish and could type with all ten fingers.

Unfortunately, he didn't think these assets were going to convince the woman who'd been playing leading lady in his recent dreams that she ought to be dating him.

His fixation had started innocently enough. Frankie's diner was *the* local watering spot. Therefore, Frankie's was where the chief had to eat. Being recognized by his townsfolk—and never mind the gossip he overheard—could only make his job easier. With three whole officers in his department, he was the law in Six Palms. If people didn't know and trust him, he wouldn't get very far.

The fact that Frankie Smith was a nubile blond exemplar of womanhood had simply seemed a pleasant perk. So what if her breasts were sweet enough to make other women's babies cry? So what if the curve of golden skin that always peeked between her jeans and shirt had a tendency to make him sweat? The slant of her sea-green eyes suggested someone in her family tree might have danced the hula, but that in itself was no reason to be alarmed.

She was just a woman, a moderately tall, racily curved, mouthwatering woman with endless, athletic legs. Leching after her was harmless, a way of easing himself back into long-overdue circulation without risking anything. For one thing, she had a boyfriend, with whom she appeared happy. For another, he doubted she knew he was interested. Jack had at least ten hard-lived years on her. Even when he started to watch more than the twitch of her butt in her low-slung jeans, even when he started to *like* her, it didn't seem dangerous.

Truth be told, he was in too deep almost before he knew he was in at all.

Bit by bit, he'd added up the evidence of who she was: a fighter who wouldn't buckle at the first punch, a loyal and fair employer, an affectionate friend once her trust was won. He suspected she had a temper, but she kept it under control.

He could see she was working hard to keep it there today.

Everyone knew why, of course, though he'd had trouble believing the rumors when they'd begun to swirl a week ago. The Calvin Klein underwear boy had left her. She was holed up in her house crying into her beer. No, she was holed up in the diner's kitchen, her eyes so red she'd bought fresh Visine from the pharmacy.

All this might be true, but from what Jack could tell, no one was going to see this woman fall apart in public. She came back from the pass-through now with her ex-boyfriend's order, head high, chalk white, her pretty shoulders straight and stiff under her *Frankie's All U Can Eat* apron. Her platinum ponytail bounced behind her like a flag of pride.

She even talked to the new girlfriend when she set down the plates in front of them.

When she was done, she came back toward him along the aisle between the booths and counter. She nodded distractedly at those who spoke, then stopped beside him and tapped her splintered pencil on her order pad.

"So," she said, "what'll it be?"

The way her lip was trembling compelled him to squeeze her arm, despite not being a big toucher. The need to keep his distance on the job had bred this out of him, and he did it gently. Even so, the contact was enough to make his palm tingle.

"You all right?" he asked.

She drew a deep, shaky breath. "I guess everybody's wondering that."

"I could arrest him."

Frankie's smile was a little startled. He supposed she didn't expect him to joke, since he never had before. "That's tempting, Chief, but what would you charge him with?"

"How about criminal negligence?"

That earned him a husky chuckle. She looked into his eyes a second, really looked, but to his disappointment, the glance was short. She immediately got back to business. "The *huevos rancheros* are good today. I think they'd complement your usual side of slaw."

"Great," he said, wishing he could think of something else to make her laugh. His heart was pounding from that instant their gazes caught, as if he were eighteen instead of forty-two. "I'm sure I'd like them fine."

"All right," she said. "I'll get you that."

She walked away, past the red-topped stools that were beginning to get prominent billing in his fantasies. God, what he wouldn't give to see her bent naked over one. It was all too easy to imagine her smiling back at him over her shoulder, licking her lips, her sexy butt swivelling just a bit in anticipation as he approached. The picture in his head was vivid, right down to her glistening sex. It had a predictable effect. He shifted in his seat, uncomfortably aware that he had a burgeoning erection, one his uniform trousers weren't up to hiding.

Idiot, he told himself—though he wasn't sure if this was because he was thinking of pursuing her, or because he hadn't found the balls to yet. With a woman as fine as Frankie, his window of opportunity was bound to be small.

It was even smaller than he thought. The sexual tag team who owned Pete and Dave's Garage turned as a unit from their post on the last two stools. Matching grins went lasering from them to Frankie. At some point during their friendship, the pair had discovered they could more than double their odds with women if they joined forces. Since Jack had accepted the job of chief from the mayor a year ago, he'd watched these yahoos cut a swath through no less than eight females, one of whom had been married. Pete and Dave were charming, and so far no one had complained, but Jack couldn't help disapproving. In his opinion, a man ought to aspire to being more than an erotic novelty act.

As to that, he thought a woman ought to want more, too.

He thought it even harder when Frankie shook her head and laughed at them.

"You keep clear of me," she said, but not as if she were angry. "I am still not interested."

"But you're *available*," Dave pleaded in a puppyish way.

"And *hurting*," Pete added. "It's gotta be time for a Marvin Gaye interlude."

"Believe me, guys, the last thing I need is to be another notch on your shared bedpost."

"We're good," Pete said, apparently the alpha gigolo of the pair. "I'm sure we qualify as rebound therapy."

Though she sighed at them and rolled her eyes, Jack noticed with no small irritation that she was smiling.

Chapter 3

It was the midafternoon lull. Frankie had swept the floors, filled the salt shakers, and was now eating a plate of mesquite-seasoned fries before she keeled over in a hypoglycemic faint.

This day had definitely been one for the record books. She hoped Karen had enough sense—or sensitivity—to steer Troy somewhere else for dinner. Frankie didn't think she could face another encounter like this morning's until she'd had a solid night of sleep.

She smiled to herself unexpectedly, remembering how "Team Boys" from the garage had suggested she cure her romantic pangs. Pete and Dave were obnoxious, but they were cute. Certainly, they were better for a dumpee's ego than the constant pity everyone else was dishing out. Hell, even the law was beginning to ask if she was all right.

Her fingers hovered over a fry as that memory went through her with a weird tingly pleasantness. Chief West had what romance writers liked to call whiskey eyes—not brown but gold—a fitting match for his vaguely gangsterish mug. Thinking back, she remembered being intrigued by what had burned beneath his coal-black brows, a low, hot fire that had nothing to do with concern. She didn't understand why Jean kept calling him "nice." "Intense" was a much better description. Frankie hadn't thought about it before today, but Chief West was a sexy hunk of testosterone.

Before she could decide how she felt about this, the street door jangled and a man walked in.

He was tall and rangy, with shoulders a mile wide. Though Frankie was certain he'd seen her, he looked around without speaking, taking in the empty booths, the jukeboxes on the counter—in essence, giving the place his own reconnaissance. Appropriately enough, he wore an olive-drab T-shirt and black fatigues. When she saw the big worn duffel that hung from one arm, she decided the outfit wasn't a fashion choice. His hair, which was medium brown, was jarhead short. It was only when he turned to face her that she realized how young he was. Mid-twenties at the most, with a weary, deeply tanned, clean-shaven face.

His eyes were brown like his hair, real brown. They squinted at her, wary and cynical, but underneath their obvious experience she sensed a trace of vulnerability.

"You open?" he asked. His tone was oddly careful, as if he was consciously trying to sound nonthreatening but didn't quite remember how.

Frankie wasn't threatened, just curious. She swallowed her last bite of fry. "We're open enough to get you a burger. My cook—that is, my backup cook is having his siesta, but I can handle the grill."

"A burger would be great if I'm not keeping you from your meal."

"Snack," she said, noting how he'd relaxed at her acceptance.

Perhaps he'd expected to be turned away. "To keep me from collapsing during the dinner rush."

"Sounds like a long day."

"One of the joys of ownership." She wiped a place on the counter in invitation, suspecting he needed one. "You want a soda or coffee while you're waiting?"

"Orange juice, if you've got fresh squeezed. I've been missing that." He set his duffel on a stool, then took the seat she'd been suggesting he was welcome to.

"You're in luck," she said. "You just out?"

He rubbed his bristling head the same way Chief West sometimes did. A buzzcut thing, she guessed. As he did, she noticed a snake tattoo spiraling from his wrist and up his well-developed arm. His muscles were so ripped, he might have had his fat suctioned out.

"Yeah," he said, snorting a little as if at a private joke. "I'm just out and about."

Perceiving this conversation required a pause, she set him up with his juice, then disappeared into the kitchen. When she came back with his burger, he was doing his recon thing again. He continued doing it through his first few bites. Frankie enjoyed watching him enjoy her food. He swallowed and wiped his mouth on a napkin.

"I did short order for the Marines," he said with a casualness only pride and empty pockets could create. "In case you were looking for a not-backup cook."

Frankie's smile came from a very deep species of understanding. She'd had a few proud, broke years herself. "I might be willing to try you out, but I have to warn you, I'm not looking for a roll-through. I need someone I can count on for a while."

"You like how I cook, I'm your man."

She liked how he met her eyes, steady but not pushy. Hiring someone new was always a judgment call. Her mom had taught her to go with her gut and hope for the best. Shrugging to herself, she asked what was for her the most important question. "You surf?"

He looked startled. "Is that a requirement?"

"More the opposite. My regular cook has a tendency to take off every time the waves are *bitchin'*, as he puts it. My name's Frankie, by the way, same as the neon up on the roof."

He shook her hand more gently than he had to. His calluses were impressive. "Michael True. People call me Mike. And as far as the surfing goes: not so much."

"Okay, Mike." Maybe it was helping someone else that did it, but she felt better than she had since she'd been dumped. "Why don't I show you the kitchen and see what you've got."

He had more than she expected. A few questions about the menu and the supply room, and he was good to go. The burger he made was better than the surfer boy's, and he was much quicker than she was. Her presence didn't rattle him at all. She imagined him loading machine guns with the same methodic efficiency. Allowing her optimism to rise, she let him handle dinner on his own.

She was right to trust him. Apparently, the dinner rush at Frankie's was a cakewalk compared to serving hungry Marines.

She was preparing to lock up and composing speeches in her head for firing his predecessor when the wall phone rang. It was not a caller from whom she had longed to hear.

"I'm so sorry to bother you," Karen Ellis said, "but I lost my favorite sunglasses, and I think I must have dropped them in the diner this morning. I don't suppose you could look around."

Frankie squeezed her temples with one hand, feeling them begin to throb. If Karen had been a kid with a lost teddy bear, she'd have had a shot at getting Frankie to look right away. As it was, spending what was finally *her* time searching for Troy's new girl-friend's shades was not a priority.

"No one's turned them in," she said as civilly as she could. "I'm about to go, but I can check first thing tomorrow. Maybe have the counterboy drop them by your office."

"Oh. Sure," said Karen, seeming to understand the hint to give eating at the diner a temporary pass. "I'll keep my fingers crossed."

Frankie cursed at herself as she hung up. She knew this was go-ing to hurt Troy's feelings, but Frankie was damned if she didn't deserve more of a break before she had to see him again. Hell, Karen didn't have to network here. She was a member of the yacht club. The lovebirds could eat with the muckety-mucks for a while. With luck, they'd both get food poisoning.

"Problem?" Mike True was in the doorway to the kitchen, his shoulders filling it, slowly drying his hands on a cloth. He'd stayed for her final cleanup, though she hadn't told him he had to. His knuckles had old white scars, as if he'd been in a lot of fights. The sight reminded her that her life wasn't half as tough as it might have been.

She sighed. "No problem. Just a little hiccup on my path to perfect happiness."

He nodded, not moving from his post, looking like he had all the time in the world to help her mop . . . which he might, come to think of it. He *had* lugged that heavy duffel into her place. If it didn't contain all his earthly belongings, she suspected it must come close.

"You got a place to stay, Mike?"

He rubbed his chin uncomfortably, the rasp of brown stubble audible in the quiet. His face was a study of lost boy fighting with hard man. A twinge of maternal feeling tightened her ribs, though she knew not to let it show.

"I'll take that as a 'no,'" she said dryly. "There's a room above the kitchen you can use for now."

"You don't have to do that. I've got enough for a hotel."

He might have enough for that, but she didn't think he had much more. "Believe me, it's nothing fancy. It's got a bed, a chair, and a toilet with a shower stall. I stayed there myself when I first bought this place. Sank every dime I had into it."

"Well," he said, shuffling his feet without actually lifting them. "I'd appreciate that a lot."

"Like I said, it's nothing fancy. Let me get the key and take you up. Make sure it hasn't been swallowed by the dust bunnies."

She was aware of him behind her as they climbed the narrow wooden stairs. His height cast a wavering shadow, and she could tell he was being careful not to rush her with his longer stride.

"I had arranged to stay with a friend," he said. "His neighbor told me he took off for Mexico. Didn't even leave a note."

Frankie said nothing, figuring another assurance that he was welcome would only make him more uptight. Anyway, she understood the message he was sending. He wasn't some homeless nutcase who had just showed up. He had a reason for coming to the area. He was trying to get his life together as best he could.

Reaching the top, she pushed open the stained old door and let out a gust of musty air. Mike walked past her, his shoulder brushing her as he went. The sun had set, and she flipped the switch to turn on the ceiling's one bare bulb. The width of his back was something to see, a wedge of pure Marine muscle beneath his khaki T-shirt. He looked from the single window to the tiny bath.

"This is fine," he said. "Really nice."

Now *that* was polite, Frankie thought with a crooked smile. He dropped his duffel on the sagging bed and then bent to lift something from its covers.

She was watching the tendons flex under his tattoo and didn't register what he'd picked up until he dangled it from one finger with a boyish grin.

"Not yours is my guess."

He'd found one of Troy's athletic supporters, which Troy only wore when they went biking. The day he'd left it here came back to her in a rush. The sweaty ride up the coast. Feeding the seagulls. Him swearing he couldn't survive the final push up the hill to her house. He'd coaxed her in here, supposedly to shower, then surprised her by making love. *I'm never too tired for this*, he'd said. *Especially when I've been ogling that gorgeous ass of yours the whole damn day.*

Her breath caught in her chest. She could smell Troy all around her, cologne and salt and his personal pheromones. She felt his hand stroking her hair after they'd both come. He loved her blondeness, even if it came from a box. Suddenly she was sobbing as hard as if the wound were minutes old.

"Shit," she said, her fingers pressed to her mouth. "I really didn't want to do this."

"Uh," said Mike, clearly taken aback. After a moment to pull his intent together, he crossed the room and took her in his arms. He held her loosely, stroking her back awkwardly. "It's okay, Frankie. Whoever he was, I'm sure he isn't worth crying for."

"He left me *last week*," she said, her face buried in Mike's chest, her hands curling into fists beside his spine. "He brought his new girlfriend into my diner this morning."

"Oh. Well. Then he really is a moron."

She didn't move away, and Mike didn't seem to want her to. She felt almost peaceful as her sobs quieted. He was warm, and he smelled different from Troy. The way his hand traveled slowly up and down her back was comforting.

It was so comforting, in fact, that her final sob came out a wistful sigh. He lowered his head enough to rest his cheek in her hair.

She supposed he was just relaxing like she was, but the change reminded both of them they were strangers. His breathing shifted,
his hand pausing midstroke.

"Uh," he said, letting his hand move again as if he couldn't
help himself. This time, his palm drifted past the small of her
back—not quite far enough to cup her buttocks but obviously
flirting with the idea. "Maybe you'd better let go. It's been a while
since I held anything prettier than my AK."

One thing was sure: he wasn't going to let go himself. His hold
settled on her waist, not exactly pulling her closer, but making her
aware of what was swiftly rising between their hips.

At the feel of that, Frankie's breath came faster, too. She knew
she shouldn't be reacting. She'd barely begun to get over Troy.
Then again, didn't people say the best way to get over someone
was to get under someone else? Something inside her decided before she knew she was going to. She tipped her head back to find
his eyes. This must have encouraged him. Without moving his
hands, his fingers settled over the first curve of bottom and gave a
squeeze.

"You are exactly what I've been dreaming of," he said with
husky softness. "Every night in those tents. Every day in those
damn Ranger graves. I'd be digging foxholes and fantasizing
about some nice girl who'd suck my tongue for hours. Some
warm, pretty-breasted woman who'd be strong enough to let me
bang her straight through the wall."

"I guess—" Frankie cleared her throat, which didn't seem to
be working right. The tips of her reputedly pretty breasts felt like
beads of fire where they brushed his chest. "I guess there aren't a
lot of opportunities for hanky-panky in an Arab country."

"Not unless you're an Arab." Though he smiled, his eyes
weren't amused. Instead, they were mesmerizingly hungry. "I
want this job, Frankie, but I want to fuck you even more."

Her hands had somehow found their way to his rock-hard pecs. His shirt was thin, and his nipples were beaded, too. When her fingers trailed around the little points, his cock lurched higher inside his pants. Frankie swallowed as she suddenly, helplessly, imagined herself biting them.

"Make up your mind," he said, rasping it out. "I am so not in the mood to be messed with."

"Okay," she said, which made him blink.

"Okay?" It seemed he hadn't read the significance of her breathless tone.

"Okay, I'm not messing with you. Lean down to me. I want to kiss you like you said."

He started to come closer, then stopped. "I didn't really mean you should kiss me for hours . . . unless you want to fuck me at the same time."

She smiled, because he honestly seemed to think she might have misunderstood. "I want the wall, though you probably shouldn't bang me through it since you're sleeping here."

"Oh, boy," he said, really breathing quickly now. He kissed her once, hard and with a bit of tongue, but too fast for her to return it. Then he pushed back.

"Take off your clothes," he said, already peeling off his shirt. "Once we start this, I don't want to stop."

The sight of his chest stunned her for a moment. As deeply tanned as his face, it looked like something out of an X-rated anatomy manual. Every muscle was delineated, every rib clear and strong. Her gaze snagged on the thin brown line leading down to and around his navel, then stopped for good at the arching hump of his erection. Her mouth went dry. That was some cock he had, a genuine two-fister raring to go.

She decided he was lucky those black fatigues weren't tight.

"Clothes," he reminded, his hands already on his zipper.

Despite the tempting show that was in the works, she shook herself back into motion. Her manager's uniform—according to her—was a knotted white blouse and jeans. She undid the tails, then the buttons, then shucked both off. Mike stopped what he was doing to look up.

"Oh, man," he said in a tone of awe. Her underwear was her usual white cotton bikini panties and matching bra, but she guessed he liked the way they fit. His jaw had literally dropped.

"I'll trade you," she said, enjoying his stupefaction and almost giddy with the crazy thing she was doing. "You take off mine, and I'll take off yours."

Speechless, he gestured for her to turn around. Stepping closer, he undid her bra hooks with shaking hands. He knelt to slide the panties down her legs, groaning softly as he rubbed his face back and forth across her bottom cheeks. Even with his stubble, it felt nice.

She put her hands over his where they clasped her hips. His knuckles were rough from the scars she'd noticed earlier. "What are these from?" she asked, stroking the spots lightly.

"Knuckle push-ups." His voice was muffled by her flesh. "Some guys did them until they bled—to prove they were tough sometimes, or because there was no other way to work off the tension."

"Fear tension? Or this kind?"

He kissed the hollow where her spine met her bottom. "Both. There's not a hell of a lot of privacy out there."

He stood then. She turned to face him but sensed he didn't want to talk about "there" any more. This was the moment he wanted to be in. His gaze went down her nakedness and up again. From the way his jaw clenched, he was in the grip of some conflict. Wanting very much to ease it, Frankie reached out her hand.

It wasn't hard to figure out where she was heading.

"Be careful," he warned, panting it. "I'm not sure I can stand it if you touch me."

His boxers were olive-drab like his T-shirt, and they revealed the source of his concern. His erection was stretched to its fullest length. The crown of his penis was poking through the front flap, so swollen and red it looked as if it were sunburned.

Immediately tempted, Frankie's fingers curled into her palms. "I think touching you is going to be very difficult to resist."

"Please, don't. It's been too long. Eighteen months, Frankie, since anyone helped me out but me and, like I said, there wasn't a whole lot of that, either. I'm about ready to explode."

The heat that welled inside her made it hard to speak. Eighteen months and hardly even jacking off. Boy, did she want to be the one to break his fast! "Do you have protection?"

"In the side pocket of my duffel."

Well, that was convenient. He'd been hoping for the best, she guessed. "Let me put it on you, and we have a deal."

"You won't tease me?"

"No," she said, because putting it on *was* the tease. "I'll slip it on as gently as I can and then you can do what you want."

"I can take you against the wall?"

"On the ceiling, if you can reach."

He stared at her, face flushed, breath soughing in and out. "Do it," he said. "I'll hang on."

His gritted teeth and fisted hands made him look like he was facing a firing squad. She pulled out the waist of his boxers, easing them over his erection without touching anything. When the shorts dropped to his ankles, he stepped out. His arousal forced the step to be gingerly. His balls were already high and tight, his shaft long and thick. She wanted to run her hands over him so badly she could taste it. She settled for rolling the condom ever so carefully down his length.

He shivered as she reached the bottom, but not because he was cold.

"Can I kiss you now?" she asked.

"Not there," he clipped out, because she was still kneeling.

She stood and smiled agreeably, though she had indeed intended to kiss his cock. Relaxing just a fraction, he surrounded her breasts in his hands, caressing them with firm, strong strokes. His thumbs flipped over their tingling peaks.

It seemed he hadn't forgotten how to do this.

"Kiss me now," he said, bending to her. "Kiss me slow and deep."

Their lips settled together just as he pulled her nipples for the first time. The tug sent a twang of feeling to her core. Though he'd told her to kiss him, he pushed her tongue into her mouth and moaned. Warmth and sensation ran through her flesh. Not wanting to let him down, she forced herself to remember what he'd said about being sucked.

He hummed with pleasure when she did it and louder when she pulled again. His arms tightened around her, bringing her flush to his front.

She wasn't ready for the fierceness of his body heat. He felt as if he had a fever. He seemed afraid to rub himself against her, but he certainly hugged her close. His erection was squashed between them, head up, silky skin blazing. She tasted salt as perspiration dotted his upper lip.

His bare feet sidled between hers, nudging them apart. A draft of cooler air between her legs made her aware that she was hot herself. The mute request to widen her stance was sexy all by itself.

"I want to touch you," he said against her mouth. "I need to know if you're wet."

The words made her throb. She kissed him deeply in answer,

pulling on his tongue, thrilling to the low, soft moan that broke in his throat. Whatever his distraction, he didn't forget his mission. His hand was gentle as it reached around her from behind, his fingers warm and slightly damp. Two attempted to slide inside her before he tried again with one. She was more than wet enough for that. She squirmed as he pushed his finger all the way in. It felt good, really good, and she could tell the way her pussy tried to draw him up excited him. His heart was abruptly thundering in his chest.

"God," he whispered, beginning moving his finger in a testing circle. "Are you always this tight, or are you just nervous?"

"Always." She licked his raspy chin. "I'll ease up once you get inside."

His erection jumped at her answer, and he caught her mouth again, sucking her with an intensity of focus that made her understand why he liked it. They both were gasping when he broke free. "Would it be easier if I made you come before I try to take you?"

"Do you want to?"

He hesitated, then shook his head. "I want to get you off with my cock—if you think you can."

"I don't think you have to worry. I'm relatively easy when it comes to coming, and you've got me pretty hot."

He grinned at that, the boy in him flashing free. His finger slid gently out of her, his hand still damp when he gripped her beneath the arms. He lifted her without apparent effort, showing off his strength by doing it slowly.

He laughed at her widened eyes. "Put your arms around my neck. You're going to want to hold on."

She did as he asked, after which her thighs found an easy mooring around his waist. She locked her ankles behind him as his hands slid down her sides to support her ass. He caressed her there as if he liked what he felt.

"You smell so good," he said, his eyes briefly closing. "You smell so sweet."

"I smell like a side of fries."

"Unh-uh." He kissed her in negation, with that same delicious deep slide and pull. "You smell like a sweet woman."

Holding her tightly now, he shifted her position so his shaft rubbed between her folds in a long, slow glide. Up and down he rubbed until the head of him bumped her clit perfectly. There he circled the tip of her with the tip of him, a meeting of their most sensitive parts. His groan told her how much he enjoyed this, and also that he wouldn't be doing it for long. Stopping, he shifted his cock's position, his crest now pulsing against her gate. Frankie's body went even more liquid.

Though she knew his control wasn't the best, she couldn't keep herself from wriggling against his heat.

He gasped at the sensation. "Ready?" he asked, beginning to push a bit himself, perhaps because he couldn't wait. The flaring rim breached her pussy's mouth.

"What about taking me against the wall?" she managed to say.

"I'll get there. After I'm inside."

"Boy, you must have one strong—" The word *back* was swallowed in a groan as he pushed himself halfway in. Her neck sagged with bliss like it was made of rubber, and his hands tightened on her bottom to shove again. He halved the remaining distance and groaned himself.

He felt like heaven—hot, hard, throbbing man-heaven.

"More," she pleaded in a throaty voice. "I want it all."

He cursed and—despite his vow that he was going to wait—he stepped to the wall. He must have decided he needed leverage to finish this. With her body braced, his hips rolled forward, once, twice, pushing her bottom into the sky-blue paint. He shuddered when he finally reached full penetration. Frankie's reaction was just as strong. Her sheath rippled over him with sheer delight.

"Lord," he said, his weight and muscles pressing her just right. "You're gonna kill me. You're a fucking fist."

"You can move," she said, though she hardly had breath to speak. "I'm ready for it."

The sound he made then was a cry of need. He moved, slowly at first, but quickly faster when he saw he wasn't hurting her. He took her in sweet, strong jabs, shifting her up and down in search of some ideal friction for some magic spot on his cock. He must have found it, because soon enough he was simply hammering her into the wall, growling with utter mindlessness. The time he'd gone without was adding up all at once. He slung himself in so hard she felt his testicles swing.

His fingers on her bottom were curves of steel.

"Sorry," he gasped, though she was mewling with pleasure. "I can't stop this. I need it too much. Oh, fuck. Oh, God. I'm going to go."

He thrust up hard and came like a fountain, too soon for her to follow, but with a ferocity and a force she would have been sorry to miss witnessing. It was a long ejaculation. His face twisted with it, his eyes screwed shut, his hips beating against hers uncontrollably. A guttural groan, like an animal in pain, rolled from his throat. Then he sighed, long and low, his relief impossible to hide.

"Sorry," he repeated, his breathing ragged but beginning to even out. He drew out to his rim, hesitated . . . and then thrust back in again.

He had slackened from his release, but the long, slow push rehardened him. By the time it finished, he was almost as thick as before. Frankie was so wet he slid in without effort. She didn't mean to, because she thought it would sound like a complaint, but she whimpered and clutched his broad shoulders. Now that she'd finished watching him, she really did want to come herself.

Fortunately, he knew it. He leaned his forehead on the wall to bring his mouth closer to her ear. "Can you go over if I keep this up?" he asked. "I don't think I'm ready to stop."

He was moving easier now, steady and piston smooth, definitely catching his second wind. With every pass, her body quivered with readiness.

"Oh, God," she said, which wasn't really an answer.

"How about if I do this?"

He stretched his thumbs between them from either hip. The instant he pressed the root of her clit, she convulsed. The orgasm was so deep and sharp, she actually kind of screamed.

"Whoa," he said, laughing a bit as she came down. "I didn't expect that to work so well—or so fast. Do you think, maybe, you'd like to do it again?"

He was so sweet she had to kiss him the way he liked best. He let her have her way with his mouth for a good two minutes, not trying to take control, just moaning in encouragement. His passivity made Frankie feel strangely powerful.

"Lay me down in the bed," she said huskily when she had his pulse racing. He shivered as she ran her hand along his tattooed arm. "I love having a man over me."

It was an innocent enough kink to confess to, but he flushed as darkly if she'd said she wanted to be spanked.

"I like doing what women want," he confessed in return, hitching her off the wall so he could carry her with him inside her. "I love knowing I'm turning them on."

Oh, my, Frankie thought as she hid her grin in his shoulder. This was going to be a pleasant night.

Chapter
4

Frankie wasn't sure what woke her—a noise, maybe, or a movement of the light in the service alley the single window overlooked. She didn't know how long she'd dozed after making love that third time. She stared at the ceiling, trying to guess. Mike slept with his back to her, his narrow butt just touching her hip. The contact was nice, trusting but not possessive.

She began to close her eyes when she remembered.

"Crap," she whispered into the dark.

"What?" Mike sat up quickly enough to startle her. His voice was froggy, but otherwise he seemed totally awake.

"It's nothing," she said. "I forgot to lock up. I'll go down and do it now. You go back to sleep."

"Are you crazy? It's the middle of the night. I'm coming with you. Anyone could have walked in."

He was already pulling on his pants . . . without underwear, but she shoved that memory away and swung her legs over the bedside. This was as far as her sleepiness let her go.

"I can lock up for you," he offered as she sat there rubbing her face.

"No, no, I'll do it. It just takes me longer to get going than you soldier guys."

She fumbled into her clothes, both flattered and self-conscious that he watched. She thought it was sweet of him to insist on coming with her, very protective alpha male. Unnecessary, most likely, but still sweet.

Mike waited at the door until she was ready, then padded soundlessly down the stairs ahead of her. All this skulking made her feel very special ops. She smiled at his back but couldn't doubt he was taking this seriously.

"Don't turn on the light," he murmured as they reached the diner itself. Streetlights filtered in through the front windows, highlighting the deco patterns etched in the glass. The place was silent, empty from what she could see. She locked the front door as quietly as she could, then gestured toward the kitchen with her keys. Mike nodded, understanding she needed to lock the alley exit as well.

The kitchen was as empty as the front and smelled of the thorough cleaning Mike had given it. Still leading the way, he stopped at the door to the storeroom. In contrast to the rest of the diner, this area was pitch black.

He looked back at her, his profile sharp and clean.

"Stay here," he said. "The light on your loading dock must be out."

Something in his voice made her shiver. He seemed different, a true stranger, alert to signals she knew nothing about. She hugged herself as he melted like one more shadow into the dark.

Only an idiot would have bothered telling him to be careful.

Farfetched though it was, he must have memorized where the

shelves and boxes in the storeroom were. She heard nothing—no bumps, no curses—until the metal alley door creaked open. A minute passed with no more sound. She began to think she ought to join him. Then, just as silently as he'd gone, he reappeared. The muscles of his face were tighter than they should have been.

"Call the police," he said. "There's a body in your alley."

"What?" She pushed past him. It wasn't bravery but disbelief.

"She's dead," Mike said. "There's nothing you can do."

She? Frankie thought. A terrible presentiment clutched her chest. She knew who it was as surely as a child feeling guilty for angry thoughts. She ran to the door Mike had propped open with a broom.

She cried out when she saw the body. It *was* her. Her sleek brown bob gleamed in the security light that shone from behind the copy place next door. She was lying on the sandy asphalt just beyond the concrete platform where Frankie's delivery trucks unloaded. A pink pearl necklace glowed incongruously on her neck. She looked as if she had laid down in her tasteful Marc Jacobs suit and gone to sleep. Sort of, anyway. Her eyes stared at the stars, and her mouth was slightly open. Frankie saw no obvious signs of injury, but her face had a strange, dusky color.

She gasped in shock just as Mike caught her arm.

"Oh, no," she said, now close enough to see the truth. "It isn't her. It isn't Karen. It's Tish Whittier!"

Jack West turned the black-and-white police car into his driveway and prepared to go 10-07. He'd had a long, boring day during which he'd had too much time to mull over his little crash-and-burn that morning with Frankie Smith. Jack worked a split shift, eight to twelve and then four to eight. A meeting with

the mayor to discuss an uptick in graffiti had kept him on duty
late. Now he wanted a beer, a plate of carb-loaded pasta, and his
bed.

Modest though his fantasy was, it was not to be. He'd loosed
the seatbelt and opened the door when the dispatcher from
County crackled over his radio.

"Hey, Chief," said the voice he recognized as Myrna Brown.
"We've got a 911 for a possible 187 a mile from your house. Female DB found in an alley behind a diner called All U Can Eat."

Adrenaline flooded him so swiftly his hands went cold. A 187
was a murder, and All U Can Eat was Frankie's place. His imme-
diate instinct was to ask if they had an ID, but this was information that shouldn't go out on air any insomniac with a police
scanner could pick up. Palms clammy, he keyed the handheld to
speak. "I'll be there ASAP, Control. Notify the ME, and have Officers Rivera and Dewey meet me on scene."

"10-4, Chief. Call if you need more help."

He wasn't sure how he did it, but it took him three whole minutes to reach the spot. He blocked one end of the alley with his black
and white, unholstered his gun, and got out. He scanned the area
swiftly. Rivera and Dewey weren't here yet, but he wasn't going to
wait. He could see the body from where he stood, oddly doll-like in
the harsh alley lights. His heart gave a funny stutter and then began
to slow. The corpse was too short to be Frankie Smith.

He knew he didn't need to, but he still bent to check the
carotid for a pulse. The triple strand of pearls the victim wore lay
over a nasty ligature mark. The necklace hadn't been what strangled her; it would have broken under the strain. He looked to
where her hands had been placed one atop the other on her stomach. The bauble jewelers liked to call a right-hand ring glinted on
one finger, reinforcing his conclusion that robbery hadn't been
the motive for this.

He ran his gaze up again. The victim was slim and soft, her pink angora top increasing the kittenish impression. Her face was familiar, but he couldn't put a name to it. She was no transient, that was for sure. More like Six Palms' tippity-top drawer.

The mayor was going to forget all about graffiti when he heard this.

Jack's neck tightened suddenly with alert. An overhang had been shielding the diner's loading dock from the light, but now a figure appeared on the edge.

"Freeze!" he said, his gun up as fast as thought. "Hands behind your head."

The minute the figure's shirt slid up with the motion, he knew who it was. Only Frankie's navel could be that cute.

"You, too," he barked to the man who'd just stepped beside her. "Hands up! Turn and face the wall!"

Jack was up behind them in seconds. He didn't recognize the man, but he sure as hell knew the tattoo that wound up his arm. It was a well known gang mark from South Central LA. "Hands in the small of your back," he ordered before cuffing his wrists.

"Chief West!" Frankie protested, taking a step closer.

"Stay where you are," he ordered, not as loudly as before but still firm. "It's my job to do this."

"But he called it in. Mike's the one who found her."

He gave her a look to keep her where she was, made a mental note of the name, then patted down the guy he'd cuffed. Frankie's friend bore it in stoic silence, obviously knowing the drill. Jack didn't particularly like observing that he only wore black fatigue trousers, or that his very buff bare back sported some scratches of the type that could not be mistaken for defensive wounds. He had a switchblade in one pocket, which Jack confiscated and tucked in his belt.

Great, he thought. The woman he had the hots for had been intimate with an armed suspect.

"I have to frisk you, too," he said to Frankie, noticing only then that her cheeks were tear-stained. "Put your hands higher on the wall."

Her eyes widened, but she obeyed. "Mike couldn't have hurt her," she said over her shoulder. "We've been together all night."

He had nothing to say to this, even if it had been appropriate. Her hair was down and tousled. She was shaking as he ran his hands down her sides, tight little tremors that shook her sleekly muscled frame. He was more than close enough to smell her, and she reeked of sex, radiating not only the scent of her own satisfied female body, but also that of her companion.

Jack's libido didn't care that she'd been with another man. With no hope of stopping it, lust roared through him. He was aching hard in seconds, the big erection throbbing awkwardly in his uniform. The reaction threw him so off balance he almost couldn't bring himself to frisk the inside of her legs. Her jeans were worn thin as silk, and the firmness of her calves and thighs wasn't at all calming.

She was clean, of course, at least so far as weapons went.

"Sit," he said gruffly, gesturing her toward a dirty white plastic chair. "I need you to stay here. Don't touch anything until I have time to question you."

She sat as if her strings had been cut. He turned to the man she'd had sex with. He was young enough to be called a kid, no more than early twenties. All the same, the hard, cool eyes that challenged Jack's were old as the hills. Jack had a few inches on the guy and more than a few pounds, but he knew he'd been right to treat him as a threat. This Mike, whoever he was, wouldn't hesitate to take him on.

"You can wait in my squad car," Jack said.

"Hey!" Frankie said, offended again.

To Jack's surprise, it was Mike who soothed her. "It's all right," he said. "He's just being careful. Plus, he has to be sure we don't . . . accidentally coordinate our statements."

Yeah, he knew the drill all right. Jack didn't bother thanking him, just walked him by the elbow down the alley to his car.

Rivera and Dewey had arrived in the meantime. Rivera, as always, looked starched and pressed. She was a single mother, as responsible and detail-oriented as an atomic clock. Dewey was her wise-cracking, pizza-eating opposite. Though he was the one who'd been on duty when the call came in, his hair was standing in all directions, his uniform as creased as if he'd slept in it.

Judging that the chief had his person of interest under control, Rivera had her kit out and was beginning to tape the scene. Dewey waited by the car. Jack supposed the thought of investigating a real murder had his junior officer overawed. For once, he didn't greet Jack with a off color joke. Hoping Dewey could handle the pressure, Jack handed Mike to him.

"Take his name and have Dispatch run him. I'm betting they'll find a record, but we'll figure out what that means as things unfold. For now, he stays cuffed." As Dewey settled Frankie's friend into the caged backseat, Jack popped the trunk and took out his camera. "I'm going to help Rivera process the scene. You keep the area clear of gawkers. We'll tackle interviews when we're done."

Unable to help himself, he glanced back to where Frankie watched. She looked small in the cheap plastic chair, her hands pressed nervously between her knees. She was obeying his order not to touch anything. To his dismay, he found the pose sexy.

He sighed soundlessly to himself. Even if she turned out not to be a suspect, he doubted this night was going to improve his chances for dating her.

• • •

Frankie had been shivering ever since Jack West told her to freeze—as if only this surreal occurrence could make the truth sink in.

She couldn't believe Tish Whittier was dead. She especially couldn't believe she'd been murdered. Tish was the nicest woman most people in Six Palms knew, a shy, pretty rich girl who served with surprising effectiveness on the boards of half a dozen local charities. No one could refuse her when she asked for favors in her soft, sweet voice. More than once, she'd roped Frankie into providing food for fund-raising barbecues. The life Tish lived, the privileged world she came from, might as well have been Mars to someone like Frankie, but she'd always thought of Tish as a real lady. How anyone could want to kill her she didn't know.

She pressed her hands more tightly between her knees. If she'd thought Chief West would let her up, she would have been calling Troy. Someone had to prepare Karen Ellis for the news. She and Tish had been inseparable since high school. Half the town still called them the Bobbsey twins. Frankie's grudge seemed unimportant in the face of how hard this loss was sure to hit. No one, even if they were a man-stealing bitch, deserved to lose their best girlfriend.

Unable to do anything about it now, Frankie rubbed her thighs. The medical examiner had come and gone, thankfully taking away Tish's body in his van. Ever since, Chief West and his attractive Hispanic officer had been going over the alley, photographing who knew what, taking notes and putting objects into bags. They didn't talk much, and only in low voices, each seeming to understand what the other wanted done.

Watching them work so easily together made Frankie feel

oddly miffed, which she couldn't understand because the most personal exchange she'd ever had with Jack West was when he'd frisked the inside seam of her jeans. A flush rolled through her at the memory. The chief was really tall. She hadn't realized how tall before, because she always served him sitting down, but when he'd been behind her to check for weapons, he'd towered over her. He also had big hands—big, warm hands that had been as efficient as they were gentle.

She couldn't help wondering what it would be like to have them running over her naked skin.

She squirmed in the molded chair, abruptly not shivering. This should not be turning her on. She'd just spent the night having sex with a very hot young guy. Maybe it was a daddy fixation, because, God knew, hers hadn't been around much when she was young. Or maybe she had a thing for big, powerful males in uniform. Of course, Mike was a big, powerful male in uniform, too, so maybe having her heart broken was turning her into a slut.

That's my story, she thought, curling her painted toes up in her sandals. *And I'm darn well sticking to it.*

"Miss Smith?" The pretty Hispanic cop was standing over her, and the look on her face said this wasn't the first time she'd called her name. "We're ready to interview you if you'd like to go inside."

"Uh, sure," she said. Her knees were stiff when she got up, her jeans suspiciously damp as she tugged them down.

Chief West was at the open door to her storeroom, its surface smeared with fingerprint powder. The inside light shone on his face, revealing a watchful narrowing of his eyes. Frankie wondered if he'd been standing there while she had her little X-rated reverie. When the light glinted off his badge as well, she felt even more guilty.

"We won't keep you any longer than we have to," he said, his voice as dark and rich as hot coffee. "We just need to catch you while your memory's fresh."

It was fresh, all right. Just maybe not on the right topics.

Jack led Frankie into the diner and sat her in the last booth, the only booth without a window. They'd been lucky on the gawker front so far, and he had no desire to risk changing that. When Frankie offered to get them coffee, he and Rivera refused. To accept her hospitality would remind her this was her place. Though this was an informal interview for now, he knew it was to his advantage to have her feel subordinate.

Clearly nervous, she rubbed her thighs beneath the table as Rivera turned her notebook to a clean page.

The preparation seemed to fascinate Frankie, but not for long. Jack's nerves zinged against his will as her cat-green eyes shifted to his. She looked softer with her hair down, more vulnerable. Her lips were as pink as spring roses.

"Is Mike all right?" she asked worriedly.

Oh, it must have been women's intuition to push his buttons right off the bat. He could only hope it didn't show.

"Officer Dewey is taking his statement." Jack pulled a clear plastic pouch from his breast pocket. The evidence bag contained an ID holder made of nice buttercup leather. It was opened to reveal Tish Whittier's driver's license. Jack slid it across the table to face Frankie.

She looked at it, then at him—not flinching or tearing up, either of which would have told him something. To his disappointment, her main emotion appeared to be confusion.

"How long have you known Laetisha Whittier?" he asked.

"About two years. She rented my diner out for a party, a retrochic phase, I guess. After that, I worked a couple of her less-upscale charity dos."

"You liked her?"

"It was damn hard not to." Frankie touched license photo through the plastic, a gentle stroke with the tip of her index finger. "She was one of the nicest people I've ever met, a little down on herself, maybe, but she made you want to buck her up. Don't get me wrong, some of her crowd were snooty pains in the ass. Not her, though. She actually invited me to one of her private parties. Said she wanted to thank me for all my help."

"When was this?"

Frankie looked up, her eyes slightly reddened now. "I don't know: four Saturdays ago? She and Troy got on, so he came, too. Their great-grandfathers were friendly rivals—both railroad ty-coons, I think."

"Did you enjoy yourself?"

She squinted at him, clearly wondering why he was asking. "It was a bit more foie gras than I'm used to, but, yeah, I did. And so did everyone else. Honestly, I have no idea who'd want to kill her."

"And you don't see this as a random attack?" He leaned forward on his elbows, classic body language for establishing rapport.

"Well, do you?" she asked. Though he'd encroached on her personal space, she didn't retreat. Instead, her pupils dilated. "Whoever it was didn't take her jewelry, and her clothes were neat, so she probably wasn't, you know, interfered with."

He said nothing as Rivera's pencil scratched all this down, let-ting Frankie realize she was the one who was here to give answers. His blood was pulsing forcefully in his thighs. Despite how un-professional it was, he knew he was getting off on dominating their interviewee. It wasn't his usual response to the situation, though being in charge had always been his bedroom preference—his bedroom requirement, truth be told.

Determined not to show what he was thinking, he leaned back

against the padded seat. "Tell me about tonight. What made you come down to the diner when you did?"

She took him through it step by step, more organized than most people were when they told a story, coloring slightly when she explained that she and Mike had spent the night in bed. He liked her better for her embarrassment, though it probably was irrelevant.

"Were you aware that Mr. True used to be a member of an LA gang?"

Eyes wide, she shook her head and turned pinker. "I only met him today."

"I see," he said, unintentionally letting disapproval tinge his tone.

To his surprise, she drew herself straighter. "No, I don't think you do see. I may not know Mike True as well as I usually know my partners, and maybe he has a past, but I sincerely doubt he's a bad person. In any case, he was with me. He didn't have a chance to hurt Tish."

Jack felt Rivera go still beside him; watching him in action, he supposed, no doubt in hope of doing the same one day.

"That's not quite true," he said in his softest voice. "By your own account, you and Mr. True spent an unknown period asleep. Either of you could have slipped out without the other knowing. As a result, I'm afraid neither of you has alibis."

He didn't intend to shake her quite as much as he did, but that didn't mean he could back down. She was gaping at him in disbelief when he took his next shot.

"We'd like to search your storeroom," he said, knowing that if she refused they'd have to wait for a warrant. "We think the killer may have lain in wait in there."

"Fuck," she said, pushing back from the table. "Knock yourself out."

Her disgust was too natural to be feigned. This, more than anything, convinced him she was not involved. Too bad the evidence wasn't on his side.

"Boss," Rivera said maybe five minutes into their search.

She was pointing toward an upper shelf, where a carton of drinking straws sat half-open. The foot from a pair of cheap pantyhose straggled from beneath one cardboard flap, as if someone had stuffed them there in a hurry. Rivera reached up with her tweezers and tugged them out. The center portion of each leg was stretched out of shape and stained, as if they'd survived a hell of a fight.

"Looks like the murder weapon," she said.

"Yeah," Jack agreed, sighing inwardly. "It does."

Chapter 5

The pantyhose went to the county lab along with every-thing else. A now very surly Frankie denied knowing how the murder weapon had ended up in her storeroom, but on the strength of discovering it there, and based on the fact that a pre-liminary test matched stains on the hose to the blood type of their victim, Jack was able to get a warrant to seal up All U Can Eat as part of the crime scene.

"Mike will need a place to stay," Frankie said with an edge of not-so-subtle accusation. "I was loaning him the apartment on the second floor."

They stood outside her now taped-up door. It was a rare clear morning on the coast. Streaks of tangerine and aqua above Frankie's neon sign announced that the sun was climbing the eastern hills. Clumps of palms rustled on either end of her diner's gleaming, retro length. The recently mown slice of Bermuda grass that sep-arated the sidewalk from her parking spaces sparkled with dew. It would have been a pretty, peaceful moment any other time. In fact, if Jack truly strained his imaginative powers, they might have been saying goodbye at the end of a lengthy date.

He curled his fingers over the keys Frankie had reluctantly handed over, probably too aware of the warmth they carried from her body heat. This was no time to be thinking about kissing her.

Even if her lips looked really soft.

"Mr. True is a big boy," he said. "I'm sure he can find somewhere to sleep without your help."

Frankie narrowed her slanting green eyes to slits but didn't—he noticed with a satisfaction he couldn't completely quash—offer to house the man herself. Maybe she'd finally realized True was no stray puppy.

"You need a lift home?" he said. "I can have Rivera run you there."

She shook her head, still frowning. "It's getting light, and I live close. Plus, I doubt whoever did this is running around looking for seconds. God." She pressed one palm to her brow. "I'm never going to forget her lying there as peaceful as Sleeping Beauty. Somebody put her like that. Somebody straightened her clothes and folded her hands after they—Somebody knew her. Somebody knew her and killed her and then treated her like someone they cared about."

Jack thought so, too, but wasn't in a position to discuss theories with her. Frankie didn't seem to be waiting for him to do it. She bent, tore a weed from the springy grass, and stuffed it in her front pocket.

"Look," she said, visibly pushing away memories of Tish. "How long is my diner going to be closed? Some of my employees are going to be strapped if they can't work their hours."

She didn't seem to realize that she, and her employees, were lucky she wasn't being locked up.

"A couple days," he said. "Depending on what we find."

Her cheeks puffed out with a breath, but he could see her anger had faded. She squared her shoulders resignedly. "I know you have to do this. I know it will help you catch whoever killed Tish."

"That is the plan."

"All right." She nodded, seemingly to herself. Her eyes focused on his again. That involuntary sexual zing went through him as strong as ever—as strong as if she'd agreed to a different sort of cooperation from solving a crime. His crotch tightened dangerously. "I really do want to help. Let me know if you need anything else."

He watched her go. The view was pleasant. As eye candy went, Frankie Smith in a pair of jeans was hard to beat—though her walk wasn't her usual confident stride. She was lost in thought, or maybe simply lost. Seeing death up close could do that to a person, remind them how little they could be sure of in this mixed-up world.

She'd gone a dozen steps toward Hill Street when she turned and caught him staring. For a heartbeat, whatever she'd meant to say was forgotten in surprise. He couldn't be sure at this distance, but he thought her cheeks went a little pink. The possibility that they did made his ears feel hot.

She recovered before the heat could spread. "If you find a pair of Louis Vuitton sunglasses while you're searching, they're Karen Ellis's. She thinks she lost them here yesterday."

He nodded as if his behavior were perfectly normal. It wasn't *ab*normal, in any case. If he had thought she was guilty, he'd have been watching her this closely, too.

Six Palms' police department consisted of four less-than-palatial rooms in city hall. One room was Jack's office, one Dewey and Rivera shared with all the file cabinets that would fit, and one served as a combination dark room and mini-lab. Anything complicated—including prisoners—was sent to County, with whom they had a standing arrangement. The fourth and final room, where the three of them were gathered now, was used for conference and interrogation.

"So," Jack said, leaning back from the cheaply veneered table that pretty much filled the space. Photos and sketches were spilled across it, documenting their work thus far. His battered office chair creaked on its base. "Let's go over what we've got."

Guessing Rivera would answer first, he turned to her.

Even in a small town, law enforcement was a tough field for women to break into, and Rivera was more of a bombshell than most who tried. Jack was big enough that he could stop a barfight by showing up. Dewey, the Irish devil with the choirboy face, could joke most people out of starting trouble. Rivera strove for a no-nonsense air of intimidation that she hadn't quite mastered yet.

A naturally sensual-looking woman, Jack's senior officer did her best to play down her sexiness. Her dark hair was scraped back, her nails and face as always unpainted. Jack suspected she ordered her uniforms a size too large so they wouldn't cling. He'd seen her with her kid now and then, so he knew she could laugh, but at work she was all business all the time—with the exception of one notable occasion both she and Jack pretended to have forgotten. This morning she looked as crisp as a person could with circles under her sultry black coffee eyes.

Until this case was solved, everyone's regular hours went out the window.

"We've got a rich girl vic," she said in the voice she worked to keep from sounding too feminine. "Family money comes from both sides. The mother's grandfather was in railroads, and the dad's father founded Whittier Vineyards. The parents, neither of whom do much of anything, live in Santa Barbara near the winery. Our vic moved here after college. She's unmarried. No known feuds. The lack of defensive wounds, or anything visible under her nails, suggests she was strangled from behind, probably by whoever she was waiting for in that alley. I've got her size six Manolo Blahnik shoe prints pacing back and forth in front the diner's loading dock. The other prints look older, so maybe whoever did her was standing on that concrete step."

"And maybe whoever did her needed a leg up. Maybe it was a woman." Dewey said this with as much relish as he'd used to bite into the doughnut he'd picked up on his drive back from the county lab. Flakes of sugar glaze speckled his uniform front. The way Dewey ate, Jack was damned if he knew how he stayed in shape, though being twenty-six might have had helped. Actually, the way he kept calling Rivera a hot tamale, Jack was a bit surprised he still had his teeth. "Maybe we've got ourselves a femme fatale."

Rivera rolled her eyes at Dewey's salacious tone but didn't deign to insult him out loud. Instead, she leaned across the scattered photos to address Jack directly. "The ME will have to confirm it, but it looked to me like considerable force was used. I think our murderer wasn't taking any chances Whittier would survive after she passed out."

"And then he arranged her," Dewey said, abandoning his femme fatale theory easily enough. "'Cause nobody falls like that. She looked as tidy as if she were already in the funeral home."

"Which suggests an attacker who knew her, or maybe somebody with a compulsion to act out a particular ritual."

Rivera's dark eyes lit up as much at this idea as Dewey's had at the thought of a female murderer. Jack could practically see visions of catching a serial killer dancing through her head. Not wanting to discourage her, he didn't smile.

"We'll keep our minds open," he said. "But we probably

should find out if Whittier was the sort of woman who'd agree to meet a stranger in a dark alley. Until we do, it's probably safe to assume someone she knew called her there."

"Or she called someone," Dewey put in eagerly. "Maybe she was a blackmailer. Or sleeping with a married man. A wronged wife could have done her. Or, heck, a husband who thought she was going to expose him."

"But why meet *there*?" Rivera asked. "Why not on the beach or somewhere more private? That time of night, that service alley is relatively empty, but not completely. Which the killer must have known, because the security light looked like it was broken on purpose. The killer made sure if someone did come out, he'd have a dark place to hide."

Dewey cleared his throat and shot a quick glance at Jack as if he thought his boss wasn't going to like what he said next. "That location would be convenient for the diner owner. I know everybody likes Frankie Smith. God knows, I've eaten enough of her food myself, but maybe she and the vic were involved in some sort of girl-fight. They did know each other from Whittier's charity work. Maybe Frankie Smith slept with that Mike guy so she'd have an alibi. Seduces the lucky bastard, wears him out, and before you can say 'hard up,' he's down for the count. Then all she has to do is say she accidentally left her doors unlocked and somebody else snuck in."

"Or he did it," Rivera said, studiously not looking at Jack. "True, he does have a record. I know he was technically a juvie, but armed robbery, even when you're just the driver, isn't anything to shrug off. Even if that weren't the case, he's been trained to kill stealthily. I've got an uncle in the service. Recon Marines wear black like True did, and they're as dangerous as Navy SEALs. Maybe there's a history between him and the vic we don't know about."

Jack wasn't happy with either of them tiptoeing around him. It said his partiality for Frankie Smith wasn't as well hidden as he'd thought. He clenched his molars and fought a sigh.

"This is good," he said aloud. "We'll keep these ideas in mind when we search Whittier's house. Dewey, you're heading up to Santa Barbara to notify her family. Rivera, you're with me."

"Oh, *man*," Dewey said, his disappointment clear.

"It's not a punishment," Jack clarified. "Interviewing the family is just as important as searching the victim's house. It's your job to see what they knew about their daughter's life. Her relationships. Anyone she had a beef with or was scared of. Anything out of the ordinary at all. And for God's sake, take good notes. You want a record of anything you might have to testify to in court."

Dewey made a face but didn't argue. He'd been called to account for being sloppy in the past. "I'll cross my t's," he promised, then broke into a grin. "In fact, I'll be so anal, you'll swear you sent Rivera instead."

The office was quiet after Dewey left. Jack and Rivera restocked their crime-scene kits and met in the hall.

"So . . . I'm with you," she said while Jack locked up.

As soon as he turned from the door to her, she dropped her gaze to the mottled gray and black linoleum. He didn't know what she'd been staring at to look so guilty, and he probably didn't want to guess. Her olive coloring, along with the ancient flourescent lighting in city hall, made it hard to tell if she was blushing.

Jack found himself wishing, and not for the first time, that she'd get over her crush on him. He knew that, short of being held at gunpoint and forced, she'd never make another pass at him. That tequila-soaked party for city workers last Christmas had been a one-time thing. He doubted the state of California held enough alcohol to make her risk her pride like that again. He just wished she wouldn't look at him the way she sometimes did. He wished she wouldn't pine.

He couldn't even be flattered, because he sensed she didn't really know him. Sure, she'd probably researched his record at the LAPD, but the things he'd done and seen there, the things he'd had medals pinned on him for, wouldn't be more than words on a page to her. She was part of the "nice" world, a civilian despite her uniform. Even if he could have reciprocated her feelings, she'd want to save him or heal him or who knew what—anything but accept him for who he was.

Jerk though he could be, Dewey would have been a better match for her.

"You drive," he said, tossing her the keys to his cruiser.

He didn't normally do this, but the last thing he wanted was to have her sneaking looks at him all the way there.

Jack let out a low whistle as Rivera turned into Tish Whittier's Mediterranean-style estate. The house was set among the hills high above Six Palms. Unless there was a noise complaint from neighbors who hadn't been invited to a party, Jack didn't see places like this. Places like this had their own security—not to mention fountains splashing merrily in the courtyard behind their gilded electric gates.

"Wow," said Rivera. "Very lifestyles of the filthy rich."

A maid admitted them. She wore a uniform like a fancy hotel employee and didn't speak much English. Though Jack's Spanish was as good as Rivera's, he let her handle the explanations. Predictably, partway through, the maid, whose name was Maria, began to cry. From what Jack could tell, her tears did seem to be for the death of her employer, rather than the impending loss of her job. She clutched a wad of tissues to her nose.

"Miss Whittier was so nice, so *bonita*. I can't think who would want to hurt her."

Jack eyed the giant modern painting that hung over most of the stucco wall in the two-story foyer. The thing was so abstract he couldn't be certain what it was meant to be, but to him, it resembled a bloody drawn-and-quartered deer. If "Miss Whittier" had chosen it, some part of her wasn't nice at all.

He cut into the maid's tearful exclamations, asking where to find her employer's private rooms.

"Join me when you're done here," he said to Rivera.

As he'd expected, their vic had a suite of rooms in her monstrosity of a mansion—a house within a house. It consisted of a gargantuan bedroom, a closet and bath, a combination sitting room and office, and one more room that opened off the others through a broad, round arch. This final space was devoted to watching movies. Every one of the plush white seats faced a big high-definition screen. Since he'd passed another media room on his way up, this intrigued him.

What, he wondered, did the rich girl save for her viewing pleasure when she was alone?

Later for you, Jack thought to the space and turned back to the kitten-soft bedroom.

"So much white," Rivera breathed ten minutes later when she came in. Like him, she'd pulled on latex gloves. "Those maids are earning their pay."

Jack stood by the side of the ruffled bed. He laid down the old photo album he'd been flipping through. "You learn anything?"

"Miss Whittier had a boyfriend, or so Maria thought. Apparently, our vic was secretive about him. The maid never met him in person, and no one knew his name. Whoever he was, Maria and the other maids decided he couldn't be very nice. For the last week or so, Whittier had been crying herself to sleep."

"So maybe Dewey was right. Maybe this was an affair with a married man gone wrong."

"God help us if that's true," Rivera muttered under her breath. "We'll never hear the end of it."

"No boyfriends here," Jack said, tapping the photo book. "Just two high school girl chums in a lot of creepily matching clothes."

"Girls do that," Rivera said, picking it up for herself. "There was one clique at my school that coordinated colors for every day of the week." Rivera braced the book against her belt and turned a page. "Shit. Isn't this Karen Ellis of Ellis Real Estate? Wow, they *are* dressed alike. I wouldn't have guessed she ran with the trust fund crowd."

"Maybe we didn't know because we don't run with that crowd ourselves. Maybe Ellis's parents were just rich enough to get her into an exclusive high school."

"Arrivistes," Rivera said, causing Jack to lift one eyebrow. "It means their money was new."

"I know what it means. I'm just a little surprised to hear it coming out of a fellow officer's mouth."

"Yeah, well, you don't know everything about me," Rivera muttered.

Jack thought it best to let that conversational nonstarter drop. "What else do you know about Ellis's family?"

"The Six Palms *Courier* did a profile on her last year. Her dad was a big-deal car salesman, and I think her mom was a manicurist. Daddy dearest paid the mom a ton in alimony when they divorced. But Ellis made her own money. Went from real estate agent to owner in just five years."

"Impressive."

"Yup," said Rivera. "Some people learn to push when they're young."

She touched a picture of Whittier and Ellis in their cheerleading uniforms. The outfits were so skimpy, Jack knew his überstrict parents would have had strokes before letting his sisters get caught in them. He distinctly recalled breaking his older sisters out of the padlocked basement where they'd been "sequestered" for wearing lipstick to school. His rescue had earned him a two-week grounding, one more reminder of how well prepared he was for healthy relationships.

From the looks of it, no excess of discipline had been at work in these girls' families. The world was their oyster to judge by their mile-wide smiles. It was all very *rah-rah* and *kiss my ass.*

Rivera felt it, too. She cleared her throat as if even a photo had the power to intimidate lesser mortals. "I wonder why Frankie Smith didn't mention Whittier and Ellis were friends."

"We didn't ask her," Jack said, stubbornly watching Rivera not look at him.

"No, I guess not." Rivera rubbed her forehead, mussing the edge of her scraped-back hair. "You want me to go through her desk while you search the media room?"

"You read my mind," Jack said, a grin beginning to form despite the awkwardness between them.

"Ha," said Rivera. "I just never met a man who could resist a big-screen TV."

Like the other rooms, the one Jack stepped into was a cocoon of white. Unlike the others, this bore no hint of girlishness. This was a grown-up, sensual space, with satin pillows and silk fringe. The seating was upholstered in white chenille, the scattered tables lacquered to match. The bedroom had boasted a view of the lap pool and tennis courts, but here a thick alpaca carpet stretched to windows overlooking the town and ocean far below. In one corner, a mirror-clad bar with flowers etched into its glass held bottles of Whittier Vineyard's 2002 Pinot Noir.

Risky, Jack thought, *to drink red wine among all this snow*. But maybe the Whittiers' daughter didn't like chardonnay.

The only other spots of color were a pair of high-heeled red satin shoes that looked to have been kicked off and left beneath an end table. Jack's nostrils flared as he drew closer to the nearby couch. The scent of Chanel No. 5 and pussy perfumed the air. When he opened the end table's drawer, a powerful-looking vibrator was hiding beneath a blank journal.

My, my, Miss Tish, Jack thought. *What were you watching in here?*

That question led him to the wall of white lacquer shelving that housed the TV. Classic sex books leaned between white knick knacks: *The Story of O, Women on Top*. He raised his eyebrows at a copy of *The Joy of Gay Sex* but let it pass. Finally, he found what he was looking for.

Inside one of the lower cabinets was a small home safe. It was neither the worst model in the world nor the best. Like most people, Whittier had probably written down the combination, but Jack knew a more entertaining way to get inside. Grinning, he borrowed a whiskey glass from the bar, set it and his ear against the door, and listened to the tumblers fall.

To his slightly subversive pleasure, he cracked the thing in five minutes.

"Thank you, cousin Tony," he murmured to his safe-cracking, black-sheep relative.

He was not the least surprised to see what the hiding place contained.

Here was Whittier's private DVD collection, female-oriented porn for the most part, but in the back were at least a dozen hand-labeled jewel cases. They had names like *Blue Light Special* and *Beach Blanket Bimbo*. *Who's Afraid of Virginia's Wolf* made the corners of his mouth twitch, but it was the one simply titled *Me* that he pulled out.

He used the remote to lower the blackout shades and slid the disc into the machine.

He'd been expecting explicit contents, but even so, when the DVD began to play, his heart gave a thump of admittedly pleasurable male shock.

Tish Whittier had been a knockout without her clothes.

She was in a wine cellar, the fancy, furnished sort rich people have custom-designed for their houses. The floor was paved in terra cotta tile, a nice inlaid table invited sampling the wares, and the lighting was flattering. Whittier's lusty pose was a contrast to her surroundings. Padded leather ties bound her wrists and ankles to the wooden wine rack that formed a wall behind her. Though her eyes were big and round, she didn't appear alarmed.

She was a willing captive waiting to be fucked.

A wave of dark excitement rolled through Jack. Bondage had turned him on since he'd been a kid playing cops and robbers with the girls in his neighborhood. He hadn't been a mean playmate, and most had loved being paid attention to by a boy, despite his always wanting to be the one who cuffed and arrested them. Back then, he hadn't known what the velvet tension in his body meant. Now he did. Now he had decades of elaborate fantasies in his head, fantasies he'd never dared reveal to anyone. Seeing one of those fantasies being played out by real people guaranteed that no amount of political correctness could have kept his cock from hardening.

Evidently, he wasn't the only Six Palms resident with nonvanilla tastes.

Whittier's spread-eagled stance gave Jack an unmistakable view of how happy she was to be there. Her pubic hair had been shaved, and her pussy lips glistened like a conch shell fresh from the sea. Her clit was erect enough to peep out. Jack blinked at that, his thighs tightening uncontrollably. Her labia were as flushed as her taut nipples. She was petite and curvy at the same time;

stacked like the planes over LAX, Dewey would have said. Even more impressive, her breasts appeared to be natural. They jiggled as she tugged at her bonds.

"Oh, please," she said breathily to someone. "I can't bear it anymore. Please get me off."

She seemed to mean it. This wasn't simply role playing. Jack watched a thin trickle of moisture slide down her inner thigh.

"Not yet," said a husky male voice that had Jack's neck prickling with recognition. "You're not really ready until you're crying."

A naked man stepped into view. After a second to goggle at the gravity-defying arrow of his erection, Jack identified him as Pete from Pete and Dave's Garage.

Whittier flushed scarlet at his approach. "You're so pretty," she sighed. "Oh, please, let me kiss your cock."

"What about Dave's cock?" Pete asked. "Wouldn't you rather kiss that?"

"I'll kiss them both," Whittier declared impassionedly. "I want you both in my mouth at once."

"We won't untie you," Dave warned from off camera. "No matter what you promise."

"But I need it," Whittier said, writhing with greater energy in her bonds. "I need to be fucked."

Dave came on scene wagging an empty wine bottle—a Whittier wine bottle, Jack saw. "I'd be willing to put this inside you instead."

"You'll tease me," Whittier protested. "You won't let me come."

Dave and Pete both grinned at this, their erections bouncing in front of them as if linked to the same metronome. They had similar bodies, wiry but muscular. Dave was the darker of the two and had more hair on his chest and legs. Pete's cock was shorter and thicker. As Pete stepped out of the way, Dave slid the neck of the bottle between Whittier's legs. Though the insertion appeared gentle, it was sufficient to get Whittier going. Moaning, she tried to sink farther down on it. As she did, Dave drew it away.

"More," she pleaded. "Oh, God, move it around."

"You're not ready," Dave insisted. "I don't see you crying yet."

This time Whittier growled her frustration. The dark waves of her hair tossed as she thrashed. "You want me. You're both as hard as baseball bats."

"We want something," Pete agreed in an amused tone. He cupped her breast and thumbed its pointed nipple. "Maybe you'd like to watch me make Dave desperate while he does the same to you."

Whittier stopped struggling, her blue eyes wide. "Would you really do that? Would you let me watch while you sucked him off?"

Pete dropped a kiss to her flaming cheek. "I would, sweetheart, and you better believe Dave here will thank you for suggesting it."

Whittier looked shyly pleased at the compliment. "Oh," she said. "I'm sure I only want everyone to enjoy themselves."

The men chuckled—a deep, masculine sound that wouldn't have been out of place in a locker room. Still holding the bottle inside of Whittier, Dave turned to the side. Pete dropped to his knees on the soft-red tile.

"Can you see?" he asked their captive audience.

Whittier bit her lip and nodded. "Dave just got bigger when you touched his hip."

Pete did more than touch Dave's hip. Pete wet his mouth with his tongue, took a swimmer's preparatory breath, and swallowed his partner's prick in one long, practiced motion. Being surrounded must have felt good. Dave closed his eyes and groaned.

"Oh, yeah," he said, his hips following Pete's withdrawal. He was so intent on not losing contact that he rose up on his toes. "Yeah, suck the head."

Pete sucked it, his tongue just visible as it swirled hard around the swollen tip. Jack didn't know what Dave was doing with the bottle—assuming he had the presence of mind to do anything— but Whittier began uttering high little cries as if she couldn't contain herself.

Pete reached for her, sliding his hand up her quivering body to squeeze her breast. This, in turn, excited Dave. He used his free hand to knead his balls while Pete began to bob more steadily along his length. Dave's cock went dark with the treatment, the veins swollen enough to see all around.

"No coming," Pete ordered Dave on a pause to swallow. "Ladies get theirs first."

While Pete recovered his breath, his hands fisted up and down Dave's spit-slippery shaft, stretching it with each sure motion. The audio was crystal clear. Jack couldn't miss the sounds that accompanied the quickening strokes. Callused palms. Laboring lungs. Muffled groans of desire. These two obviously had a history of doing this, and Pete knew what Dave liked. Dave gasped as Pete's mouth covered him once again, his fist going white-knuckled on his own balls.

"Slow-er," he said, some spike in sensation breaking the word. "I can only take a bit more. Then you'll have to stop."

A bit more turned about to be thirty seconds of hard sucking. When Pete released Dave's cock, now throbbing and red with need, Whittier truly was crying.

The sobs got harder when Dave removed the bottle's neck. Clucking with sympathy, Pete rose and kissed her on the mouth, his cheeks hollowing with eagerness. Dave followed suit, his very aroused body brushing hers. Whittier squirmed at that, but Dave held most of his weight away from her by bracing his hands on the wine rack to which she was tied. Their kiss was longer than hers and Pete's, but at last Dave let her go.

"Now?" she asked hopefully.

"Pick," said Pete, and she seemed to know what he meant.

She looked from one man to the other, comparing their heaving chests and flushed faces before dropping her gaze to their erections. Both were very hard, but Dave looked ready to burst.

"Dave," she said, but with a hint of uncertainty.

"Are you sure?" Pete asked. "He'll be even more desperate if he has to watch us first."

She nodded. "Yes, please, I want him now."

"Told you," Dave said as if he'd won a bet. He hummed in admiration as he parted Whittier's dripping labia with his thumbs. Jack didn't think he'd ever seen a woman quite that wet. Dave laughed as his touch—which was obviously pleasurable but not satisfying—made her cry some more.

"Primed and pretty," he said. "But I think Pete needs to pinch your nipples before I shove in. I'm not convinced they're sharp enough yet."

Pete did as Dave suggested while Whittier wriggled and groaned. Her nipples did get longer—and redder, too. She was panting when Dave positioned himself. Because she was so short, Dave had to bend his knees considerably to find the spot. Jack knew the instant his cockhead touched her, because Dave's buttocks clenched as if they had a cramp.

"Yes," Whittier urged as Dave trembled there. "Oh, God, push in hard."

He pushed, grunting, while she wailed in delight. Jack thought she'd come, but if she had, she wanted more. Dave seemed happy to oblige. Sounds of gratitude broke in her throat as he pounded into her. Bottles rattled in the racks, but none of the trio seemed to care. Pete was fisting himself as he watched them, starting and stopping so he wouldn't shoot. His eyes were glued to the sight of Dave going in and out, to the increasing wildness of his business partner's thrusts. In contrast to when Pete had been going down on him, Dave wasn't even trying to control himself. Faster and harder he went, gripping Whittier's buttocks, lifting her off the floor for easier movement.

Jack sensed that, at that moment, achieving orgasm was the absolute center of Dave's existence.

"Yes," Whittier groaned, her face dark and straining.

Then Dave gave it up and came with her. His shout of climax echoed through the room.

"Jesus," said the one voice Jack had forgotten all about.

He spun around, his face gone equatorial with embarrassment. Rivera had stopped in shock at the door. Jack had never taken a seat. He stood in front of the TV, close enough to have touched it if he reached out. His cock was thick and throbbing, the ache like molten metal between his legs. His zipper felt like it was bent double. He prayed Rivera would be too polite to check him out.

New moans trailed from the speakers. Jack wondered if Pete was taking his turn.

"Um," Rivera said, shifting her mortified attention from the screen to a stack of papers she held in her hand. "I guess this explains all the checks Whittier wrote out to Pete and Dave's Garage. She wasn't getting a lot of tune-ups. She was being blackmailed."

Jack swallowed and hoped his throat would work. For that matter, he hoped his brain would. Rivera must have found Whittier's bank statements in her desk. A responsible chief would want to discuss other alternatives besides blackmail before jumping to conclusions. Unfortunately, right then, Jack didn't think he could pull off responsible.

"I'm going downstairs," he said, determinedly pretending he wasn't hoarse. "I want to see if that wine cellar is in this house. Pack up the rest of the discs. Someone can go over them at the station."

"Right," she said faintly. She looked at the open safe as if it held a nest of snakes. "I'll, uh, box them up while you're gone."

• • •

Jack drove back to the station. To hell with worrying about Rivera watching; he needed to feel in control of something, if only the damn squad car.

His reaction to that recording had been unexpected—overwhelming, in fact. Yes, bondage was a thing for him, but that scene with Whittier and the men had shifted his understanding of himself in some deep and inexplicable way. He'd been aroused by what Pete and Dave had done to each other. He didn't think he wanted to do it himself, but he definitely hadn't minded watching.

The mere idea of people acting out their fantasies in real life had hit him harder than a train.

He'd gone over and over it all the way down the main staircase. Replaying Whittier's cries. Seeing Dave's buttocks tighten as he pistoned into her toward the end. When he found the wine cellar—in the flesh, as it were—he'd been rooted to the floor. The place was spotless, the camera gone. No sign remained that the cellar had been used for anything but storing wine. Still, he'd felt compelled to touch the rack where Whittier had been tied, to stroke the braces up and down with his shaking hands.

Would Frankie have liked being tied in Whittier's place? Would she let Jack wrap those padded leather straps around her slender wrists? If Frankie had promised not to struggle, he knew he'd much rather use his cuffs.

A spasm had gripped his cock at the thought, so sharp he felt like he was coming inside his pants. He could see Frankie so clearly in his imagination, naked, bound, her fingers curling helplessly into her palms. Close to panicked, he'd yanked down his zipper to fist himself, but his hands weren't functioning right. He could barely get his briefs out of his throbbing erection's way. Once he had, six long, hard pulls had been enough to bring him off. The orgasm that burst from him was so strong you'd have thought he'd spent hours working up to it.

He'd had to grit his teeth against his need to moan.

It was kind of climax he only had when he was seriously worked up, the kind that usually took some time with his favorite fantasies to build up to. He was shocked at himself for having it here. He could hardly have done anything less professional.

He cleaned up after himself, then sat for a minute at the tasting table to clear his head.

He'd felt better by the time he returned upstairs to Rivera, too much better maybe—like he'd had a vitamin shot. His groin was humming with aftershocks, still heavy despite being emptied out. It wouldn't have taken much to get him stiff again.

He began to stiffen now as he parked the cruiser at city hall. He popped the trunk and clenched the steering wheel. Without a word, Rivera undid her seatbelt and opened the door. She began unloading the boxes of evidence they'd brought back.

Relieved to have a moment to pull himself together, Jack knew he didn't dare think about what he'd witnessed until he was alone again.

Chapter 6

Without her diner to go to, Frankie hardly knew what to do with herself. She'd slept—but mostly on account of her body going comatose as soon as her butt hit the bed. She woke a few hours later at ten A.M., and immediately felt guilty because, on a normal day, this would have been very late.

"No more normal days for you," she muttered to herself in the roaring shower.

Groggy as she was, the bruises on her hips and backside stumped her until she remembered what she and Mike had been doing before this began. He'd been gripping her really tightly when he humped her against that wall. In spite of everything she'd been through since, her sex went soft and warm at the memory. A pulse began to tap like fingertips between her legs.

Aware of this with the conscious corner of her mind, she soothed the marks with her soapy hands. The lingering tenderness was oddly arousing. Troy was a careful lover. Only occasionally had he been aggressive in bed, usually when she went out of her way to get him going, a feat that rarely required more than a black push-up bra. Even then, he'd never been as rough as Mike.

Well, of course Mike was rough, she scolded herself. *He's an ex-gang member.* Jack West had made a point of telling her that.

Without thinking, she cupped her mound, her fingers sliding back and forth to either side of her swollen clit. She could feel how wet she was even through the soap. Thinking about Mike, and Jack, was turning her on.

Unnerved, she adjusted the water cooler and finished rinsing clean. Criminal or not, she hoped Mike hadn't spent the night sleeping in his car. If he had a car. He'd said he had money for a hotel, but that was before Tish's murder had put a kink in his job prospects. Frankie suspected he'd needed that first paycheck and hoped he hadn't been reduced to sleeping on the beach.

Knowing she wouldn't rest until she found him, Frankie shoved a couple breakfast bars into a backpack and rolled her bike out of the garage. Her dinged-up old Camaro glared at her from beneath its tarp, but cars were for thinking through problems. Bikes—especially when you had to chug up and down hills—were for shutting down your brain until you could actually do something about whatever was worrying you.

Her brain shut down pretty well until she spotted Mike coming out of the Sands Motel, a rundown but popular make-out spot on the edge of town. Frankie didn't know why locals kept coming here for quickies. Everybody knew the Sands did the bulk of their business with horny adulterers and teenagers. But who knew, maybe the hope was that if the guy in the next room over had something to hide, he wouldn't rat on you.

Mike had a room on the lower level next to the parking lot. Ironically enough, as he pulled the door closed behind him, he looked less suspicious than the usual clientele. He was wearing old, faded jeans and a white T-shirt—civvies, she guessed. He looked good in them: ordinary, except for the snake tattoo and the fact that he was incredibly well built. He turned when Frankie's brakes brought her to a squeaking halt.

His reaction wasn't what she expected.

"Hey," he said, breaking into a happy smile. "You're all right, and you're here! I drove by the diner earlier, but they had crime-scene tape across the door."

Being greeted this warmly threw a wrench in her plans to confront him about deceiving her. She rubbed her sweaty palms around the handlebars. "They found the murder weapon in my storeroom."

"Man," he said, sounding genuinely concerned. "I'm sorry to hear that." He jerked his thumb toward his room. "Why don't you come in for a minute and we'll talk."

She meant to say they ought to talk out here, but then he touched her shoulder and kissed her cheek. His lips were soft and he smelled of lime aftershave. The kiss's hint of morning-after shyness made it impossible to insult him by refusing. The best she could do was shut her gaping mouth.

"Let me get your bike," he said. "I've got a pot of crappy drip coffee if you want some."

His room was typical of any roadside motel: small and dingy and just barely clean enough. The latest Harry Potter lay face down and open on the unmade bed. Criminals these days sure had strange reading tastes, though maybe Mike was expressing those tendencies through his failure to protect Harry Potter's spine.

Feeling even more awkward than before, Frankie turned to watch him maneuver her lemon-yellow ten-speed through the door.

He seemed to forget all about the coffee once he had it leaning on the wall.

"My God," he said, looking her up and down. "You are seriously sexy in those shorts."

Frankie looked down at them in surprise. Her bike shorts were plain-old gray, a zillion years old, and streaked somewhat embarrassingly from where she'd perspired around the bicycle's padded seat. Her top was an equally disreputable heavy white jogbra.

"I'm dripping wet!" she said in disgust.

He smiled like a lustful Cheshire cat. "I wish," he said, with a huskiness that made her sex tighten.

She stepped back as he stepped closer. "Men are so weird."

"And women worry way too much about how they smell."

They definitely had their wires crossed here. His grin broadened as he grabbed her beneath the arms, tossed her high enough that she shrieked, then caught her and kissed her with an almost businesslike thoroughness. Far from minding her sweatiness, he held her close enough that she felt each incremental lengthening of his erection against her bare belly. The denim that contained him grew stretched and hot. It was getting very difficult to remember what she'd wanted to talk about—what with the lack of oxygen to her brain and all.

"I'm so glad you came by," he murmured a second before sealing whatever she might have said with his mouth and tongue.

She gave in and let him kiss her senseless, since he was so good at it. Slut that she was lately, soon she was making purring noises into his mouth and running greedy hands up and down his long, muscled back.

"*Do* I smell?" she asked when he broke for air.

He laughed and bent closer. "You smell like pussy," he whispered, and laughed again when she blushed.

Then he carried her into the bathroom and turned on the shower. The tile was fifties-style pink and black.

"Don't worry," he said. "I cleaned the whole stall myself."

This was reassuring until he began to remove her clothes.

"Hey!" she said, trying to reclaim her nonslut status, but he was peeling the jogbra over her head, which led to him sucking on her naked breasts, which led to her forgetting everything except holding the bristly back of his head closer.

He tugged the shorts just as handily down her legs. For some reason, the only response she could think of then was toeing off her shoes.

He pulled back to admire her nakedness.

"Damn," he breathed in praise. He dragged the back of his fingers down the center line of her body. When he reached her pubis, he cupped it and slid one finger inside her at the same time. When the finger began to move, Frankie had to catch his arms to keep her balance. She truly was dripping wet now.

Feeling her reaction, his eyes lifted and locked on hers. "I've been dreaming about how tight you were ever since the last time I was inside you."

His gaze was so intense it embarrassed her. "I shouldn't be doing this."

"No?" His thumb started moving, too. He was dragging it down the length of her clit toward where his longest finger stroked. When that almost came out of her, he pushed both digits the opposite way. The trick stole every scrap of starch from her spine. All she could do was bite her lip and try not to moan. "Let me tell you, Frankie, I've done lots of things I shouldn't have."

The shower and she both being warm now, he lifted her into spray. He tore off his own clothes in record time—even for a guy—and stepped in after her. The curtain he yanked shut was pink, the stall just big enough to leave a foot between them. Frankie simply had to look him over. His erection shuddered with the blood that was pumping through it, its thickness somehow more impressive in the light of day. When he reached back out and grabbed a condom from a strip on the top of the toilet tank, there was no mistaking what he intended to happen next.

"Mike," she said, but he was such a beautiful animal, so male and aroused, that it was hard to object any more than that.

Certainly, Mike wasn't in the mood for objections. His hands slapped the dripping tile on either side of her head, effectively caging her.

He was leaning closer, almost doing a push-up on the wall. Frankie had an urge to bark at him to "give me ten," but he wasn't smiling or playful now. His face was as hard as the rest of him, not angry but definitely serious. Maybe she should have been frightened, but all she could feel was amazingly aroused. Her thighs were taut with anticipation, her nipples beaded up like stones. From the corner of her eye, she saw his tattoo flex on his bunching arm.

"I know you have a record," she gasped out.

His eyes went flat, and, for a moment, she was frightened.

"That cop told you."

"Yes."

He pushed an inch farther away from her and stopped. "I was seventeen," he said, the words coming out crisp and clear. "I did a deal with the DA to go into the Marines instead of serving time. I've kept my nose clean ever since."

Water streamed off his shoulders and onto her. He wasn't moving; he was just holding her with that challenging stare. Her neck felt stiff from tipping it back to see his face.

"Uh-huh," she said, because some response seemed required.

A muscle jumped in his jaw. "I'm sure you can guess why I didn't tell you."

"You thought I wouldn't hire you if I knew."

"Would you have?"

"Maybe," she said, honestly enough.

"Fuck." Beside her ear, he curled his right hand into a fist. She didn't know if he was cursing her answer, his choice to hold back the truth, or maybe the inequity of life in general. Whatever the reason for his anger, she reached for his wrist before he could punch the wall and hurt himself.

With the same instinct that had told her to hire him in the first place, she knew he'd rather split his knuckles than strike her.

"Don't," she said. "I won't fire you just for that."

"Yeah, but you won't trust me again, either. Not like before."

His eyes held raw, youthful despair. She cupped his face in one hand. "I must trust you some. I am naked in your shower."

He cursed again, but she felt the angry tension leave his arms. He was looking down now, at her body and breasts sparkling with spray. The cheap pink curtain cast a glow over their bodies, deepening the flush already on their skin. His prick was downright rosy and as hard and hungry as it had been last night. Groaning, he dropped his forehead to hers. "If I had any pride, I'd tell you take your pity and get the hell out of here."

Frankie smiled and slid her hands down his sides to his waist. Her thumbs fanned forward over sleek, tanned skin, reaching toward his navel. His breathing deepened flatteringly at the touch. "You could go yourself."

"Don't want to," he mumbled, his knees beginning to bend. They sidled hers apart, his hold moving down her back to her bottom. "I'm still too hard up, and you're still too pretty."

She thought he was pretty, too. She found his hardness and stroked it, loving the way it flexed and throbbed beneath her caress. When she drew all five fingers together over his tip, he shivered in enjoyment. "I could kiss you here, the way you wouldn't let me last night."

He shook his head, apparently still not trusting his hair trigger. "I want to be inside you. I want your cunt sucking hard at me."

But he didn't move to make it happen. He stood there letting her stroke him, stiff and ready, restlessly shifting his weight from foot to foot while his palms massaged her buttocks in slow circles. Was he waiting for her to give him permission? She moved her hands to stroke his chest soothingly. At that, he spoke.

"Frankie?" he said. "You don't think I killed her, do you?"

"Please." She used her best you-must-be-kidding tone. "If I thought that, I wouldn't be here. No matter how hot you are."

He smiled at the compliment, water-dotted lashes shuttering his eyes. Then he lifted her in one quick motion. His strength and aim were admirable. With her legs clinging to his hips, he turned her to the wall that had no knobs, tilted his pelvis, and pressed her back into the tile. His erection slid straight into her, slow but sure. His low, soft moan told her how good the penetration felt to him. Frankie had lost her breath, but she held on tight.

"One more push will do it," he whispered, and swivelled and pressed again.

It took two more pushes, but that was fine. Frankie kissed him once he was in, his weight trapping her easily. Secured as she was, she was free to run her palms up and down his spine. She could tell he liked that, but rather than begin to thrust, he just shoved deeper and groaned. The sound seemed to contain an actual bit of pain. Frankie hummed in question.

"My thighs are stiff from last night," he confessed. "I'm afraid they're going to give out."

And here she'd been thinking Marines were do-it-standing-up machines. "There *is* a bed in the other room."

He made a face that said he didn't think that was very creative. Instead, he dropped a towel on the closed toilet seat, stepped out of the stall, and sat on the john with her still attached to him. Happily, her legs were long enough to reach the fresh-scrubbed floor. She was immediately more comfortable.

"Mm," she said, wriggling around him to get used to this new position. "That's better."

He thought so, too, or maybe he just liked that she'd eased up and got hotter. He swelled inside her to fill up every smidgen of extra room.

"I can touch you when we're like this," he said, his hands cruising up to find and shape her breasts. "I can watch you while you ride me." His voice got deeper and softer. "There's a mirror on the door behind you. Your little ass is the sexiest thing I've ever seen. The only thing that could make me happier is if I could bite it while we make love."

Frankie laughed at how easy men sometimes were to get going. Mike was a change from Troy, anyway, who might have been more interested in his own reflection.

Pleased with her current partner, she smoothed her hands across his shoulders, wishing she knew the names of all his fine muscles.

"You might be surprised to hear this," she said, "but I know a few more ways to make you happy than getting bitten."

She rose up from his lap until his cock nearly left her body, the rim of him tugging at her pussy's mouth. Then—in a twist on the usual sort of pole dancing—she spiraled her hips around him as she sank down.

When she tightened her sheath as well, his eyes nearly crossed.

"Uh," he said, one hand leaving her breast to curve around her bottom. "Yeah, uh, if you could do that again, that would be good."

She did it until sweat glittered on his forehead and he gasped for breath. She did it until her thighs told her she'd be sorry tomorrow. It was fun to watch him go all flushed and quivery, but he must have known the trick was doing more for him than it was for her.

"Boy," he breathed, gripping her tighter with both arms. "I think that's all I can take before I explode. Hold on. I'm going to tip you back on the floor."

He was too sure of himself for her to object. Without jostling her in the least, he laid her down on another towel, then rearranged her legs so her feet were braced—one on the opening of the shower and one on the opposite pink-tiled wall. Then he flattened his palm on the mirrored door behind her and began to pump.

She groaned at the instant increase in feeling. Flipping his switch had gotten her readier than she'd realized.

"Oh, yeah," he said, switching angles to rub against her a little higher. It felt so good she gasped and clutched his back. "Pull at me, Frankie. Pull at my cock and show me how much you want me here."

She couldn't have stopped herself from doing it to save her life. She squeezed him with her inner muscles and rocked up at him with her hips until they both began to make desperate noises. Oh, she needed this, if only to erase the events that had ended their other night. Clearly, he shared her urgency, though with the lack of floor space, neither had much room. His thrusts were short and quick—uneven, she thought, until she realized he was doing it on purpose. Maybe he only meant to keep himself from the edge, so he could last until she was done, but the choppy rhythm did the same for her. She couldn't go over without a hard, steady stroke.

Groaning, she tried not to gouge his back with her nails.

The sound of their flesh slapping together echoed off the tiles.

"Close?" he asked, the shorthand of breathlessness.

"Yes." She answered through gritted teeth, his thundering heart telling her how close he was.

"Faster?" he gasped.

"And deeper," she moaned. "Please."

He cursed, but he shifted his knees and found a way to do it. Pleasure charged into her with every thrust, deeper, sweeter. Then, in one of those rare new-lover moments, they both crashed over at the same time. The orgasm took hold of her and shook her for at least a minute, her hips shaking close and tight against his.

His groans of pleasure were a long, low song.

When it was over, he didn't have room to collapse. He pulled himself from her body, sighed, and heaved himself back onto the toilet. Frankie realized his jeans and T-shirt were pillowing her head. She pushed them into a more comfortable position and smiled up at him. His cock was flaccid, wet from having worn the rubber, but still interesting to look at.

"You ruined my shower," she observed. "Now I need another one."

He snorted and smiled back. "You're a hell of a woman, Frankie Smith."

She twinkled at him. "What a nice thing to say!"

"I'm trying not to get fired."

"I wouldn't worry about that. You're a hell of a cook."

He took her lolling foot from the wall, put it in his lap, and began to rub her arch. His hand was strong and warm. Frankie's insides began to tingle pleasantly. "So . . . I've got a second chance?"

"Just don't keep things from me that, as your employer, I have a right to know."

"As my employer," he repeated and kissed her toes.

"I am kind of on the rebound," she said, sensing she'd hurt his feelings.

"Right. So we're not starting anything serious."

"Right," she agreed, a little surprised that she meant it.

He seemed okay with her answer, though she knew with some men it was hard to tell.

"Do you need an advance on your pay?" she asked. "Until the diner opens up again?"

His chuckle was soft and wry. "You know," he said, wagging her foot back and forth, "as my employer, right this minute might not be the most appropriate time to offer me money."

Chapter 7

Pete and Dave's Garage appeared abandoned. Glad he'd left Rivera back at the department, Jack ducked under the half-lowered door to the central bay and looked around. Someone's tomato-red Hummer was on the hydraulic lift, with a pan of dirty motor oil sitting on the dropcloth beneath it. Tires were stacked by the wall, parts in boxes, tools old and new. The greasy wall clock said twelve fifteen, so maybe Pete and Dave were out to lunch.

Yeah, Jack thought, willing his unaccustomed nerves to settle. *And maybe they've lined up a nooner with someone's wife. Maybe that Hummer's owner is getting her own lube job in the back.*

As if to confirm the theory, something metallic clattered from the direction of the walled offices. Jack drew his gun, pointed it at the ceiling, and went silently toward the sound. Better safe than sorry, he figured, though he didn't bother radioing for backup.

He passed the front office with the windows—which was empty—and continued down a dim cinder-block hall to a door marked PRIVATE. NO ENTRY. Despite the warning, the door wasn't closed. Light angled outward through the gap, gold on the concrete floor. A shadow moved, causing Jack to tense, but the movement was followed by a groan that had him rolling his eyes and putting up his piece. That groan had nothing to do with robbery and everything to do with sex.

He had walked in on a nooner, after all. As it turned out, though, the participants weren't quite who he thought. It sounded like Pete and Dave were going it alone.

"Right there," he heard Dave praise with great sincerity. "Oh, yeah, keep your cock going right *there*."

"You need more lube?" Pete gasped. "You feel kind of tight."

"Just do it. Just go. You're running right over the good spot. Oh, fuck. Oh, Jesus. I'm gonna blow."

Except Dave didn't blow. He groaned some more and encouraged Pete some more, and Jack began to wonder just how embarrassing it would be to interrupt. He could leave and come back, he supposed, but there could conceivably be some benefit to catching them in the afterglow.

"You better come soon," Pete said in a tight, tense tone. "I'm getting way too close to keep this up."

"Five more minutes," Dave pleaded. "I'm all uptight from the news. I want to come hard today."

"Five more—! That's it." Pete's tone was pure disgust. "I'm wanking you in my fist. We've got a job to get back to."

"No!" Dave said, but flesh slapped flesh and his moans got louder and higher in pitch. Apparently, the threatened wanking was effective. Soon Pete's grunts and cries joined the sound of thrusting, which was obviously speeding up.

"Oh, God," said Dave, and, "Oh, fuck," said Pete, and then the cacophony really let loose.

It sounded as if they were doing it over a metal desk, and that they were now screwing so violently its legs had begun to squeak. Something else clanked to the floor in the frenzy, after which their breath burst from them in explosive huffs. The noise could not be mistaken for anything but climactic extremity. One of them—Dave, he thought—murmured something prayerful. Finally, everything was quiet except for them trying to get their lungs to work right again.

"Man," Pete panted. "You're too horny for your own good. It's not like we aren't getting any. We really shouldn't need to do this every damn afternoon."

The complaint held a note of admiration. Before Dave could respond with his own endearment, Jack rapped his knuckles on the door frame.

"Chief West," he said as sternly as he could manage. "Six Palms P.D. I need to talk to you two."

"Shit," Dave hissed. "Where are my pants?"

Jack gave him time to find them and himself time to compose his imperturbable cop face. Even with the delay, his breathing was a little shallower than it ought to be. Luckily, Pete and Dave were more uncomfortable than he was.

They were also sweaty and red-faced, and the desk they'd just been lying over looked like it had been shoved around by an earthquake. Evidently, when these two went at it, they didn't do things halfway. A puddle of something Jack didn't want to know about was dampening a stack of receipts that had slipped to the floor.

"This isn't what it looks like," Dave said. "We're not gay."

"Oh, for God's sake," Pete snapped out, as if this were an old argument. "What do you care what it's called?"

"But we're not," Dave said and crossed his arms.

They both wore navy "Pete and Dave's Garage" uniforms. The clothes made them look more alike than usual, two pervy peas in a grease monkey pod. Pete made a face at Jack as if to say, "What can you do with these guys?" Jack rubbed his brow. Despite his best efforts, he suspected he did not have the upper hand. Hoping to reclaim it, he pulled out his official notebook.

"Look," he said. "I need to talk to you about Tish Whittier."

"Oh," said Dave. "We heard about that on the radio. Totally sad. We were, um, kind of cheering each other up. For a second there, I thought you were arresting us for sodomy."

"Unless you were doing it while you strangled her, I really don't give a damn."

"While we—Hey!" Pete looked aggrieved. "We *liked* Tish. She was our friend."

"Yeah? Then why were you blackmailing her?"

"What?" said Pete and Dave at the same time.

"We found regular payments from her account to your garage and a rather incriminating DVD of her having sex with you and a wine bottle. I'm willing to bet she didn't want that getting out at the country club."

"She paid us to record that," Pete said. "It was her idea."

"Everything was her idea," Dave added earnestly. "She said women would love being seduced by two men. She said we'd be swimming in pussy if we worked as a team. She even said some of them would, you know, enjoy watching us get it on together. Before that, we'd never tried that stuff."

Pete shot him a disapproving look. "You thought about it before she brought it up. You used to check me out every time I took off my shirt."

"All guys do that. It's like when you're standing at the urinal, and you want to know how you measure up."

"Guys," said Jack, deciding he'd better cut this short. "Can you actually prove that making those DVDs was Whittier's idea?"

"Actually," said Pete. "We can." He hunkered down and pulled open the bottom drawer of a putty-colored file cabinet. He removed a plain manila folder and handed it to Jack. "She drew up a contract so we'd all have some protection. She wanted everybody to understand the rules."

"Well," said Jack, feeling blindsided. "That was bizarrely responsible." He flipped through the pages, noting the signatures and date. "This says she keeps all copies of the recordings."

"Right," said Pete.

"And you never snuck one for yourselves? Maybe put the squeeze on another of your lovers for extra cash?"

"If we'd done that," Dave said with a sharpness Jack didn't expect from him, "wouldn't someone have tried to kill *us*?"

He had a point, but this whole thing was such a tangle, it didn't mean they had no motive. Who knew what other scams these three had going?

"I need to know where you were," he said, "last night between seven P.M. and two."

The two looked at each other. "We drove down to Dana Point. Spent the night with a friend."

"A female friend," Dave interjected.

"We might still have gas receipts."

"I wish we *had* been with Tish," Dave added mournfully. "Maybe she'd be alive."

"Tish was nice," Pete said.

This seemed to be the one thing everyone agreed about, though it didn't rule her out as a blackmailer. Jack smacked the folder that contained the contract across his palm. With secrets like these hidden under her kitten-soft, charity-princess exterior, chances were no one had known Tish Whittier as well as they'd thought. Jack was going to have to view all her recordings. See who else might have been embarrassed by her activities.

He would have felt better if he hadn't, in some depraved corner of his soul, been looking forward to the show.

"We didn't judge her," Pete said, maybe thinking he saw a re-proof for her in Jack's face. "Everyone has their kinks."

No kidding, Jack thought with a wry grimace toward his notes. He was beginning to wonder just how many of his own kinks he'd come face to face with before this was through.

Dewey and Rivera were eating lunch on the steps of city hall, facing the long green rectangle of Six Palms Park. They weren't talking, but their body language was comfortable—if a little tired. Jack was glad to see them pulling together. When he was close enough, Dewey tossed him a burger from a fast-food franchise that was a fifteen-minute drive away. Rivera was picking at a fruit cup she didn't seem to think much of.

"We'd better solve this fast," Dewey said, his cheek bulging with his latest bite. "I'm already missing those All U Can Eat mesquite fries."

"Chicken salad," Rivera sighed, "on a nice fresh bed of greens."

Jack stifled a laugh and sat. "What did you find out in Santa Barbara?"

Enjoying his moment in the spotlight, Dewey wiped his mouth ceremoniously on his napkin. "First," he said, "remind me never to be volunteered for anything like that again!"

"You run into traffic?" Rivera cooed in mock sympathy.

"I ran into parents, and a more clueless pair you could not find. I don't think I've ever met anyone more ignorant of the basic facts about someone they gave birth to. They had no idea their daughter was on the boards of six charities, they were 'certain' she didn't have a boyfriend, and they couldn't name a single one of her girl chums—with the exception of 'that pushy Ellis girl whose father was a car salesman.' The mother, who by the way had more plastic surgery than Cher, insisted Ellis wasn't a friend at all, merely an 'old acquaintance.' Worst of all, they didn't cry."

Jack sat straighter. "They didn't cry?"

"I informed them their daughter was dead—used my best funeral home manners, too—and all they did was say, 'oh, dear, how?'"

"Did they seem relieved she was dead?"

"They seemed like they were on too many prescription meds. I'm pretty sure the work gene skipped their generation. They've left the vineyards management to an outside firm. The last two years weren't so good for them profit-wise, but the manager claimed that's turning around."

"Did the downturn affect their daughter?"

"Not so far as I could tell." Finished with his burger, Dewey brushed crumbs from his shirt and thighs. "Whittier's trust fund came from both grandfathers. Apparently, it was too big to run through even if she tried. I've got my contact at the bank checking how it was set up, see if maybe the parents could have been embezzling, but—honestly—I think they're just tools.

"It makes me mad," Dewey confessed. "Whittier's parents ought to be busting on us to find whoever killed their daughter. Instead, we have to bust on ourselves."

"We did get some preliminary findings from the lab," Rivera said, as if to prove *she* was self-motivated. "Estimated time of death is one thirty A.M., shortly before she was found. Death by strangulation, from behind and slightly above like I thought. The ME can't say if it's a male or female perp, but somebody with good upper body strength. There was some fiber transfer from that angora top Whittier was wearing to the hose, and he says we'll probably find more on whatever the doer was wearing at the time. He says angora is as good as cat hair for hanging on."

Dewey nudged Rivera's shoulder. "Tell him the best part."

Rivera broke into a grin that made her look more girlish than she would have liked had she known. "Our vic probably had sex no more than an hour before she died. Consensual, it looks like, because there's no bruising, but whoever it was didn't wear his overcoat. His little swimmers were still sprightly. I mean, the donor isn't necessarily the one who killed her, but it would be good to have a Last Seen By."

"It would," Jack agreed. He bit into his burger and chewed thoughtfully. There could, of course, be more than one donor. He didn't necessarily disbelieve Team Boys' story about spending the night in Dana Point, but it might be handy to have their DNA on file. Gas receipts could be faked a heck of a lot easier than genetic material.

With this in mind, he shared what he'd discovered at the garage. Dewey listened with lifted brows.

"So Pete and Dave are swinging at everything that's pitched their way," he mused. "Male or female."

"I believe as far as males go, they're only swinging at each other," Jack said. "But that's just a guess."

"Maybe they thought Whittier was going to out them as fancy fruits."

Jack shrugged. Dave had seemed uptight about his sexual identification—whatever it was—but not enough to kill someone. What concerned him more was that Dewey was surprised by the news of Pete and Dave's relationship. This could only mean Rivera hadn't told him about the discs they'd found at Whittier's house.

"Why don't you grab a kit?" he said to Dewey now. "We'll head back to the garage and see if they'll agree to give a voluntary DNA swab."

Rivera seemed to know why Jack had sent Dewey off. She clutched her knees and stared at a pint-sized skateboarder who was swooping like a surfer around the park sidewalks.

"Dewey's part of the team," Jack said once they were private.

"You can't keep important evidence from him just because you know he'll have obnoxious things to say."

Rivera hung her head. "I know, boss. I just couldn't face it today."

"You're not going to be working in Six Palms forever. At least, I don't think you will. Dewey's nothing compared to some of the men you'd have to deal with in a big department. He might be a jerk to you now and then, but I think you know he'd never cross the line beyond that. It's not fair, but sometimes a woman on the force has to suck it up."

Rivera stood and frowned at her sensible black cop shoes. "I know," she said. "It's just sometimes . . . being a woman really sucks."

Jack let her go without comment. Her mood was darker than he understood. Maybe because she was a woman she was identifying with the victim. Maybe she didn't like the suggestion that she wouldn't always work for him. Asking which wasn't a good idea, considering Jack wanted her to keep a safe emotional distance.

I need a nap, he thought, sagging back to let his elbows rest on the steps.

To his dismay, he immediately thought of sharing one with Frankie Smith.

Chapter 8

After she left Mike's hotel room, Frankie felt simultaneously wired and exhausted, as if she'd been at a long, noisy party and didn't know how to settle now that she was alone.

When a slice of sapphire-blue ocean caught her eye at an intersection, she turned her bike toward the public beach. She locked it at a stand, pulled off her shoes, and stepped across the boardwalk to the sun-warmed sand. The long, crescent-shaped beach was empty except for a mother and daughter digging a fort farther on. Frankie was glad for the solitude. At the edge of the water, she dug her toes in and heaved a sigh.

Squeezed between two stone jetties, the Pacific foamed and rolled like a quiet monster hissing at her feet. As she stood there, watching, listening, her body pulsed from its recent tryst. The warmth low in her belly was impossible to mistake for anything but arousal.

She'd thought her mind was empty, but as the ocean soothed

her, she realized she was thinking about Jack West, about the way he'd patted her down in the alleyway. She could practically feel him doing it that very moment, as if her brain cells weren't the only place that stored memories. The looming warmth and height of him behind her had been a kind of threat, a threat she found oddly relaxing now. The careful passage of his hands seemed imprinted on every single nerve of her back.

She couldn't help wondering what it would be like to sleep with a man that physically imposing.

You're looking for distractions, she told herself. *You don't want to dwell on Tish or Troy, so you've decided you're going to lust after every man you meet.* It was a Thanatos/Eros thing. Life surging up in the midst of death. No way had she given Mike the brush-off because she thought she might want to stay available for the chief.

Not sure she believed this, Frankie frowned at the wave that had just rolled across her ankles. It was cold and gritty and made her want to step back. She looked up the shoreline. Troy's beach house wasn't too far from where she stood.

Though Troy had been living with Frankie for the last five years, he'd never given up the slightly ramshackle house he'd bought with money he'd earned modeling. The place was a salty, wind-scoured, shingle box, with a little wooden porch whose steps led straight to the sand. It was too square and plain for Frankie's taste, but she'd understood Troy's need to have a sanctuary of his own. Although he usually was cheerful and easygoing, Troy did have a broody side—thoughts and feelings he didn't share with anyone. Frankie respected this. She liked privacy herself.

Of course, the first time he'd cheated on her—he'd had two brief affairs that she knew of before Karen—Frankie had thought very seriously about encouraging him to sell. She knew having his own house made it easier for him to keep secrets, and the last thing she'd wanted was for anyone, herself included, to think of her as an easy mark. In the end, though, she decided asking him to give it up wouldn't gain her anything. He'd confessed, he'd apologized, and he'd asked sincerely for another chance. She either gave it to him or she didn't. If she tried to keep him on too tight a leash, he'd resent it. In fact, knowing Troy, he'd probably use it as an excuse to stray.

She shook her head. For all her supposedly mature decisions, she'd ended up in the same place.

Sometimes a woman couldn't win for losing.

Oh, poor thing, she scoffed at herself. It wasn't as if someone had murdered *her* . . . or her best friend.

Reminded of Karen, and the person whose shoulder she'd likely be crying on, Frankie realized she ought to check in with Troy. If the news of Tish's murder hadn't reached him yet, someone needed to tell him, if only to give him a chance to prepare himself to support Karen. The thought of being the "someone" who did this made her feel slightly ill, but she knew it was the right thing to do.

Her mother would have done it without a second thought.

God, God, God, she prayed as tramped determinedly across the dunes. *Help me do this like a decent human being should. Don't let me get angry. This is so not about me.*

To her surprise, Troy was sitting on his weathered porch steps, rocking back and forth and weeping into his hands with the heartfelt openness of a kid who'd lost his dog. Troy had known Tish, of course. She and Karen had been inseparable. But Frankie hadn't realized her death would hit him this hard. Maybe she'd underestimated how attached to people her ex could get.

"Hey," she said.

He lifted his head, gasping for air through his sobs. When he saw who it was, his face crumpled. "Oh, God," he cried, a naked picture of despair. "What am I going to do?"

"Oh, baby," she crooned, squeezing up close beside him to hug his back. "You're going to do what you have to. You're going to be there for her."

His mouth fell open, and he blinked at her with red-rimmed eyes. He didn't look like a supermodel then. Mostly, he looked confused.

"Honey." She gave him another squeeze. "I know Karen is pregnant. When she hears about Tish, it's bound to be bad. She'll have . . . extra hormones and things."

"You know she's pregnant?"

"Well, I know that can't be the only reason you're marrying her, but, yes, I did put two and two together."

Troy swallowed and seemed to gather himself. "I love kids," he said, with a hint of defensiveness Frankie didn't understand. "I always thought I'd want a few someday."

Frankie looked at the hand she'd clenched unconsciously on her thigh. Funny how he'd never felt seriously enough to mention his love of kids to her. *This isn't about you*, she reminded herself. *Keep your mind on the cute and probably really nice baby that two-faced bitch is going to have.*

"Right," she said, trying to focus. "You're bound to be a good daddy, you being so mellow and all. So you just have to forget how sad you are and help Karen get through this."

"I don't know if I can," Troy whispered.

Frankie took his face in her hands. "*I* know you can. Think about it, Troy. Wouldn't Tish want you to take care of her best friend? Wouldn't she want you to be strong for Karen's kid?"

Troy's blue eyes welled up again. "Yes," he said huskily. "Tish had the biggest heart of anyone I know."

Frankie let him go. "So you know what you have to do."

Troy looked down, took a breath, and then looked back up. "Will you help me?" he asked, the barest, most unabashed plea she'd ever heard a grown man make.

"Troy . . ." she said, already shaking her head.

"I know. It isn't fair to ask you. I broke up with you—and in kind of a shitty way—but I really, really need you to still be my friend right now."

"Then I am," she said, ignoring the way her stomach clenched. "Just don't expect me to organize a baby shower."

He laughed shakily and wiped his face with both hands. Then, before she realized what he meant to do, he pulled her into a lung-squeezing hug. "I love you," he said, low and rough. "I really, really do. Even if you end up not being able to keep your promise, I'll never forget you agreed."

Frankie returned the hug just as tightly, a tear slipping down her cheek as something snarled and ugly inside her loosened just a bit.

Naturally, Karen showed up right then.

"Troy?" she said, no more than five feet away on the sand. Her face was streaked with drying tears. She looked pale and small in her bright fuchsia power suit, drained of the energy that made her a powerhouse.

She looks haunted, Frankie thought. *As if she knows her life will never be the same.*

Troy pushed back with a curse.

"We weren't—" he said, sounding guilty despite there having been nothing sexual about the hug. "Frankie came over to tell me about Tish, but I'd already heard. I . . . I guess you did, too."

"It was on the radio." Karen's voice was strange. Floaty. As she distractedly pushed back her hair, her eyes went from Troy to Frankie. "I heard it on my way to show a house."

Recalling how she'd found out seemed to suck the last of her strength. She staggered, going to her knees in the sand. Troy froze for a second, then jumped up to help her. They both ended up kneeling with Karen sobbing on Troy's shoulder. He looked back at Frankie helplessly. Not wanting anything to do with this, Frankie rose and swiped sand off her bottom.

"I'll, uh, be going," she said. "You can—" No, she shouldn't say Troy could call her if he wanted to talk. That was bound to put Karen on edge. "I'll . . . I'll be around."

Telling Karen she was sorry for her loss didn't seem quite right, either, so she left without saying more. The sense that she shouldn't do this, that she'd forgotten something, made her look back a dozen steps later. Karen was clinging to Troy, her face hidden in his shoulder. It wasn't a pose she'd ever expected to see the real estate mogul in. Though Troy stroked Karen's back, he was watching Frankie. *Numb* was the only word she had for his expression. Feeling awkward, she gave him a half-wave and continued on.

Still friends or not, he was going to have to handle this on his own.

Jack didn't get his nap for another three long hours, which were pretty evenly split between calming the mayor and handling the media. Because of Tish's connection to the famous Whittier winery, the murder was now national news.

While talking to reporters wasn't Jack's favorite thing, he could do it. He was reasonably confident he'd balanced the need to keep their progress under wraps with assuring people they were making progress—or, as the mayor succinctly put it, "For God's sake, Jack, don't let them think we're sitting out here with our thumbs up our butts!"

Knowing he couldn't function much longer without some

shut-eye, Jack stretched out on the brown pile carpet in his office and closed his eyes. Since he lay on his back, he wouldn't sleep more than an hour—a trick that had served him well in the past.

The only problem was, sleeping on his back didn't guarantee he wouldn't dream.

Per usual, Frankie was the star attraction of the one he had. She was dressed like Betty Boop in a heart-shaped neckline and short, ruffled skirt. With the logic only dreams could have, she was waiting for him in the back of Pete and Dave's Garage.

"Give me a kiss," she said in a high, sweet cartoon voice, "and I'll show you what I've got under my skirt."

When she pointed to the right side of her face, he gave her an obedient peck.

"Oh, my," she said, the Betty Boop voice falling away. "Your lips are soft as silk."

He looked at the desk behind her, at the scatter of papers across the top. He remembered what Pete and Dave had used it for. His cock got so hard it hurt.

"You need to be tied," he rasped. "I can't take you unless you're tied."

She wagged her brows at him, but she turned and bent her torso over the desk.

"How's this?" she asked cheekily.

She flipped up her polka-dotted skirt. She had nothing under it but her. The sight of her naked bottom mesmerized him. It was so pretty, so round and feminine. It took a moment before he noticed pink satin ties had magically appeared on her outspread legs and wrists, a stretchy web that bound her to the desk without hurting her.

"Oh, God," he said, his breath coming almost too hard to say the words. "That's absolutely perfect."

He dug his cock out from his trousers as she twisted her head over her shoulder to watch. Her eyes glowed like green Christmas lights and the stretchy webbing doubled, now criss-crossing her back and hips.

"Stroke yourself," she said. "I can't touch you, but I want you as big and hard as you can get."

He stroked himself, first with one hand and then with two, until he was as big as one of those crazy Aubrey Beardsley illustrations where men carted their pricks around in wheelbarrows. His size didn't matter. Somehow he knew she'd take him—just as he knew he wouldn't come until she did. He could stroke himself all he wanted and he'd hold on.

"A little more," she urged breathlessly.

He had to stretch his arms to reach the hugely swollen knob. A great drop of pre-come slicked the action of his busily rubbing hands. He slid his hold to mid-shaft, tipping himself down to show her the results.

"Oh, good!" she said. If her hands had been free, he knew she would have clapped. "Now come give me another kiss."

The way she wiggled her bottom in the webbing told him where she wanted the kiss to go. He knelt behind her, between her legs, his huge erection pressing between him and the desk. He tugged it higher until somehow, impossibly, it and his mouth touched her sex. Her whimpers urged him onward. He licked her, then sucked her, his lips finding the slick swelling of her clit. Suddenly she smelled so good a spasm of pleasure tightened in his balls. He groaned with pain and desire.

He'd thought he could hold out, but maybe he was wrong. Maybe he was going to spill right now.

"Hurry," she gasped, sensing what was happening. "You've got to be inside me before you come."

He leaped to his feet and pressed the great head against her. It began to slide into her tight, humid passage. She moaned with greed as it did. Fire licked over him—his, hers—in ever-increasing waves. He had to push. He had to get all the way inside her now. His clothes were gone, and he was naked. His bare feet dug into the floor for the big effort . . .

"Excuse me," said a sharp female voice.

He shuddered, his mind trying to fit the intrusion into his dream.

"Excuse me!"

With the second shudder, Jack's eyes snapped open. Jesus, was his subconscious ever perverse! Still trying to push off the dream, he sat up much too quickly for the current state of his groin. He fought to hide a wince.

"Chief West," said the familiar-looking woman standing at his door. She had her hands on her hips and was wearing a crisp black linen suit.

"Sorry," he said through his froggy throat. "Long day. Just grabbing forty winks. It's Ms. Ellis, isn't it?"

"Karen," she said in a softer tone. "I'm sorry to interrupt your rest, but there's something I really need to speak to you about."

With a muffled groan, he creaked to his feet and took the old metal swivel chair behind his desk. He didn't usually use the desk as a barrier, but considering the hard-on he was sporting, it seemed like a good idea.

It was difficult to get the citizenry to respect you when they caught you on the floor of your office dreaming about sex.

Ellis smoothed her skirt behind her thighs and took one of his two green visitor chairs.

One thing Jack had learned over the years was that grief took everyone differently. Ellis looked pale and a little shocky. He restrained his urge to offer her orange juice. Instead, he folded his hands and waited for her to speak. After shifting in the chair and crossing her legs, she did.

"I don't know if you know this," she began, "but Tish Whittier and I were close friends."

Keeping his mouth shut was working so far so he decided to stick with it.

"I knew her very, very well. Ever since high school, we told each other everything." Ellis looked down to brush a bit of nothing off her skirt, clearly gathering herself for something difficult. She pressed her lips together before facing him again. "I don't think anyone *could* have killed her. Tish didn't have enemies. She wasn't afraid of anyone. She wasn't involved in anything shady."

She held his eyes earnestly, willing him to believe, and Jack did his best to keep his face expressionless. Whatever Ellis's claims, he had no trouble imagining Whittier would keep her and Team Boys' activities to herself. He was going on looks and manner alone here, but Karen Ellis didn't strike him as a nonjudgmental friend.

He tapped the top of his desk. A little prodding seemed in order. "You're saying you don't think your friend was murdered?"

"I'm saying I don't think Tish was the intended victim."

Jack raised his brows for her to go on.

"I know it might sound crazy, even self-engrossed, but I think the killer meant to murder me. Tish and I look a good deal alike and . . . and I was supposed to be there."

"Behind Frankie's diner."

She nodded in gratitude. "I lost my sunglasses there. People heard me talking about it. They're nice Louis Vuittons with diamonds on the earpieces. I could have replaced them, but I wanted to check myself."

He leaned back in his chair. "You wanted to check the diner for your sunglasses at one in the morning."

She flushed, and he thought there might have been a touch of anger in the reaction.

"I'm a night owl," she said. "I wasn't thinking about the time. I knew Frankie sometimes stays late to clean up. I thought I'd drive by and see and if she was there."

"But you didn't drive by."

"Tish and I had dinner together. Girl talk. Wedding talk. She offered to go past the diner on her way home."

Jack chewed his lip and mulled this over. It could be true. The maid had said Whittier went out around six, but they hadn't had a chance to track her movements beyond that. If she had done Ellis this favor, it would provide at least a slim excuse for being where she was.

"Where was your fiancé during all this?"

This question made Ellis stiffen. "He was in his beach house. Sleeping, I'm sure."

Jack nodded and made a mental note to check this out—and to get a report from Dewey and Rivera on whether Troy was part of Whittier's DVD collection. He'd been thinking the subjects would all be women, but considering what he now knew about Pete and Dave's erotic flexibility, maybe not. It wasn't that big a stretch to think a former fashion model might walk both sides of the runway.

Ellis must have misinterpreted his silence, because, "Even married couples don't sleep together every night," she said huffily.

Jack knew that from personal experience. Sometimes husbands and wives didn't sleep together every month.

"So," he said, "you think somebody—a client, a coworker—heard you talking about your missing sunglasses and decided to lie in wait for you on the off chance that you'd show up."

Karen Ellis looked at him like he was brain-dead. "Somebody with a *reason*," she said. "Somebody with a grudge."

Ah, he thought. *Somebody like Frankie.* Who wouldn't have had to lie in wait because she would already have been there. Frankie had, so far as they could tell, no reason to kill Whittier, but her motive for killing Ellis would have been the oldest in the book. Karen Ellis had stolen her man. That had driven plenty of women nuts.

Shit, he thought and tried to restrain a sigh. He didn't believe it, but he knew that on a professional level he also couldn't dismiss it.

Then again, maybe Ellis was just looking for attention. Maybe, despite having won the "prize" in her and Frankie's competition, she still felt threatened by her boyfriend's ex and was hoping Frankie was guilty. The underwear boy probably wouldn't run back into the arms of a murderer—and couldn't if Frankie was in jail.

"That's a very serious thing you're suggesting," he said quietly.

"I know." Ellis's lower lip wobbled. "I'm sorry to have to say it. I'm sorry to even think it, but Tish is dead. If there's even a chance that . . . that Frankie did it, I have to speak up. You will check it out, won't you? You won't just blow this off?"

"This department will check out every remotely credible lead we get. That's our job."

She nodded, looking teary and grateful. Then she collected her purse and stood.

"You might stay close to your boyfriend for a while," he suggested, noting a tiny tightening of the skin around her eyes. "In case you're right, and you were the intended victim."

"Yes," she said, her stylish black clutch bag held to her stomach. "Thank you. I will."

Jack was still rubbing his temples when Dewey stuck his head in the door. He was waving a lab report and grinning with all his teeth.

"Looks like my girl-fight theory is alive and kicking. Frankie

Smith's fingerprints matched some partials on that pink pearl collar our vic was wearing. I know it wasn't the murder weapon, but Whittier was arranged, and whoever arranged her might have touched the necklace."

Dewey was so delighted by this development he seemed to have forgotten all about his fondness for mesquite fries.

"Good," Jack said a little heavily. "We'll have a new tack to take in questioning Frankie Smith."

"Can I come?" Dewey asked, actually bouncing on his toes.

Jack didn't want to let him but knew he couldn't go alone. His attraction to the diner owner wasn't the secret he wished it could be. For the sake of the integrity of the investigation, he needed a witness to the interview.

"Where's Rivera?" he asked, hoping against hope.

"Busy!" Dewey exulted. "She's running background checks on the other people we found on those tapes."

"Was Troy Wilcox one of them?"

Dewey's eyes widened. "No, he wasn't. Is he a suspect?"

"Everyone's a suspect. At least, everyone Whittier knew."

"Excellent," Dewey said with the heedless energy of youth.

Jack shook his head but waved to him to lead the way from the office. In the corridor, the mayor's staff were beginning to go home. They were older women, mostly, and their slightly dowdy outfits were a contrast to his recent female visitor, whose suit had carried a distinctive whiff of Rodeo Drive. Jack welcomed the change. These people were realer to him than rich folks. No less complicated, he expected, but reassuringly down to earth.

The mayor's secretary came out of the copy room and made a humorous genuflecting motion to him with her arms. Apparently, she thought Jack had done a good job calming down her boss. It was a small thing, a gesture of camaraderie, but it improved his mood. This was becoming his town. He'd made friends here. It had nothing to do with Frankie, but it gave him faith that he could sort out this murder and still have a chance with her.

"I don't suppose I could drive," Dewey said as they strode to the parking lot.

"You don't suppose right," Jack said and gave Dewey a grin of his own.

Chapter 9

Frankie was angrier than she could ever remember being, even angrier than she'd been the first time Troy cheated on her. She wasn't used to being mistrusted like this. She was an incredibly responsible person. A nice person, come to that. Anyone in town could have sworn up and down she was no murderess. Jack West could have sworn to it himself. As things stood, if her glare had been any hotter, the chief and his choirboy-faced sidekick would have gone up in flames.

"I thought we were done with this," she said, hands on her hips as the two policemen waited on her front doorstep. "I answered all your questions."

"You answered all the questions we had then," Jack corrected. "There have been new developments."

"And if I don't feel like being interrogated?"

Jack shrugged. "These developments could get you a chauffeured ride to the department. With cuffs, if you like."

"Fine," she said, turning on her heel. "You can ask your questions in the kitchen. You caught me starting dinner."

The other officer, Dewey, whistled when he stepped inside her soaring entryway. Frankie's house was no mansion, but its cool-factor was high. Two off-kilter pie wedges fanned out from a central cylinder to form a light-filled, sculptural space. The kitchen was in one of the wedges, and the dining room in the second. The spine for the cylinder's center was a spiraling steel staircase leading to her bedroom.

"Whoa," said Officer Dewey. "Tell me this house isn't a Moening. He was right up there with Neutra back in the fifties. He only designed, like, six residences in his whole career. Man, look at those ocean views. You'd pay a fortune to get this place today."

Frankie stopped and faced him. Her jaw was so tight it felt like it had a cramp. "My father gave me this house to make up for missing a lot of birthdays when I was a kid. He won it in a poker game. A legal poker game, before you ask. He's a professional gambler. He pays taxes on his winnings, and I paid taxes on this. But if there's anything else you'd like to insinuate about my finances, just give a shout."

"Hey." Dewey put up his hands. "I was just admiring."

To her annoyance, Jack West was smiling.

"I am not a murderer," she said as she stomped into the open angles of her kitchen.

Cool as a cucumber, Jack set his forearms on her vintage-green Formica island. "The thing is, your fingerprints were found on the pearls Tish Whittier was wearing when she died."

Frankie's mind went briefly blank. She shook herself.

"I don't think I touched her body," she said slowly.

"The prints were on the back, Frankie, near the clasp. You would have had to touch her more than casually. More than, say, to check her pulse."

His voice was gentle, his eyes patient and kind. If she had been guilty, she would have told him anything he wanted. Instead, she clenched the opposite edge of the countertop.

"Wait . . . I know what happened. Tish loaned me that necklace, a big pink pearl collar with three strands? It was for the party she invited me to at her house, the one I told you about, the thank you for doing food at her charity events. Everyone had their bling on, and she wanted me to feel comfortable. It was such a nice gesture, I couldn't tell her the necklace wasn't my style. I returned it before I left. Troy was with me. He can back me up."

Jack West drew a pattern on the Formica with his fingertips. He was watching her, but she couldn't tell if he believed her or not. "There's another thing. Karen Ellis is under the impression that she was the intended victim. She says Tish volunteered to swing by here to look for some sunglasses she lost, and that someone could have mistaken Tish for her."

"Oh, fuck those fucking sunglasses!" Frankie burst out, which probably wasn't the most innocent-sounding thing to say. She'd known Karen was kind of self-impressed, but this really took the cake. As if Frankie would bother killing anyone but Troy for what he'd done. Completely incensed, she was breathing like she'd run five miles. She had the disturbing suspicion she was about to cry from sheer fury.

It was almost a relief when Dewey's cell phone rang.

"Sorry," said the younger officer. He flipped open the phone to check the caller ID. "Shit. I gotta take this. Don't do anything exciting while I'm gone."

The reception must have been bad and the call urgent, because Dewey went out the front door to talk. Frankie doubted anything else could have dragged him away from the "excitement."

"So," said Jack, the interrogation obviously suspended for the time being. His big hands smoothed across the counter, the movement distractingly sensual. He looked around the place, at the picture windows and the furniture. Everything was clean and simple, just the way Frankie liked. After taking it all in, he looked back at her. "Your dad really won this in a poker game?"

"Yes," she said sullenly.

"It's a great place," he said, ignoring her tone. "It must be peaceful to come back to after working at the diner all day."

"It is. *Usually.*"

His mouth curved in amusement at her emphasis. "I'm sorry about your dad not being around. He missed out not watching a woman like you grow up."

The change of topic disarmed her. Frankie answered less guardedly than she might have. "He knew he missed out. Sort of. It just wasn't in his nature to stay."

He accepted her answer as simply as he'd offered his sympathy, but she sensed he'd meant what he said. Her eyes stung with repressed emotion. She felt an unexpected connection to him, as if he'd understood—in a way no one else had—both her regrets and her desire to leave them behind. If that was true, she didn't know what the hell he was doing here.

"You can't think I did it," she said, annoyed that he could confuse her this way.

Unlike her, he seemed surer of himself than ever. "Human beings do things, Frankie. When they're hurt. When they're angry. Things they can hardly believe they did afterward."

"Oh, well, as long as you only think I committed a crime of passion, it's all right."

This time, her sarcasm reached him. He came around to her side of the counter, his beautiful brown eyes sad. She didn't want to feel sorry for him when he was treating her like a suspect, but his expression tugged at her heart.

He must have seen lots of otherwise likeable people do really terrible things. She just wished he wasn't thinking one of them was her.

He leaned back with his elbows on the counter, next to her but facing the opposite way. Though he didn't touch her, he was close enough to radiate body heat. Frankie frowned. She hardly needed a reminder of how hot he was.

"It's my job to entertain all the possibilities," he said.

"Well, pardon me," she clipped back, "but your job sucks."

Her voice was too husky; she was betraying the turmoil she felt inside. He met her hurt and angry gaze with a long, probing look that made her want to slap him or jump him or maybe just scream in frustration. They could hear Officer Dewey out on the front stoop, trying to calm his caller. Slowly, as if he wasn't sure he wanted to do it but couldn't resist, Jack brought the back of his hand to her cheek. He let it rest there, his hard, warm knuckles against the softness of her skin. Then he turned his hand and cupped the side of her face in his palm.

"Yes," he said. "Sometimes my job does suck."

She saw the truth in his wistful, whiskey-colored eyes: that he wanted her, that he *liked* her, and had for some time. Despite the obvious strength of this attraction, her instincts told her he wouldn't do more than he was doing now—maybe not even after her name was cleared.

This big, imposing man had been afraid to let her know he was interested. Hard as it was to believe, Jack West was shy.

She didn't stop to think. His slouched position almost brought their heads level. His mouth was wide and beautifully cut. She touched his cheek the way he'd touched hers, laying the back of her fingers against his skin. He must not have been expecting it. He flinched, a serious jerk of surprise.

"Frankie . . ." he said, his own hand dropping, his tanned skin reddening beneath her touch.

"Shh," she said, because she felt his heat kick up another telltale notch. "I want this, too."

Their position was awkward, not quite face to face. She fixed that by stepping her feet outside his. Then she leaned in until her front brushed his uniform. Her closeness pushed him back into the countertop. He seemed frozen, but not resistant, and anyway she figured she'd warm him up. He gasped a second before she kissed him, but she didn't hesitate. Aware of the risk with his coworker steps away, and enjoying it all the same, she settled her lips on his and licked into his mouth. He let her inside with a gentleness that made her shiver. He was hot and silky and tasted of mint. His hands came lightly to her waist, indecisive but hardly discouraging. When she sucked his tongue, a low, pained sound broke in his chest.

The sound seemed to shock something awake inside him. He kissed her back then, slow but hard, taking control as his tongue pressed inward to explore her mouth.

Frankie couldn't doubt he wanted her now. She hummed in helpless approval. The surface of his lips was soft, but everything else was not. The hint of force he was using felt unbelievably good. Her sex swelled and went molten, her panties dampening with embarrassing rapidity.

Then he tilted his head to a new angle and kissed her even more aggressively.

Frankie thought her spine would melt. Something about his combination of restraint and power made this the hottest kiss she'd ever had. Chills were dancing up and down her spine, not to mention through her pussy, and his elbows hadn't left the countertop—though one of his hands did rise to touch her ribs just beneath her breast. He didn't have to come any closer; her nipples instantly drew into pulsing points.

"Jack," she breathed and slid her own hand over his endless shoulder and down his front.

He was all muscle under that uniform, all hot, tight, rock-hard muscle. Her touch seemed to make every one of those muscles tense. He was still kissing her, and his teeth clashed with her lip when she reached his groin. The bulge she found there was huge, actually startling. He rocked the prodigy up at her, rubbing it against her palm like an animal—all without making a sound. Finally, he moved his second hand from her waist to curve hers closer around his cock, pressing every inch of her fingers around his erection.

When she could count the forceful throbbing against her palm, he tore from the kiss, breathing fast but silently.

His eyes were inches away, burning gold within the coal-black spikes of his lashes.

"You should let go," he said in a rasp she could barely hear.

"You're holding me on."

He didn't stop doing it. He widened his muscled thighs and pushed her hand farther back along his trouser seam. His balls were bundled up with the rest of him, one big, juicy package she would have given a night in jail to release. It must have felt good to crush her palm against him. His jaw bunched dramatically.

"I need to hold you on," he confessed, his body beginning to shudder. He was gripping her so tightly her fingers were going numb. "I want to fuck you so badly, I probably wouldn't quit until the sun came up."

In that moment, Frankie wanted exactly that: an endless ravishment just short of pain. When he'd widened his thighs, he'd pushed her legs apart, too. If they'd been naked she could have taken him just like that. She let the weight of her hips settle more strongly behind the hand he'd wrapped around his huge hard-on. They'd be a heck of a mismatch, but she couldn't care—not when he sucked a breath and both his pupils and penis swelled.

She wanted him to fling her back against the fridge and kiss her senseless. She wanted him to put his hands all over her and press his big, hard body against hers until she was squashed. Instead, the only place he really held her was her cupping hand. Frustrated, she said the first thing that came into her head.

"What are you afraid of, Jack?"

His face changed, all his barriers clanging down. He pushed her back from him. "Don't," he said, cold and angry. "Don't act like you know me."

His reaction suggested she'd hit a nerve she hadn't known was there. She opened her mouth but didn't know what to say. He was glowering at her, only to stop seconds later and rub one hand across his rugged face. Was he regretting what he'd said? Was he thinking about explaining?

But then the front door slammed and Officer Dewey's eager footsteps approached. Jack cursed under his breath as she jumped to the sink and began busily washing vegetables.

"Sorry," Dewey said. "That was my mom. She—"

But he didn't get a chance to share whatever the crisis was.

"We're done here," Jack said. "Let's hit the road."

All Frankie could do was gape at their backs.

Yeah, and don't let the door hit your butt on the way out, she thought to herself.

As comebacks went, it didn't come close to giving her the kind of satisfaction she was hankering for.

The taste of Frankie's kiss was in Jack's mouth even as he strode stiffly out, the impression of her body against his front burning like a brand. She'd been so light, so lithe. Her nipples had been aroused. He'd felt them through all their clothes. He'd wanted to strip her naked and take her on the floor.

Christ. He hadn't expected to feel so much when she kissed

him, like fireworks exploding through every nerve. If the reaction had just been physical, he might have controlled it, but with one touch from her, the emotions he'd worked so hard to keep controlled flooded him, all jumbled together until he couldn't tell them apart. Avoiding exactly that was the one of the first rules he'd learned on the force. You don't touch the civilians, and you don't let them touch you. You can't do your job with someone crying on your shoulder, any more than you can do it if you half want to cry yourself.

Hugs were for social workers. Cops had to get things done.

Six Palms was a hell of a lot quieter than LA, but Jack still hadn't figured out how to shake off those old instincts.

For sure, this had to be a cruel cosmic joke. He'd fantasized about kissing Frankie a thousand times. When it actually happened, he'd gotten so tangled up everything came out wrong. If telling her he wanted to fuck her all night wasn't bad enough, when she'd asked if he was afraid, and he'd snapped at her. *Fear* wasn't even the word for what he felt; some part of him was terrified of truly having a chance with her.

If he'd suspected he wasn't ready for a relationship before, now he knew it. Hell, he was barely qualified to leave his house.

Grunting with annoyance, he shoved his body behind the patrol car's wheel.

Dewey eyed him curiously. "Did you find out anything else?"

I found out I'm a total idiot. "No," he said. "Her explanation was plausible. We haven't got enough to charge her."

"O-kay," Dewey said unsurely. "She did seem pretty confident that her ex would support her story." He shifted in his seat but said no more until Jack started the car and eased down Frankie's steep driveway. "Are you pissed that I took that call?"

Jack turned right onto Hill Street, letting some of his anger at himself run out. "No more than I'd have been pissed if Rivera's son had had an emergency. I trust you to know when you can't afford to split your attention."

Another pause unfolded.

"Are *you* okay?" Dewey asked then, with a sincerity he didn't usually demonstrate.

Jack sighed. "Kid, I'm as well as I'm getting for now."

"I'll shut up then," Dewey said, which suggested more intelligence than most people gave him credit for.

Glad for small favors, Jack drummed his fingers on the steering wheel. "We need to see if we can find Troy Wilcox. I've got some questions for him."

One of those questions was how the underwear boy could have been insane enough to leave a woman like Frankie. This, of course, was destined to remain unasked. Jack had a feeling he knew what Troy was missing far better than Troy could himself.

Chapter
10

Frankie had way too many free hours for dwelling on what a fool she'd made of herself with Jack West. Every time she thought of it, her face went hot. After another day without the diner to go to, she was so desperate for distraction she let Jean Yi, her waitress-slash-surrogate mother, drag her to the eight A.M. yoga class at the community center gym. *Drag* was the appropriate term. Jean showed up at her house at seven and knocked like a lumberjack until Frankie stumbled down.

"You need centering," Jean insisted when Frankie tried to say she was too tired. "Staring at the ocean isn't enough. You should straighten out your spine and get your chi flowing. Besides, the two-faced bitch won't be there. Pregnant women have to take special yoga, in a separate class by themselves."

"Great." Frankie dragged her fingers through her tangled morning hair. "Does the whole town know my ex-boyfriend's lover is in the family way?"

Jean grinned. "Not the whole town. Just women with sharp

eyes like me. Now get your butt in gear, white girl. That little instructor will frown at us if we're late."

"Three-quarter white girl," Frankie corrected as she shuffled
off to shower and dress. Her mother had been half Hawaiian, a
fact most people—including Frankie—sometimes forgot because
she'd acted like such an all-American mainland girl. She'd died
three years ago, but it was she who'd started Frankie's love affair
with diners, she who Frankie thought of every time she took stock
of her accomplishments. Frankie had never understood why her
father hadn't jumped at the chance to marry her. Mary Ellen
Smith had been warm and beautiful and full of life, a fabulous
cook with an open door who'd welcomed Frankie's father every
time he chose to roll into town between high-stakes games.

At times like this, Frankie really missed her. Her mom had
known all about staying centered, all about *mahalo* and choosing
the loving path.

To her relief, Jean was right about Karen being absent from the
class. Frankie began to relax, though she was creaky from having
been away so long. Jean was as obnoxiously flexible as ever. From
the grace and ease with which she moved through each asana,
you'd never guess she was sixty—much less that she smoked.

"Thank God this isn't LA," Frankie muttered as she pushed
her butt into the air for dog pose. In LA, she'd probably be doing
some exotic yoga hybrid, like yoga-tai-lates with kick-boxing on
the side.

Jean glanced at her just as she smiled to herself. "See," said the
waitress, "already you're feeling better."

"Right," said Frankie. "That's why my arms are shaking like
a leaf."

When the tiny instructor—or yoga nazi, as Frankie liked to call
her—finally let them sit on their heels again, Frankie noticed a new
student on the other side of the room. The woman was huffing

from the unfamiliar exertion, but she was lovely, a golden-skinned
Hispanic built like a bootylicious Bollywood star. The instructor
stopped beside her, tapping her shoulders to tell her to sit straighter.
At least today Frankie wasn't the most awkward person here—
although the stranger did have muscles.

Jean jerked her chin toward the woman. "That's the chief's
senior cop."

Frankie's gut tightened. *That* was Rivera? Frankie hadn't recognized her out of uniform. She was gorgeous—not to mention
dignified looking. Frankie bet she wouldn't kiss a man so pushily
she'd scare him away.

"She's probably here to spy on me," Frankie said. "See if I do
anything suspicious while I'm upside down."

Jean wrinkled her nose in negation. "I don't think so. She's
been too busy staring at Phoebe Atkins, the dry cleaner's wife.
You know, the one who had an affair with Pete and Dave a few
months ago?"

Frankie's knees popped as they all got to their feet. "My God,"
she murmured. "You know everything!"

Jean smiled like a Buddha and didn't disagree.

As it turned out, Jean was wrong about one thing. Officer
Rivera did want to speak to Frankie. She called to her as soon as
the crowd had thinned after class. Jack's fellow officer wasn't as
tall as Frankie, but she sure looked nice close up. Her skin was
flawless, her eyes big pools of espresso brown.

Jack works with her every day, Frankie thought before ordering
her insecurity to shut up. Anyway, it wasn't like Frankie had
needed help driving Jack away.

She was surprised Rivera seemed a little uncomfortable speaking to her. But maybe Rivera wasn't used to treating someone
who'd fed her as a suspect in a murder case.

"I'm glad I caught you here," she said softly. "I was going to call you later. We're done searching the diner. You can open any time you like."

"That's great," Frankie said, even as she thought, *Why were you going to call me?* Was the chief afraid she'd try to put the moves on him on the phone? Frankie rubbed the bridge of her nose to get her mind back on track. "I'd offer to treat you to a chicken salad in thanks, except it might be considered unethical."

Rivera was even prettier when she smiled. "Your food is more than good enough to pay for. We're all grateful you're in business here."

This bit of friendliness might be considered a vote of confidence that she wasn't guilty. Of course, it also might be Rivera and her boss playing long-distance good-cop, bad-cop.

"Thanks," Frankie said, deciding not to act paranoid. "I'm pretty grateful, too."

Though the police hadn't made a complete mess of All U Can Eat, the diner wasn't in any shape to welcome customers. Luckily, Frankie was able to reach Mike at his motel, and together with Jean they scrubbed and straightened everything.

A few curious townsfolk stuck their heads in the door, but only Mr. Atkins, the dry cleaner, seemed disappointed to find her there. He was small and grumpy, a man who lived to find things wrong with other people. Seeing her, he frowned and smoothed his wispy hair.

"I'd have thought they'd have arrested you by now," he said.

"Not so far," Frankie chirped, trying not to let what she now knew about his wife show on her face. "Better luck tomorrow."

Jean snorted in enjoyment at this, but Mike was the happiest of them all. He whistled and smiled as he put the kitchen back in order, his flexing muscles and faded jeans a cheering sight. His mood lifted Frankie's, but Jean seemed to disapprove.

"You watch out for that one," she said as they wiped the black-powdered fingerprints from the front door's glass. "He's got his eyes on you."

Frankie decided she was thankful Jean didn't know what else he'd had on her, though she did wonder why the older woman thought his interest was a bad thing. Jean usually liked hard workers. Certainly, Mike hadn't made Frankie feel like an idiot the way Jean's favorite, the "nice" chief had.

"He's a hero, you know," Jean said.

Frankie looked toward the kitchen, where—to judge by the rattling pans—Mike was straightening the cabinets.

"Not him." Jean flapped her strong, age-spotted hand. "Oh, maybe he's a hero, too; I wouldn't know. I meant that nice Chief West."

She nodded when Frankie turned to her in surprise, seeming pleased to have wrested her attention away from Mike. "Chief West—he would have been Sergeant West back then—saved five people from a burning building."

"Really?" Frankie asked, because this sounded like a tall tale, and Jean had been known to exaggerate now and then.

"Really," Jean said firmly. "He wasn't even on duty but was driving home from the station when he saw the smoke. He radioed the fire department, then decided the people who were trapped inside couldn't wait for them to arrive.

"It was an apartment building, and the way it was arranged, Chief West had to go in and get them one at a time. He didn't have a mask, and some of them were unconscious, but he pulled out every person in that building. *And* he rescued a cat!"

Jean had six cats on whom she doted, so Frankie wasn't surprised by this emphasis.

"Nobody else went in but him?"

"The neighbors stood by and watched!" Jean's lightly lined face quivered with outrage. "It was a bad neighborhood. Lots of drugs and hooligans, but he saved them all the same. The firefighters said they didn't know how he did it. The smoke should have knocked him out after the first trip, but somehow he kept on going. He got a medal and everything."

"Jean, how do you know this?"

"I have a nephew on the force." She proudly pulled back her shoulders. "He's a very good nephew. He calls me every Sunday to share the news."

Frankie couldn't keep her mouth from curving up. She wiped the last of the black powder from the silver PUSH bar on the door. "You mean he calls to share gossip."

"It's not gossip," Jean said, scrubbing furiously at the now-clean glass. "Every word I told you is true. *And* his wife left him."

"What?" said Frankie, now offended herself. "After he got a medal for being brave?"

"No, no. She left him before that. They were only married six months and—poof!—one day she packed up and left."

From Frankie's own experience with the chief, she suspected there was more behind his wife's departure than a simple "poof." Jean, however, was of a different mind.

"Imagine," she said, her fists and cleaning cloth on her hips. "Doing a thing like that to a nice, dedicated young officer."

Frankie could imagine and felt a tug of sympathy in spite of herself. She knew what it was like to have been left for no real reason you could understand. Still, to talk about Jack West as if he were a helpless victim was further than she would have gone.

"He likes you big time," Jean said in an undertone. She tapped her temple significantly. "I can tell."

Frankie sighed and tried not to sound exasperated. "Lots of men like me. That doesn't mean I'm destined to have a grand romance with every one."

Jean pursed her lips at this in the way only older people could. "I'll mop the floor now," she said haughtily. "Maybe you'll come to your senses later on."

Frankie doubted it, but considering Jean's not-so-subtle matchmaking bent, she was relieved when she left at two to attend a granddaughter's birthday. Mike came out no more than five minutes later, which made Frankie think he'd been waiting for Jean to go.

"I think that'll do it," he said, his eyes creasing with his smile. "You feel like lunch on the beach? My treat."

He must have seen her hesitate, because his smile faded.

"A friendly lunch," he clarified. "No strings attached."

Frankie had never known a man to actually mean those words. They were happy to tie the strings back on the instant you let them. Still, she was hungry, and there was a good concession stand. Right now, a big, ketchup-slathered hot dog sounded great.

"Sure," she said, which brightened him up again. "Let me swab myself down and then I'll meet you out front."

She didn't care if Jean disapproved. At least Mike didn't make her feel like a too-pushy man-eater.

It was an unusually hot afternoon. Jack had rolled down the squad car windows and was driving himself and Dewey back to the station after interviewing Troy Wilcox at his beach house. Understandably, given Karen Ellis's closeness to the deceased, Ellis Real

Estate was closed. What was less understandable was finding Wilcox by himself at home.

Frankie's ex had been distracted, to say the least. He'd been unable to remember half the things he'd been asked, and when he finally pulled himself together enough to answer, as many times as not he lost his train of thought.

"I'm sorry," he kept saying. "It's all such a shock."

He did remember the party he and Frankie had attended at Whittier's place, and mentioned the loan of the strand of pearls without prompting. It wasn't proof, but it was better than if he'd forgotten.

"That was Tish all over," he said. "She even thought the necklace looked better on Frankie than her. Said Frankie had the neck for it. She—" And then he lost the thread again, simply shaking his head mournfully.

As for where he'd been when Tish was murdered, "I was here," he said, waving listlessly around his living room. Wilcox sat slumped on the navy slip-covered couch, all long legs and flat model muscle. Take-out cartons littered the coffee table, but Jack noticed only one fork and plate. Wilcox rubbed his breastbone like he had heartburn. "I was here, and I never left."

This wasn't adding up, that much Jack knew. Even a distracted man should have been concerned about his fiancé's safety, but when Dewey brought up Ellis's suspicions, Wilcox seemed startled—not as if Ellis had failed to share her theory with him, but as if he'd forgotten.

"Karen stays here at night," he said, subsiding back into listlessness. "I look out for her then."

Jack wouldn't have rested easy letting this man look out for a pet rock, but he supposed women found comfort in funny things. Frankly, he'd have liked Wilcox to be guilty, if only because the man annoyed him. Too bad it was hard to imagine him with enough initiative to kill anyone. He seemed to have a classic pussy-whipped personality, and Frankie's whip, apparently, had been more motivating than Ellis's.

The thought made Jack grin to himself, despite his present company. Dewey had been quiet since the interview, probably still leery of his boss's mood. They were following Shore Road past the quaint bed and breakfasts and the town's one fancy French restaurant. Traffic was creeping, as if everyone had decided to leave work early. Jack was about to try a side street when Dewey sat up in the passenger seat, his gaze homing on the beach.

"Isn't that Frankie Smith? I think she's eating hot dogs with that Marine."

At the rate they were inching, Jack had plenty of time to spot them side by side on a weathered bench, laughing companionably around their lunch. They looked good together, easy. Two attractive twenty-somethings enjoying each other's company. A pang of blessings never enjoyed tightened in his throat. He'd had his wife, and he'd had affairs, but he'd never had an ordinary girlfriend. He'd never had a relationship that was simply fun. He wasn't sure he'd know how. Swallowing back his regrets, he returned his eyes to the road.

He couldn't wish Frankie unhappy because he was. Of course, this also meant he couldn't sit on his hands if there was a chance she might get hurt.

"Have you been able to contact True's old commanding officer?" he asked Dewey.

"Not yet. He's on active duty and hard to reach. I'll let you know as soon as I do."

"Good," said Jack, not feeling a lick better.

Emotionally uptight or not, right then, he would have given a great deal to have had another chance to return Frankie's kiss.

Chapter 11

Feeling better now that she had some food in her, Frankie rose from the salt-silvered wooden bench. A pair of divers were clumping out of the shallows in their wetsuits and tanks and fins. A protected reef was one of Six Palms biggest tourist draws. Mike watched the couple maneuver awkwardly onto the sand, then stood and gazed down at her warmly.

Frankie did her best to conceal how his affection made her neck muscles tense.

"We'll open first thing tomorrow," she said. "In the meantime, feel free to move back into the room above the diner."

"I won't mind that, but where are you going now?"

"Home. I've already called our suppliers, so as long as they get there early, we'll be restocked."

"I'll walk you."

"You don't have to do that."

He smiled at the cloud-flecked sky. "Sure I do. Haven't you heard there's dangerous elements in this town?"

The slant of his mouth said he knew some people considered him one of them. He beckoned her alongside him as he began to walk, and with a muffled snort, Frankie fell in step. Mike shoved his hands in his pockets, but Frankie had a feeling he'd rather be holding hers. She searched for a topic to distract him.

"I see you have a penchant for black humor."

He shrugged. "Whatever keeps you smiling through your troubles is okay by me."

Their gazes met with an awareness that, while they'd both seen their share of troubles lately, this day, here and now, was pretty good. It was a nice moment. Frankie couldn't deny she enjoyed having a man crinkle his eyes at her for no better reason than liking her company. For a heartbeat, she thought *maybe*, but Mike wasn't playing around. He might claim he was leaving the strings off, but everything in his attitude said he wanted a committed, long-term girlfriend.

Frankie couldn't blame him. He'd been through a kind of hell she couldn't imagine, even if joining the Marines had kept him out of jail. She understood him wanting stability right now. The thing was, Frankie wasn't sure she could be a serious girlfriend to him. Even if Jack West had scratched himself off her dance card, she didn't feel ready.

She hadn't been as good for Troy as she'd believed she was. She didn't want to hurt another man that way.

The thought brought her up short, coming as it did out of some subconscious left field. *Had* she hurt Troy with the way she handled their relationship? Had the break-up not all been his fault?

She was so caught up in this uncomfortable possibility that she didn't ease away when Mike put his hand on her back to usher her across the next intersection.

"Phew," he said once they finished hiking to her door. "That climb will keep your legs in shape."

He was looking down at her again. The moment was very end-of-date, and got even more so when he bent closer. It didn't take a genius to figure out he meant to kiss her.

"Mike," she said, stopping him with one hand on his hard breastbone. The instant she felt the sweat behind his soft clean T-shirt, her body wanted to say *oh, baby, bring it on.*

Luckily, he couldn't read her mind. He straightened and grinned sheepishly. "Can't blame a guy for trying." His hands rested on her shoulders, moving in a cross between an squeeze and caress. "God, Frankie. We get on. We're great in bed. I guess I don't understand what the problem is."

"The problem is, you don't really want something casual, and I'm not ready for more. Not right now."

He didn't deny her conclusion. The coaxing, upward crook of his mouth came down. "I guess you didn't buy my no-strings speech."

Glad he wasn't trying to argue, she softened her voice. "I'm afraid not. I wish I—"

"Don't wish." He cut her off with an edge of harshness. "Wishes are for chumps."

Her hand was still on his heart. She flattened it. In that instant, despite the experiences he must have been through, she felt how young he was, how close to the angry teenager who'd fallen in with bad company. "Not all wishes are for chumps, Mike. Just some."

"Right," he said and huffed impatiently. "I'll see you tomorrow, bright and early."

He kissed her cheek before he turned away. The abruptness of the contact left a little sting. Frankie watched his loping stride carry him down the hill, wishing, despite his request.

His butt was major league cute.

I am either the stupidest woman on the planet, she thought, *or the most self-controlled.*

She was certainly the most absentminded. When she stuck her key in the door, she found it already open. She must have forgotten to lock it when Jean dragged her to yoga at the crack of dawn.

As long as she shut it carefully behind her, Frankie's door was quiet, as was her recently installed bamboo flooring. She supposed Pete and Dave didn't hear her come in. When she reached her living room, they were kissing—rather enthusiastically—on her long, white Italian leather sectional.

The shock of them being there at all momentarily prevented her from taking in the details of what they were doing. Then it began to sink in. Dave's navy polo shirt was pushed up to reveal his tanned California six-pack, and Pete's hand, or at least its fingers, were wedged under the front waistband of Dave's khaki shorts. Neither button nor zipper were undone. Pete didn't have much room to move his hand, but from the giant bulge that occupied Dave's crotch, the mere presence of his fingers was having a strong effect.

Of course, the state of Dave's cock could also have been due to the fact that Pete was shoving his tongue down his throat.

Frankie was so stunned and—admittedly—intrigued that her normal anger at having her home invaded was short-circuited. She'd known Pete and Dave liked seducing women as a team, but not that they were this interested in each other.

"Ahem," she said sternly, though more than her face was flushed.

The men sprang apart. "We weren't—" Dave began.

"We *were*," Pete insisted and laid his hand on Dave's clenching thigh. Dave licked his lips unconsciously.

She noticed the zipper of Pete's new Levis was straining, too. He looked crisper than usual in a short-sleeve, button-down striped shirt. *Ralph Lauren*, she concluded, having been schooled in such things by Troy.

To tell the truth, both her visitors looked yummy, together or apart. Her body was definitely reiterating its annoyance that she'd fended off Mike True.

"How did you get in here?" Frankie asked, because this did seem somewhat important.

"We own a garage," Dave said. "We have tools."

"I'll say!" Frankie exclaimed, because both were still as hard as rhino horns.

Her laugh made the men relax.

"We thought the time might be ripe for a seduction," Dave explained. He waved toward a bouquet of at least three dozen red roses that sat in a clear glass vase on the nearby cube of an end table. It was hard to believe she'd missed them, but then she *had* been distracted.

"We'd like to fulfill one of your fantasies," Pete said in a surprisingly matter-of-fact tone. "Whatever it might be."

Frankie's body tightened and pulsed. An image, complete with physical sensations, flashed into her mind. She saw and felt herself standing behind the diner naked in the dark, being slowly and very thoroughly frisked by Jack West. She shook herself, because no way was she going to share that daydream with Pete and Dave. Better never to live it out than to have it spoiled by anyone else.

Unfortunately, she didn't hide her thoughts quickly enough. Dave grinned triumphantly.

"You thought of something," he said. "Come on, Frankie, spill."

"I don't know," she said, crossing her arms over her waist. "Taking you two on is kind of crazy, even for me."

Pete stood up, drew one rose from the bouquet, and teased it gently beneath her nose. It was a nice, smelly variety, and Frankie couldn't resist inhaling the scent.

"It's not crazy," Pete said softly. "It's fun. *Carpe diem.* A game between friends that we can joke about later on. We like you,

Frankie, and we only want to do what you want. If you like, it can be one time and no more, but if you really don't want to do this, we promise to go now and never ask you again."

"Don't say that!" Dave protested with a laugh. "Never is a long time."

"No strings?" Frankie asked. She knew Team Boys' record, maybe not as well as Jean, but enough. No woman had ever complained about being treated badly by Pete and Dave, nor had the men ever tried to turn one of their partners into a regular girlfriend.

"Cross our hearts," Pete promised, then kissed her on the lips as innocently as a child.

Frankie's mouth twitched in amusement. She knew there wasn't anything innocent about Pete's intent. The smile told Dave more than she realized.

"Yes!" he cheered, before she had a chance to agree out loud. His fist pumped the air like he was rooting for his college team. "Now tell us your fantasy."

Frankie rubbed her lower lip. She knew what she wasn't going to tell them, but hadn't decided yet what she would. She thought back to how she'd felt when she watched them kissing, to things she'd always wondered about men and men but had never had the opportunity to find out.

"Actually," she said, while the more excitable Dave held his breath in anticipation. "What I'd like is to help you two act out a fantasy."

"Us?" the pair said in unison.

A pleasurable shiver slid through her at their surprise. "Yes," she said. "I'm very interested in what you fantasize about doing to each other. Maybe something you haven't tried yet."

The men exchanged glances. Pete still stood in front of her, and Dave perched warily on the sectional. Pete touched the rose to his mouth, smiling as if he were holding back some secret. Dave seemed doubtful but very flushed. Of the two, she knew instinctively that Dave had the stronger sexual drive, maybe even an obsessive one, and that he would be the easier of the two to arouse. She filed away the information for near-future use.

"I'd be very interested in helping you act out your fantasy," she added, "if you'd be interested in letting me."

Dave seized upon this suggestion as if it were a lifeline. Evidently, he wasn't completely comfortable with his separate relationship with Pete.

"Help is good," he said breathlessly. "We love having women participate."

"Yes," Pete agreed, still smiling his secret smile. "We do."

"Then tell me what *you* want," Frankie said.

"I'll let Dave tell you," Pete said.

"Oh-ho," Frankie chuckled. "I don't think so. I think you trying to pawn this off on Dave just put you in the hot seat."

"Me?"

Frankie smoothed both hands up his warm shirtfront, delighted to find his heart thumping hard behind it. "I have a feeling Dave will be turned on by anything, whether it's to do with me or you." Having reached his shoulders, she reversed track and slid her hands back down, stopping when her fingers reached the place where his nice summer shirt tucked in. As she stretched her thumbs inward to brush the crown of his erection, he sucked a breath. Emboldened, she scratched the sensitive surface lightly with her nails. "Tell me, Pete, what deep, dark scenario would you like to play out?"

Pete's face turned so red it could have been painted. Frankie leaned up to kiss his clean-shaven cheek. "To echo your friend, I know you thought of something, so spill."

"I want to be a harem slave," he confessed in a hushed, rough tone. "I want to be forbidden to take my pleasure with anyone but the queen. I want her favorite slave to torment me, to drive me to the edge of coming even as she orders me not to."

Frankie soothed his flushing face between her palms. She hadn't expected this idea, but it pushed interesting buttons for her as well. "Am I the queen?"

Pete nodded and then said on a burst of air, "And I want *him*"—he jerked his chin at Dave—"to take me in the ass."

"Whoa." Dave took a step back.

Pete glared at him. "You can't tell me you haven't thought about it, because I know you have. Or do you think it's more 'gay' to take a man in the ass than to be taken?"

"I don't know," he said. "It's just . . . it's kind of personal."

"You like being fucked well enough," Pete pointed out. "Every damn afternoon like clockwork, or God help me if I need you to concentrate on work." This made Dave blush and raised Frankie's eyebrows. Every afternoon was a pretty strong sex drive, especially considering the other action they were getting. Pete went on. "Why worry about the labels? Just enjoy what you enjoy and be glad you can."

This seemed sensible enough to Frankie, but Dave bit his lip and looked at her.

"Well, I can't judge you," she said. "I'm the one who said I wanted to see this."

"Will you help me?" he asked.

She laughed through her nose. "Given my lack of experience in this area, you might have to tell me how to help, but what I can do, I will. Believe me, I'm happy to."

Her words must have reassured him. He sat straighter on her modern white leather couch. "So you're the queen."

"And you're my favorite."

"And Pete is the harem boy we're going to torment."

Pete appeared slightly nervous but also excited. For once, Dave and Frankie were the ones who grinned in unison.

The queen lay back on her spacious bed in her circular tower room. Her elbows were propped on an Indian pillow, her body wrapped in a square of sheer, sky-blue, knee-length silk. The abbreviated gown clung to her curves and teased every man who saw her with glimpses of the parts of her that were dark. Rose petals strewed across her cool white sheets. Her nipples were rouged, and she'd recently trimmed her thatch. Her toenails were painted chili pepper red.

Even without these adornments, she knew she was beautiful. Each night, her harem waited with bated breath until she announced who would be honored with an invitation to her bed. She forbade the chosen ones to carry tales back to their comrades, but their inevitable exhausted and blissful state told tales of its own.

Their pleasure was hers to dictate. She did not let her harem enjoy a climax with each other or by themselves. No release must ever come to them except by her will. When she did will, however, she made sure they were thoroughly satisfied.

Perhaps it was cruel of her, but the sort of slave she prized most was one who, under normal circumstances, wanted sex all the time.

Her favorite entered her chamber. David had begun as a slave but was now a trusted concubine. He was a strong, thick-muscled warrior from a northern land. Now he led in the latest object of her interest, a new slave named Peter, who had been captured in one of her victorious army's recent raids. Peter was handsome, slim, and proud. He'd been rebellious at first, and would have been dangerous still, but for the campaign she and David had engaged in to wind his needs to their highest state of readiness.

Need equaled compliance. That was a lesson the queen knew very well how to teach.

David stood behind the captive, holding him secure by the upper arms. Both men were beautifully naked, both scrubbed and pink from stem to stern. Though Peter, the new slave, struggled in David's grip, his sex had begun to thicken and lift.

Because of this, the queen was certain he must have guessed what his presence here presaged. Whether he meant to reveal his longing for release or not, he had been denied too many weeks to hide it.

"Bow to your queen," David ordered, forcing Peter to do it by pressing one hand behind his head.

The slave frowned, but his cock bobbed higher, as if the use of force excited him. Intrigued, the queen crawled closer on her bed. Despite himself, the slave could not take his eyes from her swaying nipples, red and pointed behind the silk. When she sat back on her heels, his gaze slid to the dark brown triangle between her legs. His Adam's apple bobbed as he swallowed hard.

The queen was very satisfied with this.

"You have prepared him?" she asked her favorite.

"I have, my queen."

"Tell me how. Tell me all you did."

"Every night since we captured him, I have visited him in his private cell—just as you requested. At first, I came only to bind his wounds and soothe his muscles with precious oils. When he healed, I massaged him for pleasure and to help him relax."

"Did he like that?" the queen asked.

Her favorite smiled. "He was shocked by how much he did. I had to bind him to the massaging bed so he would not touch himself. He especially liked when I teased him around the anus. I don't think anyone had ever stimulated him there. On the sixth night after his capture, he was so desperate he begged me to pull his shaft in my oiled hand. You may not believe this, my queen, but he offered to suck me off in return."

"You refused him, of course," said the queen with arrogant surety.

"Of course. Though I was hard myself from watching him suffer, I know the rewards you give to those who obey you—in bed and out."

Her favorite's voice had sunk to a husky growl, one that told her he, too, was aroused. From the sudden squirm and flush of the slave within David's grip, he must have felt the other's erection rising against his buttocks. This did not discourage his own arousal, which swelled and surged longer.

"You also knew I might be watching," the queen observed, pretending she did not notice the harem boy's increased discomfort. "Through my secret spy windows."

Her favorite bowed his head. "I know my queen likes to oversee the . . . care all her subjects receive."

"I am not your subject!" the slave, Peter, burst out.

The queen scooted forward on her knees until only a handspan separated her from the slave. Their heads were level. The harem boy's eyes glittered with emotion—most of it fiery. She drank in his vulnerability, and his desire, as if it were the world's sweetest elixir.

"Are you sure you are not my subject?" she asked, gently drawing her perfect manicure down his naked chest. Even as he tried to struggle away from her touch, his cock tried to strain toward it, frantic for any relief from its neglect. His organ was a deep, pulsing rose color, so upright it nearly strafed his belly, and so long her insides clenched at the thought of taking it. Unable to resist, she wrapped the throbbing heat in her hand.

He jerked as strongly as if her fingers were brands.

"This part of you is my subject, I think," she said, squeezing it lightly. The slave had to grit his teeth to keep from crying out, but he recovered quickly enough.

"It was his subject, too," he said defiantly, jerking his head at her concubine.

He must have expected the queen to be displeased, but she was not.

"Yes," she mused, now running her hands over his rampant maleness, over its root and balls, over its tip and shaft, watching it stretch with each playful stroke and pull. "Six nights isn't very long to be begging for the mercy of David's touch, though I admit his touch is skilled. And to offer to suck his organ in return . . ." She clucked her tongue. "Perhaps you were a lover of men before you came here, and it is only David's presence that makes you respond to me."

The slave drew back his shoulders and stood straight. "I love both sexes. Men and women. Pussies and cocks. To touch. To fuck. To kiss. To suck. To take any way I can."

The queen cocked her head curiously. "Do you like having both at once?"

The slave's breath came faster, lifting his lean, muscled ribs. He had only a scattering of hair on his pectorals, with a thin line arrowing to his arousal. "To take a woman in her pussy while a man fucks me in the ass is my oldest fantasy."

The queen tightened her fingers in surprise. The contraction around his shaft made the slave twitch and groan. "A *fantasy*, you say. Then you have not done it?"

"Never," moaned the slave with heartfelt longing. "I think I would give my very freedom for the chance."

The queen refrained from reminding him his freedom was hers to dispose of, not his to give. She gazed down at his erection, noting how it and the rest of his body trembled with his long-frustrated desires.

He shuddered when he saw what she was looking at.

"You have suffered three weeks without a release," she reminded him. "And all that time my dearest David has been teasing you sexually. Do you honestly think that, if I fulfill your wish, you will be able to obey my rules?"

The slave's mouth fell open. Clearly, he was amazed by even this much of a promise that his fantasy might at last be lived out. "I must not come until you say," he said, repeating her edicts, which every harem member knew, "no matter how much pleasure you, or your favorite, cause me to feel. Only your word grants me permission to ejaculate."

"Those are the rules," she agreed, trailing her fingers back up his torso to the tendons of his neck. "Do you think you can obey?"

He shivered as she stroked the tender skin behind his ears. "What will happen if I can't?"

"We'll lock you in your cell and chain you for a month. Nubile young maidens will make love to each other in front of you, enjoying orgasm after orgasm while you have none."

These threats made his pupils dilate.

"Will you make love to David in front of me while I'm chained?"

The harem boy had spoken in a hoarse whisper. "Perhaps," she said, smiling softly as she let him picture this in his mind. "If I think it will pain you sexually."

"He is dripping," David announced, peering around the slave's shoulder. "Even now pre-come rolls down his crown."

"So it does," said the queen, pleased to see the clear, telltale drops. This slave was very excited—and from mere talk. "You must answer me, slave. Aroused as you are, ready as you are, can you abide by my harem law?"

The slave clenched his jaw. "I can. The chance to know this pleasure is too precious to pass up."

"Then we must prepare my favorite. Nothing can proceed until his eagerness equals yours."

She swung gracefully from the bed, obliging the slave to retreat. She faced her most treasured concubine. "You are willing to take this man as he wishes?"

"More than willing," he said hoarsely.

"You think him attractive?"

David glanced at the wide-eyed slave. "Very. Too see him take my queen while I take him will be a great pleasure."

"How diplomatic you are!" The queen exclaimed with a laugh. "But now I must dress and oil you. We do not want to harm our tender virgin with your virility."

The slave colored at her comment, and so she knew she had guessed his inexperience correctly. He was breathing shallowly through parted lips. He watched his future ravisher's cock as she rolled the lambskin sheath down its rigid length, no doubt imagining how that thick, hot shaft would feel penetrating him.

The queen offered the slave the small bottle. "Would you like to oil him?"

To her surprise, the slave shook his head. "I am already too excited. Please . . . my queen, allow me to watch you oil him."

She smiled at his use of her title and poured a generous amount of lubricant into her palm. Both men's attention followed her movements as she rubbed her hands together, warming them for the first touch. Interestingly—as if to touch one of them was to touch both—they made the same low, hungry sound the instant she gripped her favorite's cock. The big erection was firm in her hand, the ridge beneath the shaft hard and hot. She pulled his thickness up and then pushed down. He throbbed impressively even before she'd oiled him enough to shine.

She couldn't help wondering if the slave's cock was pounding, too.

"Shall I also massage your balls?" she asked her favorite, not because she needed permission, but because she wanted to see if the men would react in tandem again.

"Yes," urged the slave, and "yes" said her favorite a breath later.

David widened his stance to give her access to everything he wished rubbed. She was happy to follow the wordless suggestion, and he seemed quite delighted when she leaned against his side and reached down. Wrapping one arm around her waist, he closed his eyes and sighed as she worked more oil over his scrotum and between his legs.

"God," he said as she pressed the harder swell of his perineum. "Oh, God, my queen has hands of gold."

Queen or not, she could not mind hearing this. She caressed him one more time before smoothing her slippery hands up his chest. He was hairier than the slave, rough against her palms. Gently, firmly, she pinched his tiny nipples between her finger and thumb.

David's eyes snapped open as he gasped.

"You are ready," she said. "Your cock stands as high as his."

Her favorite looked from his own cock to the other's, shuddering to see that she had spoken true. A bead of sweat rolled down his clenching jaw. "Yes," he said with more than a hint of determination. "I am ready to fuck him now."

The queen patted his perspiring cheek. "I am proud of you, my favorite. You always rise to the occasion. And now I must prepare myself. Tell me, slave—" The slave jerked his eyes from David's cock to look at her. "Do you wish to enter me from behind? Or would your rather see my face and breasts?"

"Yes," said the slave, his focus now all on her. "Yes, please, your face and breasts." His gaze descended to her darkened nipples, partially hidden by her pale blue wrap. "They are so beautiful. I have dreamed of seeing them naked since I was brought here."

"Then I suppose I must remove my gown." She untucked the sheer blue silk and let it fall. Her reward was a widening of both men's eyes.

"Oh, man," moaned her favorite. "Oh, man, oh, man."

"Come now, David," she teased. "Can it be that in all these years I have never let you see me naked?"

"Never." He gulped and shook his head. "Oh, man, you're so pretty." His stupefied ogle slid down her legs and back to her breasts. "I think I'm going to be jealous of him getting to take you."

"Your queen is gratified to hear this, though she suspects you will be adequately entertained by taking our so-eager-to-be-fucked virgin friend."

She sat on the edge of her grand white bed, her buttocks perched just behind the twined mahogany footrail. The rail was no higher than the mattress. She thought its support would serve her well.

"Take my hands," she said to the men. "Support me while I lean back."

They reached eagerly to do so, both their grips hot and sweaty and strong. When her spine settled onto the covers, she drew her legs up and apart, bracing her feet on the rail near her bottom. Her flexibility made her glad for the royal stretching exercises she did.

Both men stared and panted at what she'd revealed, their tongues nearly hanging out. Their reaction made her want to laugh, but she was grateful men found this part of women interesting. Wanting to see them as much as they wanted to see her, she propped her shoulders on her bolster.

"My queen," gasped the slave, "may I kiss you there?"

"If you wish," she said indulgently.

He was on his knees before the words were completely out. He parted her with his fingers, gently, reverently, and then sank his mouth between.

She cried out, instantly enchanted by his strength and skill. He hummed his approval at her response, intensifying his efforts.

"Softer," she said breathlessly. "I do not want to climax until you are inside me."

He eased the pressure of his lips and tongue, as adept at teasing as he had previously been at giving direct pleasure. His thumbs worked beside his mouth, rubbing firm, small circles up and down the inner surface of her outer lips. Though he did not penetrate her, this spread the magic of his mouth through other nerves. When she recovered enough to remember to open her eyes, her favorite hovered behind the kneeling slave, one hand resting on his shoulder as he peered in utter captivation at the other's method of work.

Perhaps, the queen thought in amusement, he was hoping to improve his own technique.

Amusement could not forestall the rising sensations deep in her being, no matter how lightly she was being sucked and tickled.

"That is enough," she said reluctantly. "You have brought me close. I think you should stand now and enter me."

The slave lifted his head, looking dazedly up her body. Then, with a deep, slow breath, he rose.

His cock was a long red spear thrusting from his groin.

"My queen," he murmured. "I shall not let you down."

David dressed the now obedient slave in his protective cock sheath, touching him only a bit more than he had to. Without removing her gaze from this interesting procedure, the queen reached inside her bolster for a last surprise. She hid it in the covers as the slave moved between her legs. She expected him to push at once, but he rested the knob of his cock against her without entering. His eyes met and held hers.

"Thank you," he said in a low, sweet tone. "Whatever happens,

I thank you for what you've already done. This truly has been magic. I'll dream of it for years to come."

The queen touched the muscled arms he'd braced on the mattress to lean over her. "Whatever happens, you're welcome."

Though the slave was long, he was not as thick as her favorite. He slid in like a dream, groaning with the pleasure of the sleek immersion. He was seated completely in one, slow stroke. Lost in the bliss of it, his head hung over hers. She stroked a fallen lock of hair behind his ear.

"God, you're snug," he said. "You make me feel as big as horse."

"You're perfect," she said, because he had no need to know this had been an easier entry than her usual. "Stay right where you are and do not move while David takes his place."

"I should oil his anus," her favorite said breathlessly. "I don't want to hurt him when I go in."

The queen grinned her approval.

No talking accompanied this preparation, merely jerks and huffs of breath from the captive as Peter moved his well-oiled thumbs in and out of his back entry. The queen knew many nerves were concentrated there, and the slave did indeed enjoy having them rubbed. His heart was thundering behind his ribs, his body blazing hot. Apprehension might have been part of his reaction, but excitement assuredly was as well. The part of him that was inside her was hard as rock. He bit his lip as David drew closer.

"Tell me what you do," the queen ordered her favorite. "Since I cannot see around this lovely slave."

David gasped for air before he could speak. When he did, his voice was tight. "I have the head of my prick against him. I'm ready to push."

"Do you want to?"

"Oh, yes," he breathed as if marveling at how much.

"Then do," she said. "Gently."

David's face tensed with effort as he obeyed. His entrance must have felt good. The slave groaned atop her, and then, a second later, her favorite did as well.

"Tell me what you feel," she said, though she knew that with all the sensations rolling over him, it would be hard to speak—maybe even to think.

"Oh, God," he said. "I'm halfway in. He's really smooth."

"Tight?"

"Yes. But it will only take one more push."

Without waiting for permission, his body heaved closer. Another low, rough sound broke from both the men, announcing her favorite's full entry. The slave sank to his forearms. He was trembling as David planted his palms outside his elbows. The slave's cheek touched hers, rubbing back and forth like a cat in need of reassurance.

"He's thick," he whispered next to her ear.

"Does it hurt?"

He shook his head. "Feel me inside you. Feel how hard I am."

She felt not only how hard he was but how strongly his excitement pulsed.

"Should David move now? Is that what you want?"

"Yes," he breathed. "Yes."

"You stay still," she ordered.

He smiled and dropped his mouth to hers for a slow, deep kiss. He didn't have permission for this, but she allowed it since he kissed well. Behind him, her favorite began to thrust. Though the slave's body stiffened, she could tell his tension was that of profound pleasure.

"Ah," he sighed, breaking from the kiss to loll his head back in enjoyment. His eyes were closed, his face suddenly slack. David's strokes were careful, but the queen could imagine what pleasurable territory they were rubbing back and forth.

"Don't move," she reminded the slave as his hips began to rock instinctively.

"He's pushing me into you," he gasped, his hands clenching on the sheets.

"Not that much, he isn't."

"Brace your knees," her favorite advised in a throaty tone. "Push back at me, relax, and I won't shove you forward so much."

"But moving is good," groaned the slave. "God, I feel both of you. It's fucking heaven." His eyes squeezed shut as David's cock slid over an especially good spot. "Don't you—Doesn't my queen want me to fuck her?"

"Not yet," said the queen. "For now I'd rather take care of myself."

She pulled out the toy she'd hidden in the covers, a slim, petal-pink electric vibrating wand.

"Shit," said the slave, guessing what was coming.

Behind his shoulder, her favorite's eyes went round.

"Remember," she said as she slid the smooth pink tip between her hips and Peter's, "no one comes before I say."

"But that's a vibrator!"

The queen grinned at her taut captive. "If you stay where you are, the vibrations will only touch your base. That shouldn't set you off."

"Under normal circumstances, maybe—"

"Hush." The queen cut him off. "You will obey me. You can."

The slave swelled inside her and cursed, her words as powerful as any toy. This was his fantasy come to life. He couldn't help but respond.

"Don't speed up," she cautioned her favorite. "We need not make this any harder on him."

"Right," said her concubine, sounding a bit afraid of the edge himself.

She smiled, pleased with them both, and switched the wand to low. She'd positioned it right on her clitoris. The slave gasped and shoved deeper, as if—in spite of his concerns—he wanted to get as close as possible to the buzz. He was in her far enough, and his cock was hard enough, that the leverage this created tipped her pelvis slightly off the bed.

The pressure was delicious.

"Count," she said throatily, already sensing her first climax's approach. "When I've had my sixth orgasm, you, slave, are allowed to move."

"Six," he said and swallowed. "I hope that's not going to take long."

She spasmed sweet and hard around him.

"Oh," he said, and smiled like a boy. "That's one then."

Two and three came soon after. She was so wet she missed four, but she forgave him by whispering it in his ear. At five, her favorite lifted her right leg until her calf draped his hip. His movements had slowed since the beginning, perhaps to show mercy to the slave, or perhaps to protect himself from the effects of too much excitement. Her favorite's only flaw was that he sometimes had a quick trigger.

"I wish I could feel what you're feeling," he lamented to the slave on a long forward push.

"Be glad you can't," the slave countered through gritted teeth. "You haven't got half my self-control."

Not the least bit insulted, her favorite chuckled and reached around the slave to cup the queen's right breast. He pinched its already hardened tip and then twisted lightly. She gasped at how good that felt.

"Come the last time for me," he said, and a moment later she did.

When her spine finished arching, her favorite pulled the vibrating wand from her nerveless hand.

"That's it for your toy," he said. "The rest of this show is ours." He ran his hands up the slave's back to his shoulders, squeezing their muscles in encouragement. "Your turn, Pete. Time to show our queen what a horny harem boy can do."

The slave's first stroke told her what she was in for. It was slow and hard and high, sending a lingering pressure just where she most wanted it. This stroke was followed by a second that pushed his shaft most to the right, by a third that pressed left, and a fourth—by far the longest and the slowest—that slid the under-side of his cockhead, where his nerves were concentrated, with the greatest possible firmness along the bottom of her sheath.

She could tell he liked this best. He cursed, ground his molars, and moved hastily back to the top of her cunt. She was tempted to test him by demanding he repeat the lower stroke, but then her fa-vorite began to move once more.

It wasn't long before all of them were groaning. Though her favorite was usually very excitable, tonight the other man cried out the loudest. She knew the instant her favorite found his prostate, because the slave trembled like a leaf. His cock slackened momen-tarily and then got harder.

"Not there," he gasped as her favorite did it again.

"Yes, there," disagreed his tormentor, sliding over the spot de-fiantly. "You're gonna blow, boy. You're gonna blast off like a vol-cano."

"I can't." The slave sucked in air as she moaned and came for the seventh time, her inner muscles gripping him. "She hasn't given me permission."

The queen barely had breath to and sensed he didn't want per-mission yet in any case. "Slower," she said, reaching up to squeeze her favorite's arm. "Go on . . . doing what you're doing. Just give him a chance to last."

"What about me?" Her favorite groaned. "I can't take much more of this."

"You can come when he does. And he needs at least five minutes."

"Set the alarm," said the slave in a tight, thin voice. "I want every fucking second."

The queen could only just reach it, and only after her lovers had shoved her higher on the bed. The men had their knees side by side on the mattress then, their weight more noticeable as they rocked their bodies together into her. The scent of aroused male flesh mingled with the rose petals. Both their breathing was labored, each exhale a moan of longing as it sighed out.

She loved the sound of them struggling not to ejaculate, loved the feel of them helplessly thrusting a little harder, a little faster, their physical urges taking over from their will. She almost climaxed again but forced herself to wait.

She, after all, hadn't been holding back as long as them.

"You're sure you only set it for five minutes?" David asked.

"Yes," she laughed. "I was careful to get it right."

That's when she noticed the slave couldn't speak at all. He was gnawing his lower lip and blinking sweat from his eyes.

She stroked his shoulder and kissed the corded muscles of his chest. "Not much longer," she murmured. "The instant that bell rings you can let go."

He groaned at the suggestion, stroking deep and hard into her, a thrust that started high and then dipped low. It seemed he couldn't resist rubbing his own sweet spot. He reset his elbows, then stretched his spine as if this would somehow help him hang on. His nipples were shadows above her mouth, pointy and flushed. She craned up to suck them and earned a cry.

This little extra stimulation was more than he could stand. No matter what it cost him, the slave started pumping into her like he was crazed. A second later, David pumped into him. At this added goad, even hoarser cries tore from the captive's throat.

"Bite my nipples," he gasped to her. When she did, he added, just as urgently, "Dave, squeeze my balls."

David must have done it. She was being pummeled, deliciously, by both men's thrusts. The bed squealed in protest at their fervor, but it was the slave who suffered most. His breath whined out of him, almost a sob. His whole body was rigid, his muscles clenching from groin to throat.

"Ring," he pleaded, slinging his pelvis into hers. "Ring!"

The alarm jangled its permission.

David came with a curse before it finished, but the slave was still going, his hips moving like lightning as he strove for the release he was finally allowed to take. Five strokes. Ten.

"Now," he groaned, and with two more thrusts he went.

The queen had stopped nipping his chest to watch. The slave's whole body seemed to convulse, his face dark with the blood that had rushed to its surface, his spine arching hard while tendons stood out on his throat. This was the orgasm of a lifetime. Every particle of his attention seemed to focus in on his shooting cock.

"God," he gasped, his hips pressing the last ejaculatory squeezes against hers. When they ended, all he could do was moan.

Her sheath pulsed around his softening cock, its ache more to do with hunger than the pounding she'd just taken. Even at the end the men hadn't hurt her, and she'd been so enthralled by watching Peter's climax, she'd forgotten to come that last time herself. Considering she'd had seven orgasms already, it seemed beyond rude to bring this up.

It wouldn't have done her any good anyway. Though Dave had rolled off Pete, Pete had utterly collapsed. Smiling at the memories she and her pink wand would have to enjoy later on, she ran her hands up his sweaty, relaxing back.

"You need to pull out," she reminded gently. "Before that condom stops fitting."

He mumbled something unintelligible, but he complied.

"Man," he said, wriggling himself into the space on the mattress between her and Dave. His head settled onto her shoulder as if they were old friends. "Think I need a nap."

Frankie laughed softly to herself. No matter what the fantasy, or who you lived it out with, it seemed men would always be men.

Chapter 12

When Dewey and Jack returned to their office at City Hall, Rivera was waiting at the door like an anxious mother.

"Did the lab call yet?" Jack asked, rather than let her share what was bugging her. His temper wasn't up to soothing her right now. Unfortunately, Rivera wasn't picking up his cues. She followed him into his office.

"Not today," she said. "You know how County is. Always backed up."

He pulled out his chair and looked at it without sitting down. His brain felt like it was running a couple minutes slow. He kept seeing Frankie on that bench with True, laughing like they were best buds. "That's too bad. I was hoping they'd have typed that semen from Whittier's kit."

It didn't bode well for Rivera's future on a bigger force that she was blushing when he turned back to her.

"The mayor wants to see you," she blurted, evidently what she'd been dying to tell him from the start.

Now Jack sat. "I'm not in."

"But CNN wants to set up an interview."

He stacked his hands behind his head, which made Rivera's normally lush lips thin worriedly. "I'm not in for them, either."

"But Chief—"

"Don't—" *get your panties in a bunch*, he almost said. Instead, knowing this would upset her, he tipped forward in his chair and sighed. He'd been at this—what—almost four days now, and the case was nettling him more by the hour.

"Don't sweat it," he said wearily. "Sometimes you have to dodge the bigwigs to get things done. His Honor means well, but he's inexperienced. He knows he only got elected mayor because his predecessor was a grade-A jerk. He gets to thinking he's in over his head—which he frequently is—and tries to make up for it by scheduling meetings and blustering. I'll talk to him when I've got real news. The same goes for CNN."

"Yes, sir," said Rivera, looking mollified but not happy.

"Write him a memo if you want," Jack suggested. "Summarize what we've done. Just don't give him anything we wouldn't want in a press release."

Now Rivera downright frowned.

"Fuck," said Jack, losing his patience altogether. "I'm not being sexist. Get Dewey to write it if you don't want to. Sometimes every cop has to play secretary."

Rivera's shoulders were stiff as boards. "I'll do it, sir. Dewey would never get everything straight."

Jack wanted to laugh but held it in. Rivera didn't believe anyone could get things as straight as her.

"Wait," he said, halting her at the door. "Where are the tapes?"

She looked startled. "Whittier's X-rated DVDs?"

"Yes. I've decided to watch them again. There's something in them that we're missing. Some clue to who Tish Whittier really was. If they're not the reason she was killed, they're going to tell me what the reason was."

He felt sure of it as he said it, though that might have been more wishful thinking than cop's instinct. Still, better to do something than nothing. Sometimes wishful thinking led you to the answers, too.

Rivera was chewing her lower lip uncomfortably. "They're in the dark room." She hesitated as if she couldn't decide whether to add something more.

Jack pushed to his feet. "Don't worry, Rivera. I won't make you watch them again."

"I wasn't—" She spun away without finishing. "I'll take care of the memo. I've seen enough of those things anyway."

Jack was sorry he'd been short with her, but not that he'd run her off. As he headed to their small dark room, he told himself it was just as well she was fuming. Maybe him being rude would get her over that stupid crush.

Not caring that the space was so cramped he had to prop his feet on a shelf, he stacked the DVDs beside the player they kept with the rest of their photography supplies. Happily, the developing baths were empty and didn't stink. As comfortable as he was going to get, he closed the door and began running Whittier's private porn collection, one after another, until his eyeballs felt sunburned. A few of the discs were recorded on both sides, each of which he viewed. Despite his thoroughness, no lightbulbs went off above his head. Some of the selections were sexier than others, but none played as hot, or as natural, as the one with Tish as its star.

By far the most tepid featured Phoebe Atkins, the dry cleaner's wife. She'd spent the first third of her scene complaining that Pete and Dave had refused to seduce her in her husband's actual bed.

That, she claimed, was her fantasy. If Jack had been her husband, he'd have been tempted to kill Phoebe for her whine alone, but he doubted he'd feel much animosity toward Whittier. All she'd done was make it possible for Phoebe to expose the scorn she felt for her spouse. Phoebe would do for a suspect if she'd found out she'd been filmed—though Rivera said so far her alibi was tight.

When the last image faded, Jack leaned back and rubbed his tired face. The sense that he was missing something nagged at him. He thumbed through the cases and read their labels. The tongue-in-cheek titles didn't make him smile anymore.

Who were you? he asked his unexpectedly mysterious victim. *Why did you want, or need, to record these things?* Had Whittier's clueless parents driven her to it? Was this her way of proving she existed? Maybe it gave her a sense of power to film these women unaware. He remembered Frankie's comment that Tish had a tendency to be down on herself, a tendency Troy confirmed with his anecdote about Tish thinking Frankie looked better in her pearls. So did Whittier think these women Pete and Dave seduced possessed some quality she wanted but didn't have? Was she trying to claim it for herself through the recordings, like a modern version of a tribesman consuming his enemy?

Now you're really reaching, he thought. For all he knew, Tish simply liked to watch. People did, after all, including— apparently—himself.

No more enlightened than he'd been before he began, Jack returned to his office to tackle the one big rock he'd been putting off shoving over.

Tipping it required some time on his computer and a dozen calls, but finally he had it—a link between Tish Whittier and Mike True. The summer he'd turned fifteen, before becoming an armed robber, Michael True had worked as a pool boy at a Santa Barbara country club, the same club where Whittier's parents had a membership. She and True could have met if she'd spent her first summer after graduating college with her parents. If True had been the kind of kid who looked old for his age, sparks might have flown.

"Might have," he said to himself with his hands steepled at his mouth. At least it was something to check up on, though he would have been happier if the DNA tests had come back from the county lab. If True turned out to be Tish's final lover, Jack would have felt more justified for suspecting him.

He knew too well why he wanted him to be guilty.

"That doesn't mean he isn't," he told himself.

"Hmm. Talking to yourself," Dewey said as he stuck his head in the door. "Not a good sign."

"Why don't you knock?" Jack said. "For that matter, why don't you call me 'chief' now and then?"

Dewey flapped his notebook in his boss's direction and grinned. "Too excited, chief. I've got something you'll want to hear."

"I could use good news," Jack admitted.

"Well, it's good and bad. The bad news is there's nothing funny going on at Whittier's charities. She ran those puppies like a pro. Nothing got by her, according to the accountant, despite her being a pushover most of the time."

"And the good news?"

When Dewey spilled it, Jack's eyebrows shot up. He'd had no idea just how on-topic his junior officer's revelation was going to be.

With nothing better to do for the moment, Frankie fell asleep. The men woke before her, their muted conversation drifting into her twilight state.

"You up?" Dave asked.

Pete grunted in answer. "You keep pressing that thing against my back, and I will be soon."

"I can't stop thinking about what we did. That was amazing. Frankie was amazing."

"Mmm," was Pete's sleepy response, though he didn't sound like he disagreed.

"I could do that again," Dave confessed.

Pete's chuckle warmed Frankie's shoulder. "When don't you want a second round?"

Pete's weight shifted on the mattress as he turned to Dave. Frankie smiled to hear them kissing—French kissing, from the sound of it. Her body pulsed with interest, really waking now. If those two didn't leave the room, they might be having seconds sooner than they thought.

The kissing noises stopped as the sound of quickened respiration rose.

"You know," Dave said, pausing to catch his breath, "it's a shame we couldn't tape what we did today for Tish."

Frankie's eyes flew open in shock. Pete and Dave had been taping their escapades for Tish? Like, on a regular basis? And just how many women did that involve?

"No way," Pete said to Dave before she could betray that she was awake. "Some things aren't meant to be shared."

"Maybe not, but I'd sure like to watch that a few more times. You were hot."

"You, too, buddy. I could feel that rod of yours to my throat."

Another kiss ensued at this charming and tender exchange. Frankie pressed one knuckle to her mouth, debating whether to interrupt. She was still debating when Dave spoke again.

"I feel sad for Tish," he sighed. "I'll never understand why Troy dumped her for Karen."

"Troy dumped *Tish* for Karen?"

Both men jolted up at her astonished words.

"Man," said Dave, his palm to his heart. "Sorry. I wouldn't have mentioned you-know-who if I'd known you were awake."

Frankie sat up and raked her hair from her face, now little better than a blond tangle. "I don't care if you mention Troy. I want to know what you meant when you said he dumped Tish for Karen. I thought he dumped *me*."

"Uh," said Dave, the way men do when they've put their foot in it and don't want to shove it deeper.

Judging him temporarily useless, Frankie turned her eagle-eyed glare to Pete. He gave her a rueful look.

"You aren't going to like this."

"Tell me anyway."

"Troy was two-timing you with both of them."

Frankie covered her face. Could the humiliation get any deeper?

Pete squeezed her shoulder, leaving his hand there in support. "He was just being Troy, Frankie. He's a nice guy, but not the brightest bulb in the pack. Tish and Karen looked so much alike, I think he couldn't decide at first which one he really wanted."

"He was road-testing them," Dave put in not-so-helpfully.

"Jeez," said Frankie and dropped her hands to her thighs. "Who else knew about this?"

"The three of them, I assume," Dave said. "And us. When we started planning scenes together, we got to be Tish's confidantes. God, she was crazy about Troy. They fit, you know?"

Pete snorted. "You mean they were both ditsy."

"They were in love," Dave insisted. Pete grimaced a wordless concession that this was true. With this to bolster him, Dave went on. "Tish was devastated when Troy dumped her. I mean, she felt bad for sneaking around behind your back, but Troy meant the world to her. She even told us she was going to quit recording us with other women. She didn't think Troy would understand if he found out."

"Maybe he did find out," Pete said. "Maybe that's why he traded her for Karen."

Frankie pulled the sheet over her breasts so she could think, earning herself two flattering frowns from the men.

She knew she should have been pissed at Tish, rather than just at Troy and her own stupidity. Somehow she couldn't do it. It wasn't only that Tish was dead; it was that Frankie could imagine her falling for Troy hard enough to sneak around with him and still be sincerely worried about hurting her. Tish had been insecure, and Troy was good at flattery—especially where his heart was involved. A stronger woman might have put her foot down and insisted Troy leave Frankie before he slept with her, but "Strong" had never been Tish's middle name.

"I don't think Troy found out about the recordings," Frankie said. "I saw him right after he heard Tish was dead. I didn't understand at the time, but he was acting like a man who'd lost the love of his life, not like one who'd had his trust betrayed."

"Well, Tish would be relieved to hear that," Dave said. "But then I wonder why he chose Karen over her. No offense, but if he was trying to get away from you, Karen's more like you than Tish. Tish was a cream-puff about most things. I mean, if we disagreed with her, the first thing she'd do was apologize. Karen's kind of take-charge."

"Not that *we* think there's anything wrong with that," Pete put in. "We like women who know what they want."

"Did *you two* ever sleep with Karen?" Frankie asked.

"Uh," said Pete, taking a page from his partner's book.

Frankie waved her hand. "Never mind. This whole thing is giving me a headache."

She knew the important answer anyway. Troy had left Tish

because Karen was going to have his kid. Two-timing skunk or not, he had enough of a moral center to stick by her for that. Frankie didn't want to, but she felt sorry for him again. Star-crossed lovers didn't begin to describe what he and Tish had been.

"Don't be upset," Dave said, reaching around Pete to pat her knee. "Some men don't have the brains to know what they've got."

His sweetness earned him a crooked smile.

"We could make you forget we told you," Pete suggested hopefully. Hope was enough to get him going. The sheet was swiftly tenting over his lap. From the meaningful squeeze Dave gave her knee, he was "hopeful," too.

Frankie laughed in spite of herself. These two sure did know how to raise a woman's self-esteem. "I am not wearing that blue scarf again."

"Not necessary," Pete assured her. "This time, I think we'd like to spoil you."

For God's sake, Jack carped at himself as he stared up at the precipitous modern angles of Frankie's house. *Just ring the bell and see if she's in. You know she needs to hear this even if it makes her mad.*

He couldn't let his reluctance to confront her stop him. He had a job to do. Determined to get himself off the mark, he dried one hand on his trousers, then lifted it to the bell.

Before he could press it, a faint sound caught his ear—like a woman crying out in pain. He froze, adrenaline blazing through him. Had he imagined the noise? Had he perhaps mistaken a bird for a human being?

But it came again, louder this time, from an upper window in the cylindrical portion of her house. The cry belonged to Frankie. Whether it was pleasure or pain, he couldn't say. Given what he now knew, it hardly mattered. If True was up there, she could be in danger. That was all the justification he legally needed to break in.

He didn't stop to curse or debate himself. He retreated to the edge of her front stoop, took a deep breath, and charged every one of his two hundred twenty pounds of muscle toward the wide, white door.

The hinges burst like toys, the door toppling inward and crashing down. It sounded like an explosion. Voices rang out in confusion as he charged up Frankie's crazy spiral stairs. The empty spaces between the steel treads gave him vertigo. Ignoring the effect, he bulled all the way up them two at a time to the landing he knew must lead to her bedroom.

He reached the top so fast his old football coach would have been proud.

Chances were, Coach Kowalski would have been the only one. When Jack threw open Frankie's door, the scene that greeted him was not remotely what he'd expected.

Pete and Dave's idea of giving a woman a massage was pretty personal. For one thing, it involved using every part of their bodies to massage hers. For another, it was impossible not to grow incredibly aroused.

That had not been Frankie's experience in her infrequent trips to the Six Palms Spa.

She was sandwiched, writhing, between the men while Pete's very experienced fingers worked to "relax" her vagina, and the entire front of Dave's body did its best to rub "soothing warmth" into her back. Since they'd oiled her first, Dave's impressive erection slid over her without a hitch.

"Ooh, I want my turn to be inside you," he groaned into her ear. "Sometimes Pete gets all the luck."

She started to laugh, but it turned into a moan when Pete found something especially nice to squeeze.

"Like that, don't you?" he teased.

When he extended the squeeze to her clitoris, she couldn't help crying out.

"My," she said on a panting breath. "I could get used to being spoiled like this."

"Any time," Pete promised, doing the trick again. "For you, Dave and I would make house calls."

She didn't get a chance to return his banter, because what sounded like a bomb went off on the lower floor. At once, they were bumping elbows and knees trying to sit up.

"What was that?" Pete demanded.

"Don't ask me," Dave returned.

Frankie noticed neither moved to check. Hearing pounding footsteps, she tried to grab the sheet from under the men. They'd been lying on top of the bedclothes, and now they were stuck. "Someone's running up the stairs!"

She was still tugging for coverage when the door slammed open. Frankie's mouth dropped in shock. Seeing the Hulk appear in her bedroom couldn't have surprised her more. Jack West filled the opening, huffing like a steam engine and looking twice his normal size in his desert-tan uniform.

For a long, stunned moment, all they did was stare at each other like they'd been transfixed.

Then Jack's gaze dropped to her nakedness.

He brought it up again as quickly as any red-blooded male with eyes would have done—not, however, before his face flushed dark. Torture alone could not have gotten Frankie to admit how much satisfaction this gave her.

"Hey!" Dave said in protest, and that really set Jack off.

His expression tightened. "What the *hell* do you think you're doing?"

There could be no mistaking that he was addressing her, that he had the gall to judge her for doing what she pleased in her own home. Frankie thought the top of her head would come off with anger. Naked or not, she jumped to her feet, stomped across two yards of carpet, and faced him down. "This is my house, you jerk! My bedroom! What the hell do you think *you're* doing?"

"I heard a noise."

"And that gives you the right to barge in?"

"As a matter of fact, it does, Ms. Smith. It was my professional opinion that you were in danger!"

Frankie's skin buzzed hot. The fact that he'd crossed his arms as if he were some sort of righteous avenger made her want to scream. "Oh, sure," she said, dripping mockery. "I'm certain what you heard sounded exactly like a cry of pain."

"Uh," said Dave, "maybe we ought to leave you two to settle this."

"Stay where you are," Frankie barked so forcefully both Pete and Dave fell back. "*You* are guests here. *You* have a right to take your time getting dressed before you go." Done with them, she narrowed her eyes at her intruder, her fists ready to dig holes into her hips. "*You* go downstairs and wait. I'm going to pull on a robe and then I'll deal with you. And Jack—" His eyebrows rose at her somewhat insulting use of his first name. "Don't even *think* about leaving before we have this out."

She could see Jack West wasn't used to taking orders. He glared at her just as hotly as she'd glared at him, muscles working violently in his jaw. He drew one quick breath, then turned on his heel and clomped down the stairs.

"Whoa," said Dave as silence settled over her room. "Remind me not to get either of you mad at me!"

Frankie was still seething by the time she padded down the stairs barefoot. Pulling on her favorite royal blue silk robe hadn't seemed like enough. She'd also taken a quick shower—for reasons she didn't want to think too hard about. The fact that she'd put a pair of panties and a bra beneath it would have to suffice to prove she wasn't preparing to jump Jack, too.

She found her would-be rescuer maneuvering her front door back into its opening. She could hardly comprehend how he'd knocked it down. Most times, if someone busted down a door, all he did was rip the lock out of the wood. Frankie was impressed in spite of herself. If she had been in danger, Jack was obviously the person to have called.

Feeling this attitude was a little too close to admiration, she folded her arms beneath her breasts. Though she'd been quiet, Jack must have sensed her there.

"Pete and Dave left," he said. "Shoes in hand." He pushed a screw through the splintered remains of its hole. "I told them if they'd put a camera in your room, I'd kill them both."

He turned, looking tired enough that—had he been a friend—she would have offered him a hug. His weariness was the kind that went deeper than bone and muscle, the kind that had to do with how you thought your life was going.

Not good, was Frankie's guess.

"You know about them taping stuff for Tish then," she said, relieved she didn't have to tell him. "They just broke the news to me. Bit of a shocker."

"Yeah." He jerked his head toward the listing door. "The department will pay for that."

"The taxpayers, you mean." The words came out kind of shrewish. Frankie wasn't certain if she was sorry or reassured. Being a shrew might keep him at the distance she was pretending she wanted him.

For now, her tone had him blowing out his breath. "I apologize for the damage. I honestly thought you were in danger." He hesitated and then grimaced. "I thought you were with True."

"Jeez," she said, abruptly peeved again. "How would you even know I had company? Have you been watching my house?"

"I *came* to your house because I wanted to warn you. I found out something we didn't know before, something I thought you ought to be made aware of. True has a link to Whittier. Two summers before he was assigned to Camp Pendleton, he worked as a towel boy at her parents' country club. They could have had a fling gone bad. Kids the age he was take things hard. He could have been waiting all this time to get revenge."

"*Could have*," Frankie repeated. "Are you certain they even met?"

"Not yet, but there's something else. We finally reached his commanding officer in Iraq. He said True was the stone coldest killer he'd ever seen, and this comes from a guy who commands Marines. They called him 'True Ice.' His CO said the other men on his team just about cried when he was discharged. They thought he was a good luck charm."

Frankie's stomach rolled uncomfortably. It didn't matter that she didn't plan to sleep with Mike again. She didn't want to think she had looked into the eyes of a killer and seen only a lonely heart. It was one thing to misjudge Troy, but if she was that blind, and a man like Mike was that lost, she thought she might want to crawl under the covers and never come out.

"He was a good soldier," she said aloud. "That doesn't mean he killed Tish."

"For God's sake, Frankie! Are you determined to keep sleeping with all my suspects?"

"I don't know," she fired back, insulted and hurt and angry about both reactions. "Is there some reason I shouldn't—since you seem to have no intention of sleeping with me yourself?"

His mouth fished open. "I didn't think you'd—" He stopped, apparently thinking better of finishing. He might not have known it, but it was too late. Frankie was pretty sure she could guess what he'd been about to say.

I didn't think you'd still want me to.

A prickling wave of awareness swept her scalp. Not thinking she still wanted to sleep with him was a pretty big thing to miss, considering she'd practically attacked him the other day. Even more important, his answer would seem to imply he wanted her to try again.

"Look," he said. "Whether True killed Whittier or not, his history is something to think about. He's not some harmless stray puppy."

She pressed her fist to her chest, her mind trying to process what it had just learned and also answer sensibly. "Don't policemen ever take chances? Don't they go with their guts?"

"Sure they do," he said with a bitter snort. "And sometimes their guts are wrong. When I was twenty, every cop I knew told me not to marry my girlfriend while I was still in the Academy. They said wait until she sees what being a policeman's wife is really like. But I thought, no, we love each other. This is going to last the rest of our lives."

His voice broke on the final word, and Frankie knew he hadn't planned on that. He'd planned on sounding cynical, on showing her just how wrong a person's gut could be.

He couldn't doubt he'd given himself away now.

She looked into his black-lashed, honeyed eyes. His expression was belligerent, as if daring her to say a thing. But Frankie did dare. She couldn't not. Taking chances was part of who she was.

No matter what he thought he'd been trying to do, when Jack told her this story he was, on some level, reaching out to her.

"Your ex-wife is haunting you," she said softly in understanding. "Every woman you meet, you expect to let you down like she did. You were too young when she ran out on you, and you never healed. You never let your heart grow up."

"My heart is plenty grown up," he said roughly. "You have no idea the things I've seen."

She put her hand on his chest. She remembered Jean's story about him running into the burning building while people watched. She thought of hurts her own heart had taken, and that maybe it hadn't grown up, either. Her eyes swam with tears his answered—unwillingly, she was sure—and a subtle increase in shine. His heart was pounding like he was scared. He must have realized it himself. He cursed but didn't move away. Instead, he put his hand over hers, holding it gently where it was.

Any other man would have kissed her. Any other man would have had her out of her clothes and on the floor. All Jack offered, maybe all he could offer, was this mute confession of his feelings, these few square inches where her palm connected to the beating truth of him.

"You're afraid of me," she murmured, wanting it in the open. "You're afraid if we get too close, I'll—"

"Don't say it."

His second hand came up before she realized it had moved. It gripped the back of her neck in a viselike hold. This should have alarmed her, but she was enthralled. He was taking control. He was choosing what happened. Using the grasp to pull her closer, he forced her head to tip back. His eyes were seriously glittering now, nearly spilling over. His emotion combined with his assertiveness to send her body flaring to lustful life. She was wet in an instant, fevered from head to toe. The scent of him—angry, sweaty—was more delicious than any man's she'd ever taken into her lungs.

He's it, she thought. *I want him because he's the one who matches me.*

This thought was enough to scare her, but she couldn't hide its effect. He'd been breathing so hard and standing so close that the muscled wall of his chest brushed hers. Her nipples tightened to the point of pain at the chafing of his uniform. A moan caught half-uttered in her throat. When he heard it, his gaze burned down at her like molten gold.

Then his eyes lowered to her lips and went dark.

"You don't have to say it," he said hoarsely. "I can guess what you think you know about me."

She was clutching the front of his shirt with her fists, her knees nearly weak enough to give out. "If you don't want me to say it, you'd better shut me up."

She was too aroused to laugh at her own lame joke, and he certainly wasn't laughing.

"I've wanted you since the first day I laid eyes on you," he warned her. "I've had dreams about you I wouldn't share with another soul. If that weren't bad enough, I haven't slept with a woman in so many years I've lost count. Once or twice isn't going to be enough for me. If you let me take you, I can't promise it'll be pretty."

"I've had pretty," she said, her voice husky as hell. "It ain't all it's cracked up to be."

This, at last, was enough encouragement for him. He groaned, cinched his arm behind her waist, and lifted her off her feet to his mouth. Tight as he was holding her, his kiss was almost smothering, but she didn't care. She hugged him back, throwing her whole body into it. He moaned into her mouth each time her tongue stroked his. His hand slid over her bottom. She'd wrapped her legs around his hips, and now he pressed her pelvis to him, rocking his erection into her mound in a rhythm so insistent they could have been making love already.

"Oh, God," she said, her head falling back as he trailed hard kisses down her throat. "Get me to the couch."

They made it to the kitchen, where he slammed her back against the sub-zero just like she'd wished he'd do the other day. His weight pinned her easily. Pulling her arms from around him, he gathered both wrists in one big hand and pulled them above her head. Something about his restraining her felt so good she cried out.

Her thighs hardly had the strength to hold her close enough.

"I really need this," he said, his free hand working frantically at his uniform belt, no easy task when he was trying to keep their groins pressed tight. "Please tell me you're not going to stop me."

"I . . . promise," she panted. He laid the belt, which had a gun in it, carefully on the counter behind him. Too impatient to wait, she reached between them to rasp down his zipper.

"Shit," he said, and she thought she might have caught something. But it seemed she hadn't. His cock swelled, unharmed, through the opening, still covered by his snug, white briefs but every bit as large as she'd imagined. She had a second to gasp and admire it before he swallowed her mouth again. Somehow, he'd gotten one hand between them as they kissed. He used it to cup her mound, squeezing her hot, damp panties into the folds of her sex. He covered so much of her in his hold, that alone made her blood run hot. Her robe fell open as she squirmed greedily.

"Shit," he said again, but this time he explained himself. "You've got a bra on, too. I thought you'd be naked under that robe."

"Rip everything off," she said, finally feeling sure enough to laugh.

To her surprise, he did rip her panties—and the bra as well, snapping the front plastic closure between his finger and thumb. He didn't even set her down to do it. His hand dug between them again, but this time into his own underwear. He made a little noise that sounded like relief. His cock fell against her labia, naked and throbbing and huge.

"Wait," she said, writhing so much she was almost hanging from his hold. "Let me have one hand."

"Don't tell me to wait," he said, but he freed one wrist all the same.

"I just want to touch you." She let her legs slide down his sides. "I just want to feel you before you come inside me."

He groaned at the reminder of what she expected to happen next. Suddenly both her wrists were free. Her knees gave out when his hold released, but she decided kneeling on the cold hard tiles was exactly the place to be.

His erection towered in front of her, inches away. Its heat was baking her cheeks. She had never seen a man this big, and she absolutely loved it. The sight of his thickness, of his strong blue veins, switched on something primitive inside her, something completely uninhibited. The tip of him was redder than her rouged nipples. She didn't ask permission, and she didn't want it. She clasped him between her hands and sucked him, all she could take: the fat, silky head, the first few inches of the pulsing shaft, tonguing him hard and getting him wet.

"Jesus," he moaned like a song. "Jesus, Frankie."

He stroked his fingers into her hair, surprisingly gentle for how aroused he was. His thighs had begun to shake.

"No more," he begged, even as he pushed a little farther in. "Frankie, let me fuck you now."

She let him go and kissed the salty tip of him. His hands tilted her head up. His face, so far above her, was dusky and wondering.

"Come down," she said, patting the floor. "Come down and take me here."

He sank down over her, careful again, though his knees came immediately between hers. He knew where he wanted to go even if he was being polite.

"Hold my wrists like before," she said. "I liked how you did that with one hand."

His chest gave a funny heave. "Me, too," he said hoarsely. "I like holding you down."

He did it, and her body arched by itself, a hum rolling sweet as molasses out of her throat. He breathed harder, his thighs widening to spread hers. They both gasped as his crown settled perfectly against her gate.

"Lucky," she said, stretching helplessly again. A trickle of cream ran down around him, hot from being inside her sex.

"Frankie," he murmured. He looked down between them and shuddered. He was propped up on one arm. Clearly, he could see where his big erection was poised to enter her, maybe even the glistening signs of her excitement. When he looked up again, his eyes were naked. They held concern for her and his awe that this was actually happening. "Are you ready for me?"

"I am, but—" She licked her lips, a touch of nervousness in her throat. "Go slow, okay? I'm naturally kind of tight."

"I could try getting you wetter."

She had to laugh at that. "If I were any wetter, we both might drown."

He kissed her with just enough tongue to make her lips tingle.

"Slow," he repeated, maybe to himself. He surged forward with a gentle push.

The head of him came into her and maybe an inch of shaft.

"Oh, boy," she said, her neck joining her stretch this time. "Oh, boy, that's good."

He nuzzled her hair and shoved again. "Will I be able to go faster later?"

"Yes," she sighed, her eyes half-closing. "Yes, when you're all the way in, I'll ease up."

He pulled back, pushed, then groaned as another inch made it in. His voice was a smoky rasp. "Something to look forward to." He nudged in another fraction. "Oh, Frankie, you're a freaking glove."

His long sigh of pleasure let her know this was no complaint.

"Just a few more thrusts," she promised. "And as soon as we finish this round, Jack, I *am* stripping you naked."

"Deal," he said, a little breathless from the results of another push.

Six more gentle rocks brought him to his hilt. He felt so wonderful filling her up she couldn't speak. To her pleasure, Jack wasn't much better.

"Okay?" he panted on a second try.

His cock thrummed and jumped inside her like a living thing. She smiled at his consideration in the face of his obvious eagerness. "Let my hands loose. I want to pull off your shirt."

He let her go but did it himself, balancing on one hand and then the other to wrestle out of his uniform and undershirt.

She had to stroke his chest then, had to run her fingers through his dark cloud of hair. His muscles were leaner than she expected, not bulky but impressive. Jean had mentioned once that he ran, so maybe that was why. He shivered when she scratched her nails around his flat nipples. Points sprang up in their centers, and goose bumps rose around their edges.

"Do you want to trap my wrists again?" she asked.

She watched him think. "No," he said slowly, the answer seeming to surprise him. "I like the way you touch me. I think I'll save a few fantasies for later."

"Deal," Frankie said.

They both were smiling when he set his knees to take her for real.

Chapter 13

It had been so long since he'd had sex, Jack had almost forgotten what a naked woman felt like. To have his first be Frankie, the object of his increasingly lustful dreams for the last twelve months, was enough to knock the breath out of him. Hell, his lungs had been in trouble the minute she'd appeared in that sleek blue robe with her hair a tousled cloud around her shoulders. He'd been hard while he wrestled her door back into place, his blood on fire from remembering his brief, heart-stopping glimpse of her naked breasts.

Now those breasts were beneath him, and his aching cock was buried in a pussy so snug and wet he thought he'd like to stay inside it for the rest of his life.

He knew he was lucky he'd had to be so careful entering her. It had given him time to gather his frayed control. If he hadn't done that, he'd have come ten times by now.

"Do you want to trap my wrists again?" she asked—utterly innocent of what this offer did to him.

His groin grew hotter and tighter as he thought about all the ways he'd like to tie her up. She couldn't touch him when she was bound. Only he could touch her. The thing was, he wanted her to hold him. Despite all the reasons he didn't feel comfortable being handled, he wanted her hands on him.

"No," he said, his voice embarrassingly rough. "I like the way you touch me. I think I'll save a few fantasies for later."

"Deal," she said, and smiled as if his admission that he enjoyed subduing her was no big deal.

He found himself smiling back. A knot relaxed inside him even as his cock hardened more in expectancy. He drew out all the way to his rim, letting her body tug him before surging in again. Oh, that was heaven, and she liked it, too. She made a soft, pleased noise, her hips pushing up at him. Her hands slid down his naked back, then under his trousers and around his buns.

Her squeeze felt as good as the eagerness it implied, but, "Don't hold on too tight," he said. "I need room to move."

"Do it then," she said with a grin. "Move in and out as much as you want."

"You'll tell me if I hurt you?" Unable to help himself, he asked this on a thrust stronger than the first.

She made the low, pleased noise again and said, "So far, so good."

He meant to go easy on her, meant to let her get used to his size, but she kept crooning out her enjoyment and rocking back at him with her hips. She was using her strength to do it, and recognizing this sent his excitement soaring. It wasn't more than ten full strokes before he was going at her full out. The sensation of pumping in and out of her, of pushing his erection through her tight, creamy sheath was almost enough to shut down his brain.

He caressed her clenching thigh with one hand, wanting to feel all of her, wanting to make himself savor this act he'd dreamed about for so long.

His body wasn't having it, and neither was hers. Her hands drifted up to his shoulders, hanging onto him as her pelvis jerked up the length of his shaft with increasing force. Soon her head began to thrash.

"Oh, God," she said, on the edge of a wail. "Oh, God, I can't hold it off."

He went even faster for her, for himself, and watched her beautiful green eyes glaze over a second before her sex convulsed around him in a sucking grip. His testicles drew up in warning, the pressure to ejaculate almost unbearable.

"Don't slow down," she gasped, as his last restraint was about to shred. "Oh, God, keep going."

Her nails dug into his shoulder muscles. He growled out something that wasn't quite a word and felt her come again. This time she shrieked. The sound flickered through his cock like it was being touched from the inside.

He had a heartbeat to suck a breath and then it all roared out of him—all the mornings he'd hoped she'd be the one to take his order at the diner, all the nights he'd dreamed of her in his bed, all the jealousy he'd felt at watching her with other men. Every bit of pain and frustration was transmuted to ecstasy. The relief of coming was incredible. He thrust through the whole of it, not holding deep and stopping like he usually did, because he wanted those sweet, sharp spasms to go on and on, wanted to hurt with how good it felt.

When there was no more pleasure to squeeze out, he sank down until he was cradled between her legs, settling against her soft, silky breasts. She seemed to welcome his weight. Her face turned against his shoulder, and she held him—hugged him, really—with her legs and arms. Her fingers stroked his nape gently.

The marvel of it struck him hard. These were a woman's fingers: Frankie's fingers, slim and kind.

"Oh, Jack," she sighed. There was so much emotion in her utterance of his name, so much gratitude and maybe compassion, that for a second he was a bit concerned he might cry.

No way was he going to let himself do that.

Instead, he withdrew from her and eased to the side. To his relief, she snuggled against him as soon as he made room in his arms.

"You're warm," she said, finding a place between his hairy thighs for her lightly muscled one. He pulled her closer.

"Your floor is cold."

"You smell good," she countered.

He smiled into her hair and didn't mention that a hinge from one of her work island's cabinets was digging into his butt. She smelled good, too—from some sort of tropical citrus soap. She'd taken the time to shower Pete and Dave off her. Before, Jack had been too focused on the miracle of her welcoming his desire. Now he wished he knew what her cleanliness meant.

Still, he wasn't sorry when she distracted him. With one smooth fingernail, she drew a circle around his nipple that made his tired cock immediately feel a few ounces heavier. "I hope finally having sex after your dry spell was worth the wait."

Perhaps he should have been embarrassed, but his smile returned. He knew she was fishing for a much-deserved compliment. "It was worth the wait and then some. Just don't ask me to put it off that long again."

"How long?" She pushed up on her elbow and looked down at him. "Since you divorced your wife?"

Her face was quiet, flushed from their lovemaking and so beautiful his heart ached. He remembered the compassion he'd thought he heard in her voice and didn't want to answer. Compassion was awfully close to pity. Anyway, how could he explain why he'd given up on women when the decision didn't fully make sense to him? He tried all the same. "Almost since then. I guess it stopped seeming worth the trouble. I wasn't really connecting with the women I was seeing. I was just scratching an itch. And for them, well, my job's a hard thing to date."

"But your work here isn't as dangerous as in LA."

"That's true." He cupped her soft, warm cheek, hardly able to believe she might be suggesting he could try dating her. The chance that he was mistaken made him want to tread cautiously. This was hardly territory in which he was expert. "Six Palms is much quieter."

"You're a sexy man, you know. You could take your pick of women."

Now he was confused. Did she mean he ought to be picking other women than her?

"Uh, thank you," he said.

She burrowed back down against him, smiling into his chest. "Thanks for letting me seduce you—though you must think I'm the biggest slut in Six Palms."

"I don't!" His protest was automatic and unthinking.

"You do," she laughed. "You should have seen your face when you walked in on me and Team Boys."

"That's none of my business."

Her laughter faded. "No, I suppose it's not. Anyway, I'm not going to apologize. It was probably just a rebound thing, but it was fun."

Should he be thinking of himself as a rebound thing? Ugh,

what an awful possibility! Had Mike True been one as well? He wanted to know, but it seemed too awkward to ask.

Frankie fell silent, her weight relaxed against him, keeping her thoughts to herself. He found himself wondering what they were, genuinely curious to know in a way he'd rarely been during his brief, post-divorce affairs. Rather than press her, he stroked one hand up and down the curves of her side, then slipped his hold around her to find her breast. Her skin there was melting soft, her flesh filling his hand as he'd dreamed it would a thousand times. When he began lightly squeezing her nipple between his fingers, she rubbed her nose in his chest hair.

"I should have taken more time with you," he said in regret. "I shouldn't have just fallen on you that way."

She lifted one eyebrow. "Could you honestly have waited?"

"Not one fucking second longer."

The vehemence of his answer brought a smile of pleasure to her face. Glad he'd said the right thing, he kissed the smile, and her neck, then settled in to suckle her beautiful, silken breasts. While he did this, his hands fondled at least some of the lovely lengths of her he had missed.

She sighed and wriggled as if his caresses made her too happy to be still. The way her fingers trailed across his scalp sent tingles shooting down his spine. The part of him that had seemingly exhausted itself was recovering quicker than he thought.

"Should I tell you my fantasy?" she asked. "Or would you rather that waited?"

He looked up from her breast, releasing her nipple at the last possible moment. He hadn't wanted to stop what he was doing, but the idea of *her* having a fantasy intrigued him. Whatever it was, he hoped he could do it.

As if sensing his doubt, her eyes sparkled with mischief.

"It's a fantasy to do with you," she said. "No one else could fulfill it. Not even another cop."

Her fantasy had to do with him being a cop? His cock spurted longer, obeying its own gut instinct. It knew, even if he didn't, that this fantasy was one he was going to like.

He had to shift his hips to give his erection room to come up between them. The head was pointing north again, as randy as a teenager's. He cleared his throat to speak. "Nothing illegal, right?"

Her laugh was easy and warm, a medicine he thought he could use more of. Her fingers walked teasingly up the changes she'd conjured in his cock. "Nothing illegal, big guy, though you can say no anytime you want."

The pads of her fingers drummed a rhythm on his crown, a trick that tickled and aroused at the same time.

"Boy," he gasped as the tiny percussion found a direct connection to a jangling nerve. "I don't think there's much chance of me saying no to you."

She kissed him, her delight in his answer obvious. "We're even then," she whispered, "because I don't think there's much chance of me saying no to you."

Despite their promising exchange of confessions, Jack seemed to be having second thoughts.

"I should be tracking down Mike True," he said reluctantly. "Questioning him about knowing Whittier."

Frankie frowned but tried not to give up on the moment yet. This thing that was happening between them seemed important, whether it was just totally combustible chemistry or budding romance. It wasn't every day a man could make her feel like she'd hadn't had sex in years when in truth she'd had it all afternoon.

She did, however, withdraw her hand from his erection. "Mike is moving back into the room above the diner. You can find him any time you want."

"Frankie . . ."

"Stop running," she said, tired of his indecision. "Finish playing this out with me."

"Playing?"

She wasn't sure what he was asking. "Mike's not going anywhere. He's got a job and a place to stay and, as far as I can tell, not a lot of other options."

"And let's not forget your power to keep him here."

Jack's voice was deceptively soft, almost his cop-voice but not quite.

Oh, thought Frankie, a smile forming just behind her mouth. *He's jealous. He thinks I'm playing with everyone—including him.*

"I'm not sleeping with Mike anymore," she said. "Not that that's your business, either."

This disclosure did not reassure him. His eyes narrowed.

"What?" she said, but he shook his head.

She could see that getting Jack West to open up was no job for the impatient.

"Tell me your fantasy," he said, sidestepping whatever the problem was.

"You're still in the mood to hear it?"

He took her hand, kissed its palm, and laid it gently back on his groin. His shaft was lying against his belly, very firm and thick. Their brief debate seemed not to have discouraged his interest in a second round. Considering how interested she was, she found this an extremely endearing trait.

"I'm more in the mood than you can imagine," he said roughly.

She was abruptly breathless from his intensity. "We'd have to go into my back courtyard. The hill rises up behind it. No one can see in."

"I take it we'd be naked."

"I would. You'd be in your uniform. Unless that seems too disrespectful."

"What would I be doing?" His eyes were lasers boring onto hers.

"Frisking me," she answered on a gasp for air.

She wasn't stroking him, but his cock lurched higher under her hand.

"Could I—" He hesitated. "Would you mind if I restrained you?"

"I'm hoping you will."

His pupils were big, shining pools of black, his breathing shallow. This evidence of his excitement made her ribs feel tight and her sex as soft as melting marshmallows. He looked down her body to her sharpened nipples, then returned to her eyes. When he spoke, he was hoarse.

"What would you think about me restraining you with my handcuffs?"

She thought of the cold, hard metal, of him looming hot behind her, and she wasn't even a bit afraid. Instinct told her this wasn't quite the right thing to say.

"If I struggled," she said, "the cuffs might hurt me."

He heard how husky she was, too. "Yes," he murmured soft as velvet. "You'd have to be very still."

"That might be hard. I've noticed when you're inside me, I like to move."

"I'd help you," he said. "Once I was inside you."

She leaned forward and kissed him, not holding anything back—not desire, not tenderness. She put it all on the table for him to read. He moaned as her tongue pushed into his mouth, sucking it hard and wrapping his arms around her in the tightest hug she thought she'd ever had.

"Let me do it now," he whispered next to her ear. "I think I'll die if I have to wait."

Frankie had no inclination to make him wait. She stood and shed her robe while he blinked up at her nakedness in surprise. Evidently, he hadn't expected her to comply this quickly.

"Put your shirt back on," she said, "and grab anything else you need."

After a second to gather his brain cells, he rose as quickly as she did. He removed the gun from his belt and put it in her silverware drawer. Then he dressed himself again. Undershirt. Shirt. Uniform belt. It was the sexiest reverse strip-tease she'd ever seen. The first time they'd had sex might have been erased; his erection was that stiff and straight. Watching him try to shove it back in his pants reminded her how big he was.

"How the hell did I get that monster in me?" she marveled as he struggled to zip up.

He looked up from the bulging zipper. He didn't grin. He knew he was big, but this didn't inflate his ego. His body was simply part of who he was. Frankie noticed it was twilight. The purpling light from her big back windows threw his rugged features into relief. His mouth was a slash between lean, hard cheeks, his nose a slightly crooked blade. Only his ink-black lashes were soft. They cast fanlike shadows across his high cheekbones. She'd never thought of him as handsome, but in that moment, he was as starkly beautiful as the desert at sunset.

"You're going to get this monster in you soon," he said. "And this time I'm going to pay attention to every inch of you."

He practically stole her breath. "We could wait until full dark," she panted.

At first his answer was just a growl. "We'll risk it," he said. "I'm not waiting to take you again."

A drainpipe ran down the middle of the back wall of her house, a sturdy, galvanized thing. Jack spotted it even as he tugged her into her postcard-sized, grassy, walled-in yard. An overgrown aloe, monstrous in the lengthening shadows, had taken over one corner . . . sort of like Frankie had done to his dreams.

Frankie, of course, was a lot prettier.

"Face the wall," he said, lightly pushing her. "Lace your fingers behind your neck."

She did it as soon as he asked, her exquisite body seeming twice as naked in the outdoors. He glanced up the hill behind her house, but nothing overlooked her yard but scrubby rocks and ice plants.

"What did I do, Officer?" she asked.

"Chief," he corrected, gently touching her cheek to remind her not to look at him. She was trembling, but not with fear. When he let his gaze slide down her, the inside of one thigh glistened with a pearl-like sheen. The sight was magic, more powerful than he'd dreamed. He'd gotten her so wet, cream was running down her leg. Trapped now inside his clothes, his penis pounded in sympathy.

Her excitement made him feel like a king.

"What did I do, Chief?" she asked humbly.

"You fucked the wrong man," he said without thought. The words surprised him. The role had taken over him.

Frankie jerked as if she'd been slapped, but she wasn't peeved. "Did I?" she asked softly.

He spread his hands around her ribs, lightly, just behind where her arms were raised. "Yes," he said, because the role gave him permission. "You should have saved yourself for me."

"You have me now."

His blood leapt again in his groin, his trousers increasingly un-comfortable. "Not yet, I don't. But I will."

He frisked her slowly, carefully, just as he would if she were a true suspect, passing his hands over her without being overtly sex-ual. Her breathing grew ragged nonetheless, her toes curling hard into the unmown grass.

He knelt to run his hands up and down her legs. Her calves were firm as apples, her thighs smooth and warm. Jack kissed her bottom because it was there and cute as hell. The wonderful scent of her arousal whirled around his head. He rubbed it lingeringly where it shone on her inner thigh.

"You're very wet," he said.

Frankie shuddered at his comment. Twice she tried to speak before she succeeded. "I'm wet because I haven't had enough of the right man yet."

He stood, his knees not as firm as they could have been. "Do you think it's possible to get enough of him?"

Her loose blond hair swung from side to side. "I don't know. I'm hoping I can try."

He pulled one of her hands from behind her neck, placing it firmly against the cold drainpipe. "I think you're going to have to try very hard. And I think I'm going to have to lock you onto this. You've been tractable so far, but I wouldn't want my suspect turn-ing uncontrollable."

"I don't mind," she said breathlessly. Her back arched just enough in excitement that her lush little bottom brushed the pounding ridge behind his trouser front. "I want you to have faith in me."

The way she fell so perfectly into his fantasy was almost too much. His heart felt like it was slamming inside his groin, all his blood surging there. He snapped one cuff around her wrist, passed the chain behind the drainpipe, and lifted her other hand into position.

"Ready?" he asked, one last chance for her to act on any second thoughts. After this, it would be difficult to get away—impossible unless he let her.

This, however, was not her concern.

"Do you promise to take me after I'm locked up? Do you promise to give me everything you have?"

Helpless to resist, he rubbed his erection, hard and slow, across her taut bottom. "I'll give you everything you can take, as many times as you want it."

"That might be a lot," she warned, and he clicked the final cuff into place.

The completion of her bondage surprised a little moan of hunger from her throat.

"Now you're ready," he said.

His satisfaction at her position was deeper than he could express. It felt as if he'd been straining toward this moment all his life, as if this act—with her—completed him. He stood close behind her, very aware of the difference in their sizes, of the difference in their male and female forms. Gritting his teeth in the forlorn hope of keeping his control, he slid two fingers inside her sex.

Immediately, her body worked to suck them deep and hold on. He had to put his free hand on one of her wrists to remind her to hold the pipe and not tug the cuffs. This game was pushing her buttons as much as it was pushing his. Her head fell back as he continued to move his fingers in and out of her heat, her hair whispering over his shirt front like spun silk. Her hips rolled in opposition to his fingers' movements, greedy for even more stimulation than he was giving her. Her eagerness felt like a priceless gift, magnifying his own arousal. Soon the suctioning sound of her wetness was competing with their panting breaths.

"Can I come?" she asked. "Is it allowed?"

The question sent a long, cool shiver down his spine. "You don't need me to touch your clit?"

She groaned and bore down on him, her body undulating with her need. "I don't think so. I think—" She groaned again. "I'm not sure I can stop myself."

"Try to wait," he said, taking the excuse to rub himself against her rear again, a risky thing when he was this wound up. "I want you to save your orgasm for my cock."

He watched her responses then, careful to take her to the edge but not over. When she promised she'd try not to struggle in the cuffs, he released her forearm and used his second hand to caress the curves of her breasts. That had her whimpering in no time.

"Will you put me in lockup?" she asked, gasping as he lightly pinched one long nipple. "Will you sneak into my cell and take me there?"

Arousal stabbed through his loins. He could see it: the narrow mattress, the concrete block walls, her with her legs spread and waiting for him. The lust he felt then was absolutely violent.

"I'll take you everywhere," he said, gently biting the back of her neck. "Over and over again."

"Jack," she moaned, as if she were going to die with longing if he didn't do it soon.

The sound of her hunger was more than he could take. He had to yank open his trousers, half expecting his cock to be steaming when it sprang out. He didn't dare stroke it the way it craved. In truth, he was so long and swollen the state of his erection almost frightened him.

"Push your bottom back," he ordered, his voice gone harsh. "Spread your legs to make room for me."

She spread them. "Take me," she said. "Don't do it easy. Take me hard and fast."

He had a second's hesitation, but she seemed to mean it. He took her in two strong strokes, grunting with nearly overwhelming pleasure as the second push drove him to his root. This was where he belonged: in her, filling her. His body was right up next to her, where they met a line of fire from chest to hip. He was literally in pain from wanting her, but the way they melded together was so perfect he had to stop.

"Oh, God," she said, wriggling around his hardness as much as she could. "Please move."

"I'm going to touch your clit," he warned, sliding one hand back to her breast while the other headed for her crisp patch of pubic curls. "Try not to come right away."

"Jack," she said, his name a plea.

"Try," he repeated.

He found her clitoris in a warm pool of cream. It was hard and slippery and swollen. When he rubbed the little hood up and down, she growled in frustration. He honestly thought she was going to stomp his foot to make him say she could come.

"Jack!"

"Just a few minutes longer." He began thrusting slowly with his eyes half closed. "This is too good to rush."

"Rub me harder," she pleaded. "No, wait, don't!"

He rubbed her harder and thrilled to her moan of agony. She was squirming under his weight like a live-caught fish.

"I can't wait," she said.

"Wait," he insisted, pushing in again with his own pained sound. "I can't last much longer, Frankie. I just want us to go together."

"Haven't you heard girls go first?"

He laughed, because the way she was panting told him how hard she was working to hold off her climax. He shifted his stimulation of her clitoris to a long, firm stroke of his fingers on either side. This made her arch and hum.

"Better?"

"I don't know," she said. "Mmm. That feels really good. I think it's just different."

"Hold on then," he said, taking pity on them both. "I'm going to pump hard until the end."

"Oh, yes," she said. "*Really* hard." She got a grip on the drainpipe and set her feet. Her bottom lifted back at him. "And please keep doing that rubbing thing."

He braced his own legs and gave himself with all his heart and strength to do as she asked. She hadn't lied. She couldn't wait. She came in seconds after he started and then again, her pleas dissolving into wordless cries. He knew she wanted more, knew she needed it. He went faster yet, sensation screaming inside him as he nipped her shoulder and finally took hold of the clanking cuffs to keep her still. The feel of the metal against her wrist did him in. He'd captured her. Claimed her. His climax seemed to explode from inside him, a supernova of concentrated ecstasy. Every part of him blazed with it: his palms, his heels, the skin at the top of his close-shorn head.

"Frankie," he gasped, actually alarmed by the intensity of his release.

She moaned in answer, and he felt her rippling around him in a climax even stronger than before.

He had to hold her up when it finished because she'd sagged in the cuffs. She was nearly sitting in his still throbbing lap, her body trembling from head to toe.

"Shh," he soothed against her ear. "I'll hold you safe until you can stand up."

"That was so good," she marveled, the words throaty and slurred. "I didn't know it could be that good."

It didn't make sense, but her praise alarmed him, too. "I'm glad it was good. I wanted you to have fun."

Her tremors began to relax, but he continued to hold her, enjoying rocking her from side to side. This moment was a refuge from all the thousand things that might screw them up. He realized he didn't want it to end. *That* was what had alarmed him. It frightened him to suddenly have so much to lose.

"I'll unlock you now," he said, knowing she must want it.

"'Kay," she said.

He suspected she was a single yawn away from sleep.

Chapter
14

He carried her into the house like a sleepy child, something no man had ever done for her. Frankie loved it, her bones just about turning to rubber—and never mind how nicely the flesh between her legs was warming up.

Oh, you don't have daddy issues, she mocked herself.

It was a sign of how relaxed she was that she didn't pay any attention to her own self-scorn.

He settled into the corner of her long, white leather sectional with her turned across his lap. She couldn't help but remember seeing Pete and Dave kissing here. Wisely, she didn't mention this aloud.

"I wonder what Karen's fantasy was," she said, murmuring the next idle thought that came into her dozy head. "If Pete and Dave seduced her, she must have had one."

Jack shifted beneath her. "Karen *Ellis?*"

"Yes, I'm sure that's who they meant. It wouldn't have made sense for me to be talking about any other Karen."

"And they filmed this fantasy?"

His tone was strange, the muscles of his arms suddenly tense. Frankie lifted her head from his shoulder. "I assume so, though it is weird to think of Tish watching her best friend having sex."

"We didn't find any discs of Ellis with Pete and Dave."

"Well, maybe they didn't film it. Maybe they thought, what with Tish and Karen already sharing a boyfriend, having Karen horn in on Tish's hobby would be uncomfortable."

Jack sat up so quickly Frankie was in danger of rolling off. He caught her by the shoulders before she could and locked his most serious gaze to hers. "Tish and Karen shared a boyfriend? You mean Troy Wilcox, I presume."

"Yes." Frankie was taken aback by how energetically he cursed at that. "I'm sorry, Jack. I only just found out myself from Pete and Dave. I assumed you knew. You did interview Troy."

Jack set his mouth into a thin line. "Your former boyfriend wasn't kind enough to inform me of the full extent of his conquests. For that matter, neither were Pete and Dave. Fuck." He slammed his fist onto the couch's thankfully padded back.

Then he went completely still, his eyes going back and forth as they watched some scene in the distance only he could see.

"The blue light special . . ." he said in an odd, slow tone. "I knew I'd forgotten something."

"At K-Mart?"

His eyes flicked to hers. His mood seemed both wired and grim. "K-Mart isn't the only thing associated with blue lights. Police cars have them as well." He sighed gustily. "Unfortunately, only one person besides myself had access to those discs between the time I found them and when we brought them to the station."

"Tish's discs?"

Jack grimaced and shook his head. "I'm sorry. I'd really love to stay here and be irresponsible with you for a few more hours, but I have to take care of this."

"Take care of what?" Frankie asked in confusion, not liking the suggestion that what they'd shared was "irresponsible"—even if it was.

He hoisted her off his lap and stood along with her. "I can't answer that, but Frankie—" He clasped her face between his big, gentle hands. "Thank you for tonight. You can't know what it meant to me."

I'm not done wanting to mean something to you! Frankie thought.

But he'd let her go already. He was heading for the foyer when the doorbell rang.

"Lord," Frankie muttered as she hopped up to find her robe. "I ought to charge admission."

"Do you want me to get that?" Jack offered in a tightly amused tone.

"Let me see who it is," she quipped back tartly. "Then I'll decide if I want to hide you in the closet."

This wasn't an option, even if she'd been serious. She needed Jack's help to muscle open the broken door. The person behind it was a surprise.

"Troy!" she said.

He blinked at her, equally nonplused. A number of Chinese take-out cartons dangled from his hands. "Your door is broken." He widened his eyes at Jack West and then at her crumpled robe, which at this point had no tokens of modesty beneath it. His gaze shifted back to Jack. "Uh, hi, Chief. I just came to see if Frankie was hungry."

"Now really isn't a good time," Frankie said.

Troy colored, finally getting it.

"Nonsense." Jack shocked them both by reaching for half of Troy's cartons. "It's a great time. You wouldn't believe how hungry I am. Boy, I hope that's moo-shu pork I smell!"

Even Troy knew better than to take this seeming friendliness at face value. "I don't want to interrupt your evening . . ."

"No, no," Jack insisted, steel brightening his smile. "You *must* join us. I really want to talk to you."

He took Troy's elbow before he could bolt and steered him into the living room. There, he dropped the cartons onto her low burnished bronze table.

"Sit," he said, pushing down Troy's shoulder.

Troy sat, as obedient as a befuddled schoolboy.

Jack collected the rest of the cartons from him, arranged them on the table, and peered into the single brown paper sack. "Chopsticks and plastic forks! Excellent."

"Frankie didn't invite me. She shouldn't have to put up with doing dishes."

"No, she shouldn't," Jack agreed. "But then Frankie shouldn't have to put up with a lot of things."

Troy glanced at her. Frankie wasn't in the mood to explain, but her doing it was probably kinder than letting Jack. "I found out you were cheating on me with Tish as well as Karen."

Troy began to stammer, but Jack cut him off. "Where is your bride-to-be, by the way? Shouldn't you be eating dinner with her?"

Troy was a helpless deer in Jack's headlights. "She told me to leave her house. She said my hovering upset the baby."

"The *baby*." Jack threw up his hands in exasperation. "The baby." He looked at Frankie. "Did you know about the baby, too? No, don't tell me. You assumed I knew."

"I did!" Frankie said.

"Great. Great." Jack squeezed his temples between his hands.

"It's just a tiny bit of a baby," Troy put in, obviously attempting to be helpful. "We weren't going to announce it officially until later."

"I'm not the social column at the paper!" Jack snapped. "I don't 'announce' people's private news." He shook his head and visibly tried to calm, then nudged a carton closer to Troy's knees. "Eat something, underwear boy. You're going to need your blood sugar up to answer a few questions."

Underwear boy ate a few listless bites of chicken before setting down his chopsticks.

"I can't swallow anymore," he said apologetically. "My stomach's in knots."

Jack was beginning to wonder how Troy had kept Frankie's interest for more than five minutes. Naturally, this was when she sat beside her ex and put her arm around his shoulders.

"Tell me about the day Tish died," Jack said, deciding he didn't have to be gentle since Frankie was. "Tell me about the last time you saw her, and stop leaving things out."

Troy looked down at his beautiful model hands. "Tish was happy," he said, already sounding teary. "She met me at my beach house and promised everything would be all right." He lifted his woeful baby-blue eyes to Jack's. "I really was at my house all night, just like I said."

Jack stifled a sigh. "You were engaged to Karen Ellis by then."

"Yes. Because of the baby."

"And Tish knew about the baby."

"I had to tell her, to explain why we were breaking up. Each of them knew I was seeing the other. The baby . . . the baby was an accident, but Karen wanted it and so did I."

Jack sat on the arm of the big square chair opposite the couch. "So you liked them both."

This seemed a simple question, but Troy's brow furrowed. "You mean Karen and Tish?"

Jack nodded.

"At first. But that was before I fell in love with Tish." Troy said the "L" word with an ease that, for a moment, made Jack admire him. "Karen knew it. I'd stopped seeing her a few weeks earlier, but then . . ."

"She told you about the baby."

"Right." Troy seemed relieved to be understood. He leaned forward, clearly expecting more empathy. "I didn't tell you about Tish coming to see me that night, because I thought—if it got out—it would be like rubbing Karen's nose in her not being my first choice."

Jack knuckled his forehead. "For future reference, Troy, these are the kind of things cops need to know."

"Right," Troy said and slid to the back of the sectional. He was wearing shorts, and his hands rubbed up and down his perfect Greek athlete thighs. Perhaps sensing Jack's forbearance straining, Frankie stopped the nervous gesture by putting one hand on top of her ex's. Jack tried not to stare at how close it was to his groin.

"So Tish was happy the last time you saw her," he said, returning to this.

"Hopeful." Troy decided this word was better. "I don't know how she thought she would work things out, but she seemed confident. We . . . made love. I'd promised Karen I wouldn't, but Tish was so sweet it was hard not to."

Frankie rolled her eyes at this but kept her arm around Troy's shoulder. Though Jack didn't want to ask his next question in front of her, he didn't have much choice.

"You made love to Tish without a condom."

Troy looked startled. "How did—? Oh, I . . . yes, I'm pretty sure I did. I guess, maybe, I was thinking if I got her pregnant, too, Tish would have an equal claim on me."

"Jeez!" Frankie burst out, which made her ex-boyfriend flush.

She was looking at him like he was a nutjob, which maybe he was. Jack gave Frankie credit for holding her tongue this long, but when she would have spoken again, he held up his hand to get both their attention.

He waited until Troy turned his eyes to him. "You were hoping to get Tish pregnant because you didn't believe she could solve your dilemma."

"Not with Karen," Troy said. "When she makes up her mind, she really makes it up."

He looked a little leery thinking about this, but not—Jack thought—half as leery as he ought to be.

"I'm going to my car now," Jack said. "I'm going to get my kit from the trunk and take a sample of your DNA. I want to confirm you were the last person to have sex with Tish."

"I was!"

Jack almost smiled at Troy's indignation. "I'm sure that's true, but I need to prove it. When I'm done, I want you to tell Karen that I collected it. Nothing else. Just that. She doesn't need to know I found out about you dating her and Tish, or that she's pregnant, or anything at all except that I wanted a sample of your DNA. Tell her I called you into my office and took it there."

Both Frankie and Troy were staring at him goggle-eyed. The dawning horror in Frankie's eyes told him she, at least, was beginning to suspect what he was getting at.

"You can do that, right?" Jack asked Troy. "Tell only one thing and not the rest?"

"Yes." Troy answered with an absentminded confidence that reassured him. "You called me into your office and took my DNA. I just don't understand why I have to lie."

"It's better that you don't. Murder investigations can be tricky. Only the police need to understand everything."

Troy nodded, satisfied with this. Frankie, on the other hand, followed Jack to the door when he went to retrieve his kit.

"You can't be thinking what you're thinking," she said in an undertone. "Karen loved Tish since they were kids. I'm willing to bet she loved her more than she loves Troy."

"You may be right," Jack said. "But there's no one we can come to hate quite so much as those we used to love."

Jack took swabs and hair samples from Troy with matter-of-fact ease. Troy didn't seem to realize he had any choice in the matter, and Frankie wasn't inclined to remind him that he did. She thought she'd known the depths to which Troy's self-centeredness could sink, but she'd been wrong. If he hadn't been such a lost puppy, she'd have knocked his head into next week.

"One more thing," Jack said as Troy prepared to go. "Don't leave Karen alone so much. Even if she asks you to."

Troy's mouth fell open. "You think she really could be in danger?"

"She might be," Jack said with such gravity Frankie had to marvel at his ability to lie convincingly. It was a side of him she hadn't suspected he had. "Remember, you're keeping her safe for two."

Troy nodded with a somewhat doubtful attempt at manfulness. He gave Frankie an absent peck before shuffling out the door.

"What are you playing at?" Frankie demanded after Troy was gone. "You know you don't think Karen is in danger. If she's already getting tired of him, Troy will drive her up the wall."

"He might," Jack agreed. "But the less she thinks he knows, the safer my investigation will be. And now—" He took her shoulders in his hands and kissed her—a deep, wet, all-too-short French kiss. Frankie's cheeks were warm when he released her. "I really have to go."

She put her hands on his shirtfront, the light contact enough to hold him there. "Jack, I saw Karen right after she heard Tish died. She was every bit as devastated as Troy. I don't think she could have been acting."

Jack felt his eyes sting for the lesson Frankie was learning— and for the lesson Karen Ellis probably already had. For once, he didn't try to hide his emotions. Frankie had to know how serious this was.

"People can have these reactions," he said. "And they can be sincere. The heat of anger only lasts so long. Just try not to con- fuse regret with remorse, and, whatever you do, stay the hell away from Karen Ellis. She may be getting tired of Troy, but that doesn't mean she's ready to give up her only prize for what she did. I doubt it's an accident that the murder was committed be- hind your diner, or simple convenience that led to the murder weapon being stashed in your storeroom. As for that, she may have had access to the necklace that had your prints. If Ellis was trying to frame you, she'll know by now that it didn't work. At the moment, you're looking like the last rival she has."

"But that's horrible!" Frankie said. "To have to be on your guard against someone you know."

He kissed her firmly on the forehead and held her gaze.

"Do it anyway," he said.

Jack thought he'd be angry when he confronted his senior of- ficer. Instead, he simply felt bone-tired. Rivera was one person whose morals he'd never had any doubt about.

He found her sitting alone in their combination interrogation- conference room. She was going over Whittier's case files. Even after all his years on the job, the autopsy photos inspired a visceral jolt of shock. Someone had died, and it was his job to get justice.

"Chief!" she said, smiling brightly, not seeing the bitterness of his mood. "I think I might have found a hole in Phoebe Atkins's alibi."

Jack didn't care how or why the dry cleaner's wife had lied. Phoebe Atkins probably had plenty of reasons to be deceitful that had nothing to do with Whittier's murder. In any event, he had zero desire to delay his unpleasant task.

"Where's the missing DVD?"

Rivera paled. "Wh-what?"

"The 'Blue Light Special.' The recording you removed from Whittier's collection before it could be logged into evidence."

"I . . . don't know what you're talking about."

"Jesus, Rivera, don't lie to me on top of everything else." Jack braced his hands on the table's edge, looming over her just as he would to intimidate a suspect. Cop or not, Rivera couldn't stop herself from shrinking back. "Did you use your departmental car? Did you let those two bozos do you in city property with the blue light on?"

"We were inside their garage," she gasped, trying to hold herself together in spite of being overtaken by the shakes. "No one could see in. I didn't know they'd taped it until I saw that disc." She gritted her teeth and clenched the arms of her chair. "It was nothing to do with the case. Only with me."

Jack leaned back from the cheaply veneered table. The room was so small he could now prop his shoulders against the sound-proofed wall. "I guess it didn't occur to you—while you were con-cealing evidence and obstructing justice—to check if the other side of the disc was recorded on."

"Oh, no." Her hands flew to her mouth in horror. "It wasn't."

"Oh, I think it was. It's come to my attention that Pete and Dave probably filmed a scene with Karen Ellis—one that is not among the discs we have."

"Karen Ellis?" Rivera dropped her hands and looked surprised.

"The same Karen Ellis who was rivals with Tish for Troy Wilcox's affections. The same Karen Ellis who conveniently got pregnant and won him back."

"I didn't know that. Oh, God, you think she—You think I might have had evidence that could have led us to the murderer?"

He didn't say anything, just let her work it out. Her face was a study of unfolding dismay and guilt.

"I didn't destroy it," she said, spreading her hands flat on the scattered files. "I wanted to, but I couldn't bring myself to do it."

"If what I think is on that disc is there, that may be all that saves your butt." He lifted his hand before she could ask. "I'm not firing you, but you are on probation. Plenty of cops have screwed-up private lives"—him, for one—"but if your dirty laundry happens to get into the open, you deal with it. You do not, do *not*, let it compromise your integrity on the job."

"I only went with them because—"

"I don't give a damn why you did it. It's not my business, and it never will be. My only business is how you act as a cop."

He meant the words to serve as a kind of slap, and they did. Though her eyes had reddened, she pulled herself straighter.

"Yes, sir. I'll do anything to win back your trust."

"You haven't lost it, Rivera. Let's just say the jury's out on break."

She made a face at that, trying to smile and not making it.

"Get the disc," he said, "from wherever you stashed it. I need to watch it before I do anything."

She rose awkwardly. "Do you . . . I guess you have to watch the side with me on it."

He was glad she knew that. Theoretically, with all she had to lose, she could have been a suspect, too. "I'll try to keep Dewey out of it," was the best he could offer.

"Thank you, sir," she said glumly. She tugged her uniform

shirt straight. She'd dodged one bullet, but Jack suspected she understood she hadn't dodged the last.

The first thing Jack did was check the disc and its case for prints. Both had been wiped clean. If he'd stumbled across wherever this had been hidden, he wouldn't have been able to prove Rivera put it there. Unfortunately, he also couldn't prove Tish had handled it.

Strike two, he thought joylessly.

He didn't feel any better when "Blue Light Special" began to play. Rivera hadn't simply used her patrol car for her escapade with Team Boys; she'd also asked Dave to dress up in a sheriff's uniform. He resembled Jack slightly in his muscularity and coloring. Other than that, his impersonation of an officer of the law was pretty pathetic—which did not squelch Rivera's interest. For this and other predictable reasons, Jack winced through most of the recording.

These weren't things a boss should know about his employee.

Relieved when it was done, he ejected the disc and turned it over. He didn't call Dewey or Rivera to watch the other side with him. He wanted to know if his guess was correct first.

A date from almost a year earlier came up on the bottom of the screen, not long after Jack had accepted the job as chief of police. He marveled at how little he'd known about Six Palms then. Then the scene began.

His heart jumped with validation as Ellis coyly opened the door to an unidentified residential room. She looked very different from the soberly suited, grieving woman he'd met in his office. She wore a pale-pink angora sweater over a short pleated skirt. If it wasn't the same white cheerleading skirt he'd seen her wear in Tish's high school album, it was damn close. Her feet were shod in pristine white court shoes and pink-striped socks.

In this state of relative underdress, Jack could see Ellis was attractive. She was harder-looking than Tish, as if maybe she exercised more compulsively in an effort to control her weight.

He couldn't help thinking that a former cheerleader who'd stayed in shape must have sufficient upper body strength to strangle a woman.

Blithely unaware of who was going to see this, Ellis put one finger indecisively to her lips.

"Oh, my," she said in a wispy voice that was not normal for her. "What are you two doing in my room? I'm not allowed to have boys up here."

"Like that ever stopped you," answered someone Jack recognized as Pete. "We were waiting for you to come home from school so we could have some fun." Pete stepped into camera range. He was dressed casually in jeans and a CalTech T-shirt, looking friendly but a little stern. In a pinch, he could have passed for a college boy. "Did you behave yourself today?"

"I always try to," Ellis said, crossing her sneakers' toes one over the other.

"*Try?*" Pete repeated. "Karen, I think you know trying isn't good enough."

"Don't say my name," she snapped, her displeasure clear. "We agreed."

Pete's brows went up, but he recovered. "As you like. But don't think my little slip will excuse your misbehavior."

"Of course not," Ellis agreed, all compliance now. She sank to her knees on the white shag carpet, rubbing her face back and forth across Pete's slowly bulging crotch. "Forgive me for even suggesting it."

Pete touched the back of her head, obviously enjoying this behavior. "I'm not sure I should forgive you, but perhaps if you're very nice to my friend, Dave, he will."

Ellis stared wide-eyed and soft-mouthed at Dave. He had moved from wherever he'd been before to stand beside Pete. Both men were positioned to give the camera their side view. They, at least, seemed aware they were being filmed.

Ellis scooted over to face Dave's crotch. Unlike his friend, his erection appeared full-blown. "I'd like to be nice to you," she said, her hands laid flat against his hipbones, "but I think you might be too big."

"You'll manage," Dave said without sympathy. "Or Pete will give you what for."

He opened the button of his jeans, unzipped, and pulled out his thick erection. With both hands, he steered its tip toward Ellis's mouth. Despite his warning, he didn't force Ellis to take more of him than she could comfortably. It was she who set the pace, her head soon bobbing up and down smoothly.

Unseen by Ellis, Pete reached behind Dave to squeeze his ass. Whatever the main cause of his excitement, Dave's face was flushed by the time Ellis let him go.

"There," she said proudly in her put-on baby-doll voice. "That's as good as any college girl could do. Look how big you are! Don't you think I'm the sweetest thing you've ever met? I just want to please everyone."

"You pleased me," Dave conceded. "And you'll please me even more before we're through."

"I want to." Ellis simpered happily. Then, like a cloud covering the sun, she frowned and wrung her hands. "I'm afraid I've been bad, though. I'm sure I need to confess."

"I'm listening," Pete prompted.

Ellis hung her head. "At school today, I almost let the cheerleaders vote me in as team captain."

Pete was quick enough to know how he should respond. "That was pretty arrogant of you."

"It was," Ellis agreed eagerly. "Especially since I *know* I'm not the best person for the job. I'm not even the one the other girls like the most. I think . . ." She covered her mouth with shame. "I think they must have felt sorry for me."

Pete crossed his arms and peered down at her. "And did you correct your mistake?"

"Yes, but it was only at the last minute that I caught myself and reminded them who they really wanted for team captain. The organized one. The one with the good ideas. I'm sure I ought to be spanked for my slowness."

She was running her hands entreatingly up and down Pete's jean-clad legs, but he was austere even in doling out punishment.

"I'm sure you're guilty of more misbehavior. You're hardly the perfect angel everyone thinks you are."

Ellis bit her lip. "I might have given a blow job behind the bleachers to a boy my best friend used to date, but it was the only way I could get him to notice me!"

"That's no excuse. Everyone knows you're not supposed to mess with your girlfriend's ex."

"I know," Ellis said low and mournful. "I'm just so stupid sometimes. I think you'll have to beat it out of me."

"We're going to tie you to the bed," Pete cautioned. "You won't be able to get away."

Dave had moved out of frame. Now he panned the camera—hidden in who knew what—toward a girlish bed. A poster of a young Bruce Springsteen hung above the brass headboard. This was a classic '80s princess room, replete with all the electronics and knick-knacks every sixteen-year-old *had* to have. Jack concluded they must have been filming somewhere in Ellis's house, maybe in an old guest room. Creative though they were, Jack couldn't imagine those two grease monkeys pulling this together.

"I shouldn't be able to get away!" Ellis exclaimed as Pete

tugged her by the arm toward the bed. "I need to learn to stay in my place."

Jack clenched his jaw at his inevitable reaction to Ellis being bound to the headboard rails with long white ties. When Pete tossed up her cheerleader's skirt, her bottom was bare.

"You were hoping we'd do this," he accused.

"Oh, no," she sighed. "I was just trying to make it easier for you to punish me."

"Liar," he said, "but that won't save you from my paddle."

The spanking—with a ping-pong paddle, from what Jack could tell—seemed to go on interminably. Jack soon grew bored, but Ellis periodically urged Pete on. Dave took her in the middle of it, enjoyed a loud and vigorous climax, then removed himself to let Pete continue. Interestingly, considering Ellis presumably got off on being spanked, she didn't come until the very end, when Pete moved onto the bed to take his turn.

The camera was behind Pete. Jack could just see Ellis's head where it was turned to the side on a heap of ruffled white pillows. Her face was as brightly pink as her bottom.

"Tell me I'm bad," she panted. "Tell me I'll never be as good as my friend."

Pete told her, not once but at least six times, his hips pumping steadily through it all. Each repetition seemed to bring Ellis closer to climaxing.

When she finally went over, her face screwed completely tight. She said something into the pillows he couldn't hear. Jack replayed the section at higher volume, but the microphone wasn't picking up the sound. He zoomed in on her mouth instead and thought he saw her lips form a name two times.

"Tish," she appeared to breathe. "Tish."

That's when he realized where he'd seen her fuzzy pink top before: on the body of his murdered vic. Ellis must have borrowed it from Tish for this . . . or bought a duplicate. Jack shivered involuntarily in reaction.

Karen Ellis wasn't asking Pete and Dave to punish her. She was pretending to be Tish. That's what the funny voice was about. That's why she'd acted so self-deprecating.

She was asking Pete and Dave to punish her best friend.

"Shit," Jack said, impressed with Ellis's twistedness in spite of having expected it. Then he thought about Tish keeping this tape for almost a year, most likely watching it repeatedly. If he'd been Tish, he'd never have worn that top again.

"Shi-it," he said, more drawn out this time.

Tish had known what her best friend really thought of her, had seen it clearly maybe for the first time, and—to all appearances—had stayed friends with her nonetheless.

Could Tish have agreed with Ellis's low opinion? Was that why she did nothing?

Except she had done something. Jack's brain was ticking over smoothly now. She'd done something at the end, or she wouldn't have promised Troy they'd be together. Whatever it was, it had probably made Ellis snap.

Did you try to blackmail her to give Troy back? he asked the absent Tish. *Did loving him give you enough courage to play hardball with a woman who'd been working all her life to keep you in her shade? Did you realize Ellis was probably sexually obsessed with you?*

Jack didn't have the answers, but his gut was telling him he'd find them soon.

"*Phew,*" said Dewey when the screen went black. "That may not be proof, but it sure is incriminating."

"That it is." Jack and his two officers had viewed the disc in their conference room. Understandably, Dewey was the most interested in talking about what they'd seen.

"Why didn't we have this before?" he asked. "Did you search Whittier's house again?"

Jack glanced at Rivera, who was looking at the hands she'd folded tightly around her knees. She showed no inclination of wanting to speak up.

"If it comes to the point where you need to know," Jack said, "you'll be told. Let's just say the chain of evidence was compromised on this particular disc. We can't prove, definitively, that it came from Tish's house, or that she viewed it, which we need to do if we want to make the case that she used its contents to blackmail her murderer."

"Prints?" Dewey suggested.

"When the disc came into my possession, it had been wiped."

"Drag." Dewey pushed his hands back and forth on the conference table. "We'll have to get her some other way. Trick her into confessing. Not that she seems like an easy mark."

"I doubt she'd tell us much," Jack agreed. "And while we can't use the disc to obtain a warrant to surveill her house—anything we found would be fruit of the forbidden tree—I think what I learned about the triangle between her and Tish and Troy will be enough."

"That could be iffy," Dewey said. "You'll have to send Rivera. Judge Olivos thinks she's the bomb."

Rivera was not in the mood to be teased about her sex appeal. "Even if we get a warrant, it'll take a while to get County to cough up a surveillance van."

"Well, that's your second assignment," Jack said before turning to a curious Dewey. "Did you confirm Pete and Dave's story that they spent the night of Tish's murder at Dana Point?"

"Oh, yeah," he said. "I got gas receipts and witnesses on top of the statement from their out-of-town girlfriend. Seems two 'hunky' guys in a lime green Firebird are hard to forget."

"Good, because I'd like to put their talents to better use than they've been up until now. Rivera, your job is to get them to co-operate."

"Sir!" She was breathing hard from all the objections she couldn't blurt out. Jack imagined she wasn't looking forward to seeing her partners in shame again.

"Yes?" Jack prompted with one brow raised.

She struggled with herself, but she knew she had to give in. "Yes, sir," she said, then added acerbically, "I'm sure they'll welcome the chance to redeem themselves."

"We can hope," Jack said, feeling slightly more cheerful.

"I wonder why Ellis didn't try to destroy the disc," Dewey mused aloud.

"Don't know," Jack said. "We can add that to the list of things to find out."

"At least the list is getting shorter," Dewey observed.

Jack was, for the first time since the case had started, happy to agree.

"I just have one question about that Wilcox-Whittier-Ellis triangle," Dewey added. "Did that undeservedly lucky bastard get to make horndog sandwiches with both women?"

It was a sign of Rivera's demoralization that she didn't bean him with her pen.

Chapter
15

It took Jack twenty minutes of cruising the more traveled byways around Six Palms, but he finally "bumped into" Karen Ellis the next morning.

She was stepping out of Premiere Launderers, on the opposite end of Six Palms Park from city hall. Premiere was the more expensive of the town's two dry cleaners, Atkins perhaps being too déclassé for her.

Ellis looked like she must have gone back to work. Her tailored dress was navy silk with small white dots, and her matching pumps were undoubtedly some designer brand. The dress's tasteful belt emphasized her narrow waist without squeezing it. Most interesting, at least to Jack, were the pair of expensive sunglasses that perched atop the dark, glossy waves of her hair. The brand was Louis Vuitton.

Gotcha, Jack thought but kept his smile off his face as he parked the squad car by the curb and stepped out. He tried to look as slow-witted as Ellis probably assumed law officers were.

"Ms. Ellis," he said. "I'm glad I ran into you."

She lifted her hand to tip her shades over her eyes, then thought better of it. "Do you have news about the case?"

She was less distracted than she'd been that day in his office when Tish's death was fresh. Today, her composure was complete and cool.

"We might have news soon," he said. "We caught some luck at the lab. Trace evidence. What I wanted to tell you was, I think we'll be able to release Whittier's body soon. We'll release her to her parents, of course, but I figured you might be hoping to arrange a memorial service. Her parents seemed kind of . . ."

"Out of touch?" Ellis supplied crisply. "Yes, there was a virtual army of nannies marching in and out of that house. It's a wonder the Whittiers remembered Tish's name."

"Sad." Jack gazed down the length of the park while watching Ellis from the corner of his eye.

"Yes it was. If it weren't for my mother, Tish wouldn't have had any nurturing at all."

"Mmm," Jack said, privately wondering how much good her nurturing had done Ellis. "I notice you found your sunglasses."

"Oh, yes." She took them off the top of her head as if she'd just remembered their existence. "Silly thing. They were lost on the floor of my car."

"So Tish didn't have to go to Frankie's to look for them after all."

The skin around Ellis's mouth tightened for a second before she relaxed it. "No, she didn't. I suppose it's morbid to keep them, but they remind me how kind she was."

"That's what everybody says." He pursed his own mouth and looked at the sky. Between the double line of tall Mexican fan palms that framed the park, a cloud in the shape of a rubber duck sailed in the direction of Frankie's diner. *Lucky duck*, he thought, really fighting his smile now.

"Well, if there's nothing else . . ." Ellis said, now tipping down her sunglasses.

"Just be careful." Jack let his gaze focus in on the dark lenses, never doubting that behind them Ellis was equally focused on him. "You can't assume anyone is harmless. Until we catch the guy who did this, no one in town is safe."

Her hand fluttered to the elegant diamond pendant that hung at her throat. "You're sure the murderer is a man?"

"Oh, yeah. We've got the kind of trace only a man can leave."

He left her with that to think about, knowing that she was bright enough to add two plus two equals Troy.

"Take care," he said, folding his height back into the car.

"You, too," she said faintly.

For a moment, he considered Premiere's front window. Ellis had hung onto her sunglasses. The clothes she had been wearing to strangle Tish might be in the dry cleaner's now. He could try for a warrant and have the lab run them before they were cleaned, but it didn't seem worth it to tip her off. By her own admission, Ellis had been with Tish that night. One hug hello or goodbye could explain a lot of pink angora transfer. Tish's death hadn't been bloody. That being so, he was going to have to hang his hopes on Ellis's true nature showing itself under pressure.

It was the men coming to replace Frankie's door that decided her. With all Jack West had on his mind, he hadn't forgotten her safety.

Frankie tried calling him at the station but was told he'd gone off-duty for a few hours. Jean Li was, in her all-knowing way, able to supply his home address. The information had come with a lot of wagging eyebrows and meaningful hums, but Frankie considered it worth the cost.

She had to see Jack. She had to know if their evening together was going to lead to more. She had to know what he'd meant when he said she should have waited for him.

Even if those words had come from him and not the role he'd been playing, they might not mean he wanted her to wait for him more than once.

"Since when are you so insecure?" she muttered to herself as she pulled up to the front of the small tan stucco box in which he lived. The house was doleful, but the small front yard was lush with flowering plants. The plumeria smelled like heaven, and a well-groomed queen palm shaded one side. Either Jack had a great gardener, or he spent his days off exercising his green thumb.

His police car wasn't in the driveway. She knew he always drove it home so he could be on call, so he must not have arrived. That, or he wasn't planning to spend his downtime here. Frankie turned off her ignition and bit the side of her thumb.

"In or out, girl," she ordered herself.

When she thought about it, it was funny that she felt on tenterhooks around him. Jack West wasn't cruel or careless of people's feelings, and she couldn't doubt he wanted her. Even so, he made her nervous in a way no man ever had. Certainly, Troy hadn't. She'd had all sorts of reactions to him—fond, angry, disappointed—but not nervous.

You care about Jack, she thought, preferring not to say this out loud. *It's important to you that he's serious.*

Sighing, she forced herself to leave the car. She couldn't let a little nervousness stop her. For one thing, she'd never hear the end of it from Jean.

Recruiting Pete and Dave for surveillance wasn't quite the trial for Rivera Jack had hoped. Not only were they eager to help,

free of charge, they were able to borrow a high-tech van from a re-
tired FBI agent who lived in Century City. Rivera returned to the
office looking like a hero for sparing their budget.

The mayor was going to like that.

"He consults on movies now," Pete said when Jack came to
check out the van's setup at their garage. "Earns three times what
Dave and I do in half the time."

Their friend from the FBI seemed to have put some of those
Hollywood earnings into his toy. The surveillance van was mint
condition and cutting edge. There was stuff inside it Jack had no
idea how to use, though the mini fridge and hotplate did seem like
they'd be handy. He went over it inch by inch before stepping
back into the garage bay.

Pete and Dave had closed up shop as soon as the van came in,
for which Jack was grateful. All the same, they were way more excited than he could be pleased about.

"You talk to nobody about this," he said. "Not girlfriends. Not
boyfriends. Nobody."

"We don't have boyfriends," Dave huffed predictably.

"And we're trustworthy," Pete added. "We kept Tish's secrets
even after she died."

This was a point in their favor only at the present moment. Deciding to save his breath for other arguments, Jack slid the van
door shut. The side was painted to resemble a plumber's truck.

"You know how to operate this equipment?"

"Do we ever!" Dave enthused. "We rode around with Remminger a bunch of times. You know, in LA."

"You won't be riding around Six Palms," Jack told him bluntly.
"Not without my say-so."

"It wasn't like that," Dave said. "Not like peeping. Remminger
just wanted to keep his old skills honed."

"Uh-huh," said Jack. "Like I said: not around here."

Pete elbowed Dave before he could speak again. "You can count on us, Chief. If this turns out, we'd be happy to get more work like this—with your say-so."

Jack shot a look at Pete to let him know he was being held responsible for keeping Dave in line. It was marginally reassuring that Pete didn't look worried.

"Set up as soon as you can," Jack instructed the men. "I don't want to leave that house unwatched. Officer Dewey will join you today, and I'll take the graveyard shift. You have my number if anything looks like it's developing."

"We have it," Dave said more moderately than before.

Jack left them with a tip of two fingers.

Lord, he thought as he exited the garage's oil-spattered back entry. *I hope this isn't heading for a huge screw-up.*

When Jack rolled up to his house, the sight of Frankie sitting on the concrete stoop made his heart beat twice as fast as before. She was here. At his home. That probably signified some sort of intent to start up a relationship. Unless she was here to ask more questions about the case. He should invite her in e ʰer way. Show her he wanted to see her. For the life of him, though, he couldn't remember what state he'd left his living room in.

He might have had two left legs as he walked up the flagstone path toward her. None of his joints seemed to want to bend. When he was close enough to speak, she stood, tugging down the thighs of her snug blue jeans.

He couldn't have said why that simple gesture was enough to dry his mouth. He was so flustered, he suspected his face showed no expression at all. Her first words confirmed it.

"I'm sorry. I've come at a bad time."

"No," he said. "I'm just surprised and . . . wondering how messy I left my house."

She smiled, which was much better. "I could let you have a head start. Give you a chance to stuff the chip bags and dirty socks under the couch."

"How long have you been waiting?"

She shrugged. "A bit. I was enjoying your garden. Your bird of paradise is really nice."

This made her smile, too, as if she'd discovered a secret he hadn't meant to let out.

"I like to garden," he said, trying not to sound defensive. "It relaxes me."

"Just like me and cooking!"

She was beaming at him now and, wow, was she ever gorgeous when she smiled like that! It took him a couple seconds to remember to put his key in the door.

"It's not bad," he said once he poked his head in. "No chip bags in sight."

She followed him in and stood in the middle of his very plain, very brown, paneled living room. He suddenly realized how interesting her house was, how full of light and air. His hideous indoor-outdoor carpet really needed replacing. He hadn't done much decorating since he'd moved here.

"I'm sorry my house is so—"

"I'm sorry I didn't call before I—"

They both stopped talking and smiled. "You first," he said.

"I'm sorry I came over without asking. It's seeming kind of presumptuous now."

"We did have sex," he pointed out.

"And how!" she agreed, grinning.

"Some might say that justifies some presumption."

"But I don't really know you, Jack, except that you're an exciting lover and a private person." She hesitated, and he let her. Her mention of him being an exciting lover had his ears blazing. This, after all, was not the sort of thing he was sure about. "I want to know you better, in case we . . . do it again. I feel like we ought to catch up."

"I want to do it again," he said, his voice gone low, almost harsh. He cleared his throat. "Would you like to stay for dinner? Steak is about all I cook, but it's edible."

"Let me cook. Maybe it will calm my nerves."

He had a hard time believing he could make her nervous. It seemed like a weird, backward blessing. "All right, but I might have a few questions, too."

"Personal or police work?"

"Personal, if that's okay."

"That's perfect," she said with a lack of dread he wished he could match. "Now point me to your kitchen."

She took charge of the tiny space without hesitation, pulling open drawers and cabinets until she'd figured out where what she needed was. "No kidding you don't cook much. All your stove has on it is dust."

"Microwave," he explained, and she rolled her eyes.

He watched her from a stool at his '70s-style breakfast bar, pleased in some deep and possibly immature male way. Every move she made was magical to him.

"You're the first woman I've had in this house," he blurted out. He was immediately sorry he'd said it but decided it was just as well she knew he was no playboy.

Not that she couldn't have guessed.

She paused in the act of slicing onions with a chef's panache.

"I'm honored," she said with a casualness he thought might be put on for his benefit. "How do you feel about sautéed garlic on your salad?"

"Good." He squirmed on his seat. "Why do you have a wooden oar hanging above your bed?"

She stopped slicing to laugh, instantly turning his kitchen into a foreign land. "I'm surprised you noticed, what with everything else there was to stare at in my bedroom. All right. I won't tease. The oar was my mother's. She was a competitive rower as a teenager. Outrigger canoe events are a big deal in Hawaii. My mother's team were three-time champions."

"I *thought* you might be part Hawaiian."

"Huh," she said. "Nobody guesses that. My mother was a mix of a couple things, and my dad was all Anglo."

"My best friend in college was *hapa*-Hawaiian. Your eyes look a lot like his."

"Huh," she said again. "Maybe you caught island fever."

"More like Frankie fever," he mumbled. He was sure she'd heard because her lips curved up. Her forearms corded as she chopped some more. Before this, he wouldn't have guessed how appealing a woman with buff forearms was. She was still smiling when she spoke.

"Where did you go to college?"

"UCLA."

"Pretty fancy for a cop."

"Not so much. I know a few cops with doctorates." He put his elbows on the counter, actually starting to enjoy this. "Why did your mom move to the mainland?"

"To give her daughter job opportunities that didn't involve catering to tourists." She laughed. "And what do I end up doing, but flipping burgers for the tourist trade! Mom was proud of me, though, running my own place. And she loved, loved diners.

When I was a kid, she'd scrape her money together and take us on diner tours, wherever we could get to in our crappy car. Best vacations I ever had. Mom adored talking to new people."

"Sounds like fun."

She plopped his steaks onto a stovetop grill he didn't remember owning—no doubt a gift from one of his sisters. She made sure the meat was settled before she turned her head to him. "I know it's trite, but I have to ask. What made you want to be a cop?"

This story was too serious to tell her soft, sunny face.

"I need food before I answer," he stalled. "Why don't you let me tear up lettuce instead?"

They ate the steak, which was perfectly medium rare, along with a heaping salad that tasted better than Jack had known salad could. Considering how seldom he drank, the one beer he tipped down his throat mellowed him.

As shored up as he was getting, he wiped his mouth on a paper napkin and leaned back from his plate. "That was incredible."

She laughed, but she seemed pleased. "You're easy to spoil."

He wouldn't have guessed it, but maybe he was—if she was doing the spoiling. "I'm having an almost uncontrollable urge to offer to mow your lawn."

"Noticed it was kind of shaggy, huh?"

"In passing."

They locked gazes, happy with each other, their pulses picking up at the memory of what they'd done on her unmown lawn.

This is what it's like, he thought, *when the chemistry between two people works.*

"Let's go to the den," he said. "It's more comfortable than the living room."

The den wasn't any fancier than his living room, but he had his

TV and stereo there—and one big, broken-in saddle leather sofa that a person could sink into and never come out. Frankie took one look and said, "Napping couch."

"Yes, it is. I'm afraid I have the habit of falling asleep in front of the news."

She plopped down in its middle, conveniently forcing him to sit close to her. "Just don't fall asleep before you tell your story."

He sat and pulled her against him. She sighed and swung her legs up, so he did, too, stretching out along the full length of the cushions with his neck pillowed on the arm. Her head settled naturally into his shoulder, her back inviting the stroking of his hand.

"So," she said, running her hand up his ribs. "Why did you become a cop?"

He drew a bolstering breath. She wanted to know him better. As serious as he felt about her, she had a right. "I became a cop because of my parents. They were religious—and not in a nice way."

"Did they . . . were they abusive?"

"Not physically. The worst thing they ever did was 'sequester' us in the basement for a couple hours. They didn't even yell much. But they'd tell us we were bound for hell if they didn't like what we did."

"Nice thing to tell a kid."

"Well, they believed it. I think we minded not being able to do what our friends did even more. We knew our parents weren't normal. There was no real warmth in our house, not from them. No board games. No loud music or TV. No boyfriends for my sisters."

"You have sisters?"

"Three. Two older. One younger. They were great. The first two had already set up 'The System' by the time I was born."

Frankie drew a circle around his badge. "What was the system?"

"Them against us, basically. We did a lot of things we weren't supposed to when we were kids. Harmless stuff, compared to what goes on these days, but it kept us sane. We covered for each other. We loved each other when our parents didn't know how. We were our own blue line."

"Rightfully speaking then, with sisters like that, you should be comfortable with women."

"Well, I like women." He shifted his hand up to pet her hair, needing the motion to soothe him. "But I grew up as such an odd-ball, I guess you could say I never got socially adept. When I was thirteen and my older sisters were both old enough, they convinced my parents to let them go away to college. God knows how they did it. It was a girls' college, and they went together, but it was too far for them to come home on weekends. I only saw them twice a year. With them gone, our house really did feel like hell. And I had to shield my younger sister from my parents all by myself."

"You felt betrayed," Frankie said softly.

"They called me," Jack said in his older sisters' defense, "but, yeah, maybe I did. My little sister got to visit them now and then. I remember being fairly furious that I couldn't go as well."

"And you wanted to be a cop so you could lock up your parents?"

He laughed, surprising himself. "You're not entirely off base. I wanted to be the one to say what was right and wrong. I wanted to be the law."

"And you were good at it, I take it. Jean Li told me about your being a hero, about saving those people from the fire."

"Your waitress?" Jack lifted his head to look at her. Being called a hero embarrassed him, but he did wonder how she knew.

"Jean has a nephew on the force. She also told me people from the neighborhood stood by and watched while you went into that burning building over and over again."

"They weren't trained to help. It's easy to be scared when you don't know what to do. The EMTs took care of me when they arrived."

Her brow was furrowed—worried for him, hurt for him. He sensed that, trained or not, she would have tried to do something. People like Frankie didn't understand standing around when someone needed help. People like Frankie pitched in.

Feeling too tender not to, he cupped her face. "I wasn't thinking when I did it. My brain switched into action mode. Or automatic pilot. It didn't let me be afraid."

"So you're not a hero," she said dubiously. "Even though you saved people's lives and could have died yourself."

He had to laugh when she put it that way. "I guess I don't feel like a hero. Anyway, my job wasn't usually that dramatic, but, yes, I was good at it. Police work was the first thing I'd found that I loved as much as my sisters. I couldn't give it up, no matter what, but there were things about it that changed me in ways I'm not sure were good for me."

Frankie rubbed her nose across his breastbone, the gesture oddly comforting. "What things?"

"Long-time cops tell the rookies, don't let the civilians get to you. Don't touch and don't be touched, in every sense of the word. I learned that lesson really well. I think it was a relief to learn it because of how emotionally ass-backward my parents were. All they knew was criticism, but if you don't feel, you can't be hurt. Most of all, the older guys taught me home was for escaping the job, not for sharing it."

Jack shifted beneath her, his spine uncomfortable. He made himself go on. "I think, maybe, that was why my wife gave up on me. God, we were young. She was the first woman I'd slept with, my first serious girlfriend, and I thought our marriage was forever. But she knew I had this whole other life, a *realer* life than I had with her, and I wasn't letting her in. After a while, she got tired of trying to make me."

"Maybe she should have fought harder," Frankie said to his shirt. "The friends who warned you not to marry her could have been right. Maybe, as young as she was, she only wanted to play at being a policeman's wife, and the real thing scared her off."

"You're excusing me for a lot without having been there."

Frankie pushed up on one arm, forcing him to meet her eyes. Jack fought not to wince at how very discerning they were.

"You're not an unemotional person," she said. "I never thought that about you. And I'm not the only one who likes you. You might be surprised how many people miss you when you don't come into the diner for breakfast, who say nice things about you behind your back. You might not talk much, but people here sense you care. Maybe you've been worrying you turned into your parents, but I think you're still more like your sisters."

"Jesus," he said, because his eyes had welled up with tears.

Frankie laughed and laid her head on his chest, thankfully not watching him. "Give yourself a break, Jack. Whatever you did to your ex, and whatever she did to you, it's old news. Forgive her and forgive yourself."

"Is that what you're doing with Troy?"

The question surprised both of them.

"Maybe," she said. "God willing. He certainly seems to go out of his way to try my patience. My mom would have told me to forgive him. She was very 'let bygones be bygones.' I used to tease her that she didn't know how to stay angry."

She seemed to know how lucky she was, so Jack didn't tell her. He simply ran his hand slowly down her back, starting again at the top of her spine when he ran out of vertebrae.

"I wish you could have known her," she said. "She would have liked you."

"Apparently, she liked everybody."

"Not everybody. She just gave them a fair shot."

"You've got a lot of her in you."

She hugged him with a strength that made his throat ache. "My temper is all my own."

"That's all right. I think people need a bit of fire."

"Sometimes . . ." she said, so soft and hesitant he knew she wasn't sure she ought to confess what was coming next, "I worry about following in her footsteps. My mom was the most wonderful woman, and she couldn't hold onto my dad, who—believe me—she loved. I look at what happened with me and Troy, and I think I'm really arrogant to have expected any better."

God, she broke his heart and stole it at the same time. If he wasn't careful, he was going to say something completely sappy and inappropriate. "Troy Wilcox is an idiot," he said, judging this was safe. "I don't think any man in this town doubts that."

She hummed at that, pleased, and wriggled more fully onto his front. Her weight felt like nothing against him, her breasts and belly soft beneath her white T-shirt. She was wearing a bra, but not much of one, and the memory of how she looked and felt without one was potent. He wasn't sure it was what the moment called for, but his cock began to swell forcefully.

"Jack?" she said, her nose now nuzzling beneath his jaw. "Do you think we could switch to the kissing part?"

He laughed with pure happiness, then hitched her body high enough to do it.

"Ooh," she said as one of her legs slid onto his erection. "Not a moment too soon."

They kissed until she thought she'd die if she didn't get him inside her. His kisses were exactly the kind she liked, but that cock of his was so hard, so big, and so inviting, it seemed a shame to leave it trapped where it was. At last, not caring if she was being too aggressive, she pushed onto her knees and sat on his thighs.

To her pleasure, when Jack looked up at her, he was flushed.

"I vaguely recall promising to strip you naked," she said. "And I know I haven't done it yet."

"No, you haven't," he agreed with the deadpan wit she was beginning to find endearing. "I think it might be very nice if you did."

"I'd want to touch you all over."

"I wouldn't stop you."

She bit her lip. "I might want to be on top."

He laughed until his ribs shook, until his eyes gleamed with pleasure, and his face looked quite handsome. "You can be anywhere you want, Frankie," he finally gasped. "I'm not sure anything you do could turn me off."

This certainly seemed to be the case as she stripped him, button by button, from his uniform. In fact, he seemed more sensitive than most men to being touched, maybe because he'd shut himself off from it for so long. The signs of increasing excitement were unmistakable—his ragged breathing; his heightened color; the way his toes curled when her hand reached some new and interesting spot.

"Take off your clothes," he said when she had him down to his white briefs.

She stepped back and did it, peeling off her clothing piece by piece, enjoying what watching her did to him. He was still stretched out on the couch but had rolled onto his side. One hand propped up his head while the other draped the formidable hump of his erection. He wasn't rubbing it, simply covering it as if, subconsciously, he thought its power needed containing.

She couldn't explain it, but she found that as sexy as if she'd seen the whole thing.

"Turn on the CD," he said, and Frankie smiled to herself. He was going to be in charge of this no matter who was on top.

When she turned on the music, something slow and sultry and Latin began to play.

"I could dance for you," she offered, beginning to understand that her lack of inhibition was a turn-on for him.

His chest heaved twice at the suggestion. "You have five minutes to strut your stuff, Ms. Smith, and then you'd better come ravish me."

"Take off your briefs first. I'm not doing my Salome imitation unless you're naked, too."

He stood and shoved them down his legs. The sight of his thick, bobbing hard-on was all the inspiration she could require.

"Back on the couch," she ordered, and with a grin, he laid down.

Frankie wasn't known for her shyness, but as she danced for him, she felt freer than she ever had with a man. The music thickened her blood as she ran her hands up her belly and over her breasts, the feel of her own caresses sweet. Jack's grin was soon history, as was her nervousness. His eyes followed every undulation and turn of her hips. When she plucked her nipples, he licked his lips.

Whatever his upbringing, nothing in him disapproved of her.

"Touch your pussy," he said hoarsely.

"Touch your cock," she fired back.

His mouth fell open, but he hesitated just a moment before wrapping his fingers around the base of his shaft. Only his big hand could make that monster appear normal sized. It occurred to her that, with no serious girlfriends before his wife and only a few afterward, he must be pretty experienced at pleasuring himself. She was looking forward to making up for what he'd been missing, but, for the moment, watching Jack jack himself was mind-meltingly sexy. He pulled his grip upward once, dragging the flushed, smooth skin toward the bulbous tip. The effect that it had told her he was even more revved up than she'd thought. A bead of fluid squeezed from his slit.

"Oh, boy," she breathed, her insides threatening to run out in a hot puddle.

"Come closer," he said. "Where I can see."

Her knees were shaking as he watched her fondle herself, sitting up to get a better view. With an audience like him, she didn't want to hide anything. He bent forward to kiss her stomach as her fingers worked. She'd done this occasionally for other men, but never had the sensation of masturbation been so strong for her. His attention cast a spell on her, his focus like another touch. He was only holding himself now, too enraptured by what she was doing to stroke himself.

Forgotten in his fisted grip, the head of his cock was so taut, so shiny and flushed with blood, it could have been a ripe, red plum.

"You're beautiful, Frankie," he said. "Every bit of you. Everything you do."

"I want to touch you now," she croaked from her tightened throat.

"Yes," he said. "*Yes.*"

He leaned back and lifted her over him, until she sat on his thighs as she had before. This time neither of them wore anything. This time his cock thrust free in front of her belly. She stroked its upper side, pulling it against her so its bottom ridge pressed her skin. The part of her that was all woman reveled in how firm and hot he was.

Then she did as she'd warned and touched every inch of him.

His naked body was beautiful, big and lean and muscled all over. He was writhing long before she'd finished exploring his hairy chest, was gasping when she found the sensitive spots inside the bend of his arms, and just plain moaned when she feathered her fingers over his knees.

"What's this scar from?" she asked, kissing her way around its curving length.

"Gunshot," he panted.

"Oh," she said, mildly shocked. Since she'd already kissed it, she licked her way around its trail.

"Frankie—" His voice was sounding kind of tortured.

"Just calves and feet yet," she assured him. "I'll be ravishing you any minute now."

It was especially nice to think she was probably the first woman who'd done that. She stroked gently down his legs, standing and moving to the end of the couch to get access. He took the calf part well, his eyes drifting closed with pleasure, but as soon as she started kneading his feet, his jaw went tight.

"You're not ticklish, are you?"

He groaned when she worked her thumbs into his arch. "No, not ticklish, but if you don't stop doing that soon, this ravishment is going to be very short."

"I see. Cops are like waitresses. Massage their feet and they're helpless slaves."

He was too far gone to laugh, and that might have been the sexiest thing of all.

"Frankie," he said. "Please. Come make love to me."

She really couldn't resist him. She crawled back over him and poised herself over his waiting cock. The heat of it rose in waves. He was so excited a thin rivulet of pre-come ran down his crown. Frankie rubbed it into him with her thumb, loving the way this sent a mini-earthquake through his shoulders. As eager as he was, she tipped him toward her for entry. She knew he was more than ready for that, but he stopped her long enough to kiss her, driving his tongue deep inside her mouth. Only then did he let her go and look into her eyes.

Her heart stuttered in her chest at what she saw in his.

"Frankie," he said. "I'm falling in love with you."

"Oh!" Her fingers flew to her mouth, emotion overwhelming her. "And here I was thinking I was the brave one!"

He held her wrists. "Don't cry," he said, which let her know she kind of was. "Please, Frankie. Whatever you feel, it's okay."

"I'm not sure what I feel. With everything that's happened, this is sort of fast for me. I . . . think I love you, too."

He smiled and stroked her hair from her face, catching a tear on the way. "Wait until you're sure. Then tell me again."

"Deal," she said, but her voice was shaking. "Is it all right to ravish you now?"

He took her hips in his big, warm hands. "I think now would be just fine."

Chapter 16

It wasn't hard for Frankie to pretend she was steady when Jack's sure hands were supporting her. She sank down as slowly as she could, luxuriating in every millimeter of hot male flesh that went into her.

"That's right," he murmured reassuringly. "Take your time."

She blew out her breath, willing away her shakes. The big leather cushions were easy on her knees, their texture sensual. She wondered if the leather felt good along his naked back. Something certainly did. His shaft stretched upward even as she lowered herself, his body growing more excited as it was engulfed. He murmured her name in appreciation, encouraging her to keep up what she was doing. Her progress was so leisurely and her sex so slick that, despite his increasing size, she didn't have to strain to take him.

"Boy," she sighed, when she finally had all of him throbbing inside her. "That cock of yours is like the last frontier."

He snorted his amusement and pulled her down for a nice, wet kiss. He ended it reluctantly. "I'm glad we fit. I'd hate to think I was hurting you."

"Nobody else your size could get into me. Only you turn me on enough."

She wriggled around him as she said it, letting him feel the truth in her flickering muscles and lubricious heat. His appreciative groan was deep.

"Ride me slowly," he whispered next to her ear. "I'll stroke your clit whenever you say. You can come as often as you want."

She liked hearing him say *clit*, liked how intimate it meant they were. She pushed upright, gazing into his flushed but oddly peaceful face. He'd been awkward before, but he wasn't now. The Latin music washed around them, seeming to guide the beat of their pulse. She flattened her hands on the slab of his chest, his tightened nipples poking her palms. She knew she would never forget having him beneath her this first time.

"I want to come when you do," she said.

His burning whiskey eyes darkened. "Then I'll touch the rest of you for now. You tell me when you want my hands on your sex."

"I'm in charge?"

"As much as you want to be."

She chuckled at that, because it was exactly the right thing to say. "I don't want to be completely in charge," she admitted. "I like masterful men."

"Had many before me?" The question was hoarse.

"No," she said, choosing that moment to pull her body up his shaft again. "No one ever flipped my switch like you."

He shuddered as she almost lost him, seeming to like the extra tug she gave his rim. Liking it herself, she sank down again. "That slow enough?"

"Mmm," was all he could get out.

She took him this way, one deliberate, delicious stroke at a time. His hands roved her body everywhere he could reach, hard and gentle at the same time. Her breasts felt worshipped, her thighs adored. Her body went into a trance of sensory pleasure, caressed with sensation inside and out. When he couldn't take any more of her slowness, his fingers tightened on her ass.

"Faster?" she asked on a moaning exhalation.

He craned up to suckle her breasts. "Harder," he said, sitting now. "I want to feel it when you come down."

He braced one foot on the floor, preparing to help. Knowing she needed more pressure, too, she took one of his hands from her bottom and placed it between them so his thumb curled under the top of her labia. Their eyes met, his pupils expanding in circles of gold.

He knew what she wanted and was aroused by it. She'd stopped thrusting while she repositioned his hand. Now he held her trapped where she was, watching her reaction as his thumb massaged her clit up and down. He knew the trick of it just right, quickly ratcheting up her arousal. Her mouth felt swollen from his kisses, her eyelids heavy with lust. Every time he changed what he was looking at, the place went hot.

For at least five minutes she let him watch what he could do to her—which was at least four minutes more than a red-blooded girl should be asked to take.

Her soft moan of frustration warned him his time was up.

"Go," he said. "Give us both what we want."

He still had one hand on her bottom, and that one hand was enough to deepen every thrust from then on. As wonderful as her long, slow savoring of him had been, this forceful ride had her biting her lip with the sharpness of her pleasure. She could drive his cock exactly where she wanted it, could take him as greedily as she pleased. Her nerves were screaming in half a minute and, apparently, so were his.

"God," he gasped, abruptly spilling hard into her.

His thumb worked the heart of her sensation, his motions wild but firm, as if his life depended on her pleasure. She was coming, too, then, a deep, tightening spear of ecstasy through her sex.

"One more," he said, tipping her back under him.

He shifted them so quickly she couldn't stop him from taking charge, which was exactly what she wanted. His weight on hers was exciting, his thrusts twice as strong. His thighs spread hers into a new and bewitching vulnerability. Despite her recent climax, he flipped her switch and then some. She wanted to come again, needed to. His face twisted with strain as he pumped into her, his cock still hard, but probably hypersensitive from having just come himself. She didn't have the presence of mind to worry for him. The idea that he was hurting himself to do this for her aroused her—until she almost growled with lust.

Though she held back the sound, he must have seen the change in her expression, must have felt it in the tightening of her body.

"Yes," he said, thrusting even deeper. "Go!"

It was all she needed. She moaned with relief as the most exquisite of tensions broke long and sweet.

That he definitely felt. He grunted as her body gripped him. Then, to her amazement, he came again as well, his hips shuddering against her with the surprise climax.

"O-kay," he panted above her once he had enough breath to speak. "First time for everything."

Frankie hugged him, loving the sweaty breadth of his heaving back. She started to giggle and couldn't stop. Who'd have thought she'd end up here when Troy dumped her? Who'd have predicted she'd find this? Jack West was her unsuspected ideal: absolutely, unpredictably perfect for her.

"I'm giddy," she tried to explain through her snickers. "Too much sexual happiness."

"Ha." He returned her hug. "I'm sure there's no such thing."

She was giggling still when his beeper went off. It was loud enough that it startled her into hiccuping.

"Shit," he said, reluctantly easing from her arms. "I'm sorry, Frankie. I've got to get that."

He checked the number on the beeper, then walked—still stark naked—into the adjoining room with his cell phone. Frankie was able to admire his muscular butt through the archway, but he sounded so serious as he spoke to whoever called that she didn't feel like laughing anymore.

"Is everything okay?" she asked when he returned and began pulling on his clothes.

"Everything's fine. Just work stuff."

He was all business—and all evasion. She handed him his briefs, not wanting to push. He thanked her for them and stepped into his trousers. When he reached for his gunbelt, a lump materialized in her throat. Six Palms might not be LA, but dangerous things could happen here. Tish's death was proof of that.

He finished buckling and zipping before he looked up and saw her face.

"It's okay, Frankie. Just a call I have to go on. I'll see you tomorrow for breakfast at All U Can Eat." He put a smile into this, but Frankie couldn't smile back.

"Be careful," she said. "I'm getting attached to you."

He crinkled his eyes at her, then hesitated. "I'll tell you about it," he said. "Once it's okay for me to share the story."

She knew this was a big concession for him to make, and she was grateful. She just wished whatever this call was didn't look like it was going to be worth a tale.

"I'll be all ears," she said as lightly as she could.

The chief of police kissed the top of her head and left.

Jack didn't want to leave Frankie with that worried look in her eyes, and certainly not for such a typical cop inconvenience. Even in a small town he was, for most intents and purposes, on call all the time. Frankie didn't need to have her nose rubbed in that particular reality yet.

"Leave it alone," he muttered to himself as he got into his personal car, an unmarked, five-year-old black Jeep. "Time to focus on the task at hand."

The task at hand was getting to Ellis's house as fast as he could. Ellis and Troy had arrived for the evening and were, according to Dewey, beginning to snipe at each other like a bad Spanish soap opera.

He slapped his blue light on the roof to clear traffic but took it off again once he reached Ellis's gated community. For the rest of his drive, a low profile was key.

His heart rate was up already, but not as up as it could get. The Palms Estates development was new, only two-thirds finished so far. Ellis was probably paying for her house by agenting remaining lots. Fortunately, the house across the street from hers was still under construction. The borrowed plumbing van looked perfectly at home in its rutted dirt driveway.

Jack parked his car half a block away, in front of another unsold house, using the short walk to his destination to scope out Ellis's residence. Her lights were on upstairs and down. Jack could see the house was bigger than Tish's, but it didn't have as much land. It might end up being as impressive, but at the moment, all he could tell was that it was in dire need of landscaping.

Aesthetics aside, the lack of trees made surveillance easier.

Dewey slid the van door open for him quietly. "Pull up a pair of earphones," he said. "Things are heating up in there."

Jack nodded to Pete and Dave, who were at the far end of the van fiddling with dials. Jack took the seat Dewey had vacated, pushed a Twinkie wrapper out of his way, and slipped a set of earphones over his head. The parabolic mike picked up the couple's voices clear as crystal. Pete and Dave also had live video from a long-lens camera that was trained on the upstairs media room/library.

Jack turned his attention to the monitor.

Here was a well-furnished house, even if it was too fussy for Jack's taste. Powder-blue walls surrounded tasteful furniture of green and cream. The bookshelves could have come from an English manor. Troy's blue shirt nearly matched the walls. The only spot of hot color was Ellis's satiny orange robe. The pair were holding drinks. Ellis looked like hers hadn't been her first. Her hair was tousled, and she was swaying slightly on her feet.

"You slept with her!" she said, her voice rising from its usual modulated tone. "You promised you wouldn't, but you did."

Troy dropped to the arm of a cream-colored couch that was piled with pale-green pillows. "For God's sake, what does it matter? She's dead. I'm with you."

"Yes, but you might not be with me if she were alive."

Troy ran the side of his bourbon glass across his forehead. The audio was so good, Jack heard ice tinkle. "You're having my child, Karen. You know that's important to me."

Ellis tossed back her drink and poured another. "The police found your sperm inside her. You're going to be a suspect again."

"They'll figure out who really killed her. You're not going to be left alone." His voice was so weary he almost sounded wise. He rose to where she was pacing. "I'm going to be with you through everything."

"I can't trust you," she said, drunkenly teary. "I can't trust anything."

Troy rubbed her shoulders. "I'm not a saint. I've never been that for anyone—including Tish. You just have to believe me when I say I'll be there for you."

Ellis tried to take another swallow, but Troy stopped her hand.

"You wouldn't have cheated on *her*," she accused. "You were in love with her."

"Strictly speaking," Troy said with a sigh, "I did cheat on her. Even after I broke up with you, I was still with Frankie."

"You should have left that bitch," Ellis said, swiping her fallen hair back with one wrist. "You should have made up your mind and left her, instead of hurting everyone."

"I didn't think I was hurting you," Troy said softly. "I was pretty sure you were only having fun when you slept with me."

"Ha." She pulled away from him, seeming not to notice that half her drink flew across her robe. She lifted the glass again.

"Don't," Troy said. "I know you're mad at me, but the baby doesn't deserve to be hurt."

"The baby!" she shrieked, suddenly throwing her glass wildly. The heavy crystal hit an end table and bounced off. "Fuck the baby!"

Troy was backing away. Horror seemed to be his main reaction rather than fear for himself. Ellis was too drunk to get in a decent slap.

"There is no baby," he breathed, finally getting it. "You lied to take me away from Tish."

"Oh, boy," Dewey said. "Here it comes."

"Yes, I lied!" Ellis snapped. "I lied to a lying liar, and so what?"

Troy's perfect, chisel-cut jaw dropped in astonishment. Clearly, he wasn't used to being on the receiving end of deceit. He recovered with an audible gasp. "How could you do that? Tish was your best friend. You knew she wanted to marry me."

"She had no right!" Having failed to smash her glass, Ellis threw a pillow at a table covered in porcelain knick-knacks. They fell over but didn't break, either. The effort winded her. She stumbled into a chair Jack suspected his own weight would have turned to kindling. The video was blurry, but it looked as if Ellis was weeping. Her cheeks were shiny with tear tracks. She bent in over herself, her arms hugging her belly. "She had no right to win you. She had no right to have you love her."

Troy went to her tentatively. He knelt in front of her sprawling knees. "What are you talking about? Everyone deserves to be loved."

Pete made a low, sad noise, reminding Jack that he'd known Ellis as a person, before all this.

"Come on, underwear boy," Jack murmured. "You're halfway there. Might as well figure out the rest."

"We had an agreement," Ellis said. "Tish and I had an agreement since we were kids. I came first. I helped her out of her shell when she was the biggest loser in school. I helped her feel like she belonged. She owed me. She had to come second."

"Tish never told me that."

"She didn't have to. It was unspoken. It was . . . what was right."

Ellis pushed Troy out of her way so she could stand. She went to the table that held her decanters. It was a carved mahogany bureau with a glossy top—an antique, Jack suspected. Her back was to the windows, her shoulders bowed. She looked thin and delicate. She opened one of the drawers.

"I let her have the charities," she said. "They didn't matter.

Nobody takes society fund-raisers seriously. An excuse to throw expensive parties is all they are, and I always liked expensive parties. If the charity gets a dime on the dollar, they're lucky. When she started thinking they were important, that she ought to be doing more, I told her she shouldn't waste her life catering to a bunch of silver-spooned babies' vanity. I should have put her in her place when she didn't listen. I should have known she'd forget who she really was."

"What are you trying to tell me?" The whiteness of Troy's face said he was beginning to guess. "What are you trying to say?"

Jack could have kissed him for the aptness of this lead-in.

Ellis's shoulders sagged even more. "I'm saying you aren't worth it, Troy. I'm saying you don't even come close to making up for what I had to do."

Troy was panting with shock. "What you . . . had to do?"

On the monitor, Ellis turned slowly. She had something in her hands.

"Gun!" said Dewey. "Shit."

It was a forty-five semi-automatic, the same caliber Jack used, except hers was a Beretta, and his a Smith & Wesson. The gun looked like a freaking cannon in her little hands. Despite its size, Ellis held it like a woman who'd spend a few hundred hours on the shooting range. Her eyes were narrowed, like she meant business. She definitely wasn't looking drunk enough now. If she shot that thing at this close range, she was going to put underwear boy underground.

These thoughts sped through Jack's head in milliseconds. He was already out of his headphones and his chair, already starting to shove open the van door.

"Take the back," he said to Dewey. "Go in if it's open. Break a window if it's not. Don't announce yourself until you hear me."

Dewey flew across the street like silent bat out of hell, like he'd never eaten a Twinkie in his life. He was drawing his gun as he ran.

"You," Jack said to Pete and Dave. "Call 911 and tell County we need backup. After that, do not fucking leave this van."

Their eyes were wide as saucers, but Jack didn't wait to watch them comply. He ran across the street in a crouch, across the patchy lawn, and up the three marble steps of the portico. He tried the door, but it was locked. If he broke it down, would Ellis shoot? A muffled cracking of glass told him Dewey was breaking in. No alarms shrilled, so they mustn't have been set for the night.

Jack knew he had to beat Dewey to that upstairs room. He wasn't sure his junior officer had ever discharged his gun at a human being. Jack himself had never shot a woman.

Eyeing the side of the house, he reengaged the safety on his gun, shoved it into the small of his back, and shimmied up the portico column. He tried not to groan as he pulled his weight onto the slate-tiled roof. The library window was open. Troy's and Ellis's voices drifted faintly out.

That's it, he thought to Troy as he crabwalked closer. *You keep her talking. She wants to confess to you, if only to make certain you're as miserable as she is.*

"You know what she did?" Ellis was saying. "She came to me, offering to adopt the baby. Said she knew I didn't really want it, but you and she would give it a good home. Said that baby would have every advantage a kid could dream of. Saint Tish. Better than everyone."

"You liked her," Troy responded in confusion. "I know you did."

"I *loved* her," Ellis said. "I made her. And she tried to blackmail me."

"What could she have to blackmail you with?"

"Recordings," she spat out as Jack edged his head around the window where they were. The gun was dangling in Ellis's hand, but Jack didn't like how close Troy was standing. "DVDs of me and . . ."

it doesn't matter. She said she didn't want to hurt me, but if I forced her hand, she'd send copies to every member of the chamber of commerce. She said I'd never be respected in Six Palms again."

"*Tish* did that?"

"Yes, perfect Saint Tish tried to use her kitten claws on me. Naturally, she wasn't up to it. I told her I'd agree to her terms if she'd give me the disc."

"You told her to meet you behind Frankie's diner. You tried to make Frankie look guilty."

Ellis tossed her hair. "Why shouldn't I? You didn't want her anymore. When I found the door unlocked, it was like she was begging me to plant evidence. Anyway, they both deserved it. Tish was too stupid to doubt my word.

"You should have seen her pacing back and forth in that alley, rehearsing what she going to say, how she was going to 'salvage our friendship.'" Ellis's sneer didn't erase the teary throatiness from her voice. "I watched her from the shadows, watched my best friend take her last breaths on Earth and mumble her last stupid words. When I did her, I don't think she even knew who it was. I was that quick and clean. Then I took that damned disc and tossed it down the storm drain."

You took a copy, Jack thought as Troy covered his face and moaned.

The sound didn't quite cover the click of Dewey opening the door. Karen turned toward it with the forty-five in both hands.

"Freeze!" Jack barked, his gun at the ready as quick as thought. As he'd intended, this swung Ellis back to him.

When she saw who it was, she laughed scornfully. "Bet you thought I'd confess to save him. Bet you thought I couldn't stand to see him go to jail."

Jack swung one leg over the sill. She didn't shoot him, so he lifted the other and ducked his head inside.

"Actually," he said. "I was hoping you'd do pretty much what you did . . . minus the gun."

She smiled at that, but tightly. A bead of adrenaline sweat rolled down her cheek. Jack wondered how much proof it was.

"Sir?" said Dewey from the door, obviously not certain what to do now. Though his finger wasn't on the trigger, he did have his gun aimed at Ellis.

"It's okay," Jack said, not wanting him to do any more than he was. When it came to shooting, waiting was almost always a good thing. "Karen and I are just going to talk."

"Oh, sure," she said. "We're going to talk about how nice my cell for life is going to be."

"Pleading diminished capacity might be an option."

"Right," she said, her gun never wavering from his chest. "That should shoot me to the top of everyone's invite list. You know, 'cause my story is so damn sympathetic."

Jack wondered if he dared move off the sill but Ellis's eyes were too wild. "I'm sure you can afford a good lawyer."

"I can afford an office full of good lawyers, but, thank you, I think I'll pass." She resettled the gun in her sweaty hands, firming up her two-handed grip. She couldn't have telegraphed what she was thinking any clearer. If she'd wanted to kill him, she would have tried already. Instead, she wanted him to kill her. Suicide by cop. Still in fashion on both coasts.

"Karen," he said, every shred of respect he had for life in his voice. "Our case is good, but you really do have a chance. Stop and think. Give your head a chance to clear."

She lifted the gun an inch and set her jaw. Jack curled his finger into his trigger guard.

"Karen," he said, even more soulfully than before.

"Oh, I *like* the way you say that," she said, her eyes glittering with angry tears. "You say it like you care."

"I care," Troy said in almost the same tone Jack had used.

Jack thought he meant it, but Karen's face distorted with fury. "Shut up!" she screamed, walking back toward him with the gun pointed. Her strides were purposeful, her manner absolutely fearless. "Shut up! Shut—"

Jack shot her before her finger could tighten. The impact spun her around, blood blossoming from the back of her right shoulder. She fell onto her hip without crying out. She didn't go down completely, but the gun clattered to the floor. The bullet had gone straight through her. Her now-empty right hand went to the exit wound as if she couldn't quite believe he'd done it. She smiled at him, Troy temporarily forgotten.

"You know what?" she said with eerie pleasantness. "I think you're not as good a shot as I am. Maybe I shouldn't move next time."

"Shit," he cursed as she went for her gun again.

His surprise cost him half a second, but he shot her before she could bring her Beretta all the way up. She jerked back and then forward, caught in the chest from both sides. Dewey had fired, too. Jack didn't have to see her fall to know she was dead.

"Sir," Dewey said, the second time in one night.

Jack's ears were ringing from the dual explosions. He had to read Dewey's lips to know what he'd said. Dewey began walking toward him, past the body, past an astonished Troy. Jack's head was spinning. He gripped the window frame and tried to stand but only got halfway. A strange, burning pain was shooting through his thigh. He looked down and saw that one of his pant legs was black.

"She shot you," Dewey said, catching him as he teetered. "Your leg is bleeding like a pig."

This hardly qualified as good bedside manner, but Jack's breath was too knocked out of him to complain.

"I got this side," Troy said, leaping forward to help Dewey

lower Jack to the floor. His back slid down the wall beneath the window. When his butt hit the carpet, it made a squelching sound from his blood. Troy whipped off his belt with what looked like super-model speed. Crouching, he cinched it high on Jack's injured thigh. The pressure of the belt hurt like holy hell.

"Alligator," Jack managed to gasp out. "Pretty classy tourniquet."

"Stop talking," Dewey said, then cocked his head like a hunting dog. "I hear ambulance sirens."

"Your . . . ears are younger than mine."

"Shh," Dewey ordered, putting a shaking hand over his boss's mouth.

Jack rested his head against the window sill and smiled, suddenly feeling he loved Dewey as much as he'd ever loved anyone—as much as he loved Frankie. Come to think of it, he might love Troy a little, too.

"You did good, kid," he said, closing his eyes as the sirens wailed. "You did exactly what you were supposed to. I'm gonna . . . buy you . . . a truckload of doughnuts first chance I get. Then I'm gonna buy . . . underwear boy . . . a new alligator belt."

"Is he delirious?" Troy asked worriedly.

"No," Dewey said. "But I'm glad the EMTs are here to keep him quiet. This is no time for him to be learning how to tell jokes."

"Strain might . . . kill me," Jack teased. He had one last glimpse of Ellis's broken body before he passed out.

Chapter 17

Having no excuse—or invitation—to stay at Jack's, Frankie returned home. Once there, she curled up on her bed to watch her remastered DVD of *Casablanca*. Humphrey Bogart had just told Sam that if Ingrid Bergman could stand to hear him play it, so could he. Frankie started to sniffle when a pounding came on her brand-new door.

She looked at the player's clock. It was only nine-thirty. Could Jack have finished up his call?

She hurried down the spiral stairs, but her visitor was Jean Li. She looked more upset than Frankie had ever seen her, her steel-gray hair sticking out in odd tufts and arcs.

"Thank goodness you're here!" she exclaimed before Frankie could speak. "I heard it on my police scanner. The chief has been shot!"

Frankie gasped and covered her mouth.

Jean grabbed her elbow and tugged. "Come. My car is out front. We must go to the hospital and pray."

Jean was as big a believer in praying as she was in the su-
periority of cats over other pets. Still unable to move, Frankie
looked down at herself. She'd been calling it an early night. She
was wearing bright green flip-flops and her favorite tropical fruit
pajamas.

"Never mind that," Jean said. "Grab a sweater and you'll
be fine."

She seemed so certain, Frankie obeyed.

"Shot how?" she asked as Jean pulled her stumbling to her car.
"Shot bad?"

Jean was already praying in Chinese. "A little bad," she said,
shooing Frankie into the passenger side. "But if we pray, he'll
be fine."

Jean's face was grim as she peeled away from the curb. She was
always a fast driver, and now her car's wheels were squealing.
Frankie didn't think it was a good sign that she'd left the engine
running when she came to Frankie's door.

"Did you mean it when you said he'd be fine?" she asked, beginning to cry. "Or are you just hoping?"

Jean glared at the road and ignored the question. When they
reached the town limits, halfway to the nearest hospital, she
slapped Frankie's knee in scold.

"Stop that noise. Praying is useful. Crying is not."

Frankie choked out an "Our Father," which was the only
prayer she knew all the way through. Tears were still running
down her cheeks, but Jean seemed mollified.

Please let him be all right, she prayed in her heart. *Even if I
don't get to keep him, You keep him safe.* She thought about Jack's
parents "sequestering" him and his sisters in their basement for
nothing worse than being a normal kids. She thought about his
older sisters leaving him behind, about his wife, about all those
years he'd spent too knotted up to reach out for love. He'd been

through so much and stayed a good person. He deserved a chance to be happy and, damn it, Frankie wanted to help!

"He's not dying," Jean interrupted in annoyance. "He probably just lost some blood."

Frankie nodded, not knowing whether to believe her. She dried her face on her sweater sleeve.

The hospital Jack had been taken to wasn't big, but it was modern and well staffed. Frankie and Jean followed the milling LA County Sheriff's personnel to the appropriate waiting room. Frankie did a double-take when she saw Troy slumped in one of the vinyl chairs. His face was haggard, as if he'd lost ten pounds since she'd last seen him. Equally surprising, Pete and Dave were there, too.

She didn't get a chance to ask why. When Troy saw Frankie, he rose and put out his arms.

"Frankie," he said, hugging her to him. "It's okay. Chief West is going to be all right. He's still unconscious from the drugs, but they're saying his condition is much better."

She squeezed him hard, grateful that he knew what she needed to hear. When she released him, Pete and Dave told her what had happened—not in every detail, she suspected, but enough to get an idea. While they shared the story, Troy creaked back into his chair and stared at the floor. Worried for him, Frankie sat next to him and took his hand. His fingers were cold and limp.

"She killed Tish," he said dully. "Because of me."

"Not because of you, Troy. Because of her own problems."

He looked at her when she cupped the side of his jaw.

"Not because of you," she repeated. "You *know* Tish wouldn't blame you for what Karen did."

This bucked him up enough that at least some of the hopelessness left his eyes. She patted his hand encouragingly.

"I'll go find coffee," she said, knowing there wasn't much she could do for anyone beyond that. Maybe when she came back, she'd have Jean teach her a Chinese prayer.

Instead, a nurse was waiting when she returned. Nervous, Frankie set down the coffees on an end table.

"That's her," Dave said, pointing.

"You're Frankie Smith?" The nurse had a funny smile tugging at her lips.

"I am." Frankie put her hand to her heart. "Is something wrong?"

"No, no," the nurse assured her, her smile growing broader. "We've been hoping you would show up. I'd like to ask you to stick around if you could. You see, in the operating room, when they were putting Chief West under so they could remove the bullet, he said your name a couple . . . hundred times. The anesthesiologist started to think he was giving him the wrong drugs."

"Oh," said Frankie, her heart racing for a different reason now. "I guess . . . I'll stay until he wakes up."

Jack opened his eyes for the second time since being shot and immediately felt like a new man. He was propped up on a pile of pillows, and Frankie was sitting by his bedside. Frankie was holding his hand.

This was so much better than the trip to the bathroom with that nurse.

"I'm sure now," Frankie said, her pretty green eyes catching the light from the window in his private room.

Jack saw it must be nearing noon. He wondered if he and Frankie had been having a conversation he'd forgot.

"You're sure?"

"That I love you," she said. Despite the calmness of her tone, this made all the nice new blood he'd been given feel a lot livelier. "I cried all the way here. Jean was about to slap me."

"Jean was."

"She drove me. I think she keeps a police scanner by her bed. I've never been as terrified as I was when she told me you were shot. So now I'm sure I love you."

Jack wasn't one to look a gift horse in the mouth, especially this one, but he had a responsibility here. He carried Frankie's hand to his heart. "You're emotional right now," he said. "You thought I was going to die. It's natural to think you feel more than you do."

Frankie narrowed her eyes at him. "The nurses told me how you acted in surgery."

"How I acted?"

"You were saying my name—'Frankie, Frankie, Frankie,' like a broken record. The nurses got quite curious to see who I was."

"Shit," he said, his nice new blood having its first blush. He wasn't a fan of blabbing his business to the world.

Frankie's raised eyebrows said she was waiting for a better response than this.

"Well, *I* know I care about you," he said, "but are you sure you want to be a cop's girlfriend after all this?"

"I love you," she repeated. "I'm not just whistling Dixie when I say that. The question is, can you have faith in how much I mean it?"

"I want you to be happy. I don't want you to have to be afraid for me."

Frankie's face softened. She squeezed the hand that was holding hers. "I can't promise never to be afraid, Jack, but I promise never to let my fears turn me into a coward. If things don't work out between us, it won't be because of that."

"I want them to work out."

"Then promise you'll believe in me as a girlfriend, that I'm not going to wimp out on you and let you down. You can trust me, Jack, with all of you."

"Whew," he said, breathless from a sudden upsurge of nerves and hope. "I think I believe you."

"Yeah, well, let me know when you're sure." She drew her hand back and laid it on his arm instead. The warmth and gentleness of her hold told him what she meant. "By the way, you've got more visitors if you're up for them. Troy fell asleep on one of the couches in the waiting room. He wants to thank you for saving his life."

Jack had to snort at that. "I guess he hasn't figured out I'm the one who put his life in danger."

"He may never figure that out."

Frankie didn't appear terribly outraged, but Jack felt he ought to explain himself. "I honestly didn't think Ellis would hurt him, but I admit I was counting on him driving her around the bend enough to slip up."

"That is Troy's special gift." Frankie shook her head guiltily. "I shouldn't say that. Troy lost a lot when Tish died, things he'll never get back. I'm not sure how important Karen trying to kill him seems in the face of that."

"You have to treasure what you have," Jack said softly. "Every minute it's yours."

She smiled. "That's the plan, Chief."

Jack's eyes stung as he smiled back. "Frankie."

"That's my name, Chief. Don't wear it out."

"If you're done sniggering at my expense, I vaguely remember a nurse helping me brush my teeth this morning. You could kiss me instead."

Frankie leaned over the bed rail. "Sure you're up for it?"

He ran his hands up her arms, only then realizing that she was dressed in a pair of very fruity pajamas. She truly had flown to his bedside.

"Absolutely," he said. "I can tell they put the important blood back."

Once they'd started kissing, Jack couldn't stand to stop. It felt so good to hold her, to hear her call herself his girlfriend. She had the best mouth for kissing: bold and strong, but also girly where girliness was good.

The little mewls she made were certainly inspiring, and the way she ran her hand up and down his side wasn't bad, either. He undid the middle button of her pajamas and slid his hand inside to her breast. He cupped her warmth with a sigh of pleasure. Her nipple was pointed but smooth as silk.

"Jack," she breathed in the husky tone that was an aphrodisiac. "If you don't stop that, I'm going to stick to this chair."

Oh, she knew how to get to him. He realized the doctors had in fact replaced all his blood, because every freaking drop was trying to squeeze into his swollen cock. He was as rigid as if he hadn't had a climax in weeks, instead of twenty-four hours.

"Boy," he muttered. "Must be that brush-with-death-is-a-turn-on thing."

Frankie pushed back and stared at him.

"Sorry," he said, trying to explain. "You're right. We'd better stop this if I'm going to have other visitors."

"Ohh," Frankie said, her gaze descending to the evidence that was speaking louder than words. Her teeth sank into her kiss-flushed lower lip. "I see."

Being as big as Jack was could occasionally be an inconvenience, but with Frankie, he was beginning to see it was also fun. Her eyes were wide with interest as she took in how he'd increased in size. She reached out, carefully, and stroked the tented sheet along his throbbing shaft.

He had to admit it felt pretty nice.

"That's not going to help," he said.

A mischievous sparkle entered her eyes. "I do have a bottle of lotion in my purse. Jojoba. Perfect for *sensitive* skin."

"Frankie . . ."

"Come on, Jack," she laughed. "You can't tell me you've never had a fantasy about getting a hand job in a hospital."

"I've had fantasies about doing you over the stools in your diner. Maybe we could wait until I'm out of here."

She'd already taken out the lotion and was squirting a big, clear puddle into one palm. She rubbed it lasciviously between her fingers, which Jack found himself utterly unable to look away from.

"Mmm," she teased. "Feels like wet pussy."

Jack stifled a groan as his erection lurched another aching inch stiffer. "You could block the door . . ."

"Nobody will come in here. They think we're having a tender reunion. You'll just have to refrain from groaning suspiciously."

One of her warm, well-oiled hands slid under the sheet and found him. The lubrication did indeed feel like a woman's sex.

"Stop," he said faintly.

"Stop?" she said, actually doing it.

Her fist gripped his swollen base, preparing to slide up to the tip and bring him to heaven.

"I think my thigh might be cramping. I don't want to strain the stitches."

"Oh," she said. "Sorry."

Before she could pull away, he clamped his hand over hers.

"Wait." He forced himself to breathe deep and slow, forced his toes to uncurl and the creeping tension to release his leg. "Okay, go ahead."

"You *do* want this," she said, beginning to look amused.

"Oh, yeah. I think I might bust if you don't get me off."

"I want to use both hands."

"I have no objections."

"And I'm going to try to make it feel as good as I can."

He couldn't hide his anticipatory shiver. "I'm up for that, too."

She laughed at him and brought her second hand into play.

He was up for it, but he sure wasn't prepared. Her oiled hands were hot and supple. She pulled them, tightly, one after the other up his erection, a smooth, hand-over-hand motion. She didn't go fast enough that he blew right away, but the sensations got incredibly strong incredibly quickly. His balls began to tighten with readiness.

The only way Jack could keep his thigh from tensing up again was to repeatedly blow out his breath.

"Want me kiss you?" she asked.

Her cheeks were beautifully pink. He knew she didn't mean kiss him on the mouth. Not caring how reckless it was, he dragged the covers down and saw her holding him for the first time. That was a sight he wanted to remember.

"Keep your hands on me," he rasped. "Just suck the knob."

She met his eyes, her lips parted for her quickened breaths. She didn't speak, only nodded and bent down.

He bit his lip to keep from groaning when she reached her goal. She licked and sucked him at the same time, taking him into her mouth from just under his rim to his weeping tip, swirling over every sensitive curve and dip. The inside of her mouth was fantastically hot and wet, her tongue eager to tickle every nerve he had.

"You can suck me harder," he panted. "You're not hurting me."

When she did, she practically sent him through roof—and that was before her oil-slick fists began to twist on his shaft, each in opposite directions. The index finger of her top hand rubbed the coin-sized sweet spot beneath his head perfectly.

It was too much. His body couldn't catch up to this sudden multiplication of its pleasures. His pelvis jerked, trying to come that instant. She sucked him harder, wetter, wanting to help. Her hands screwed faster over his shaft. A tortured sound broke in his constricted throat.

She moaned softly in response, right against the head of his penis. The little vibration was all it took. Sensation swept up from the base of his spine like a rush of heated, tingling water from a garden hose. He toppled over into release, squeezing, gushing . . . and probably sighing too loudly to count as discreet.

Frankie came up smiling like the *Mona Lisa*. He felt warm all over, as if his skin were painted in sunshine.

She ran her tongue across her upper lip. "You look relaxed now."

"If I could remember how to speak, I'd tell you how relaxed I am."

Clearly pleased with herself, she pulled the covers back to his waist. "Just call me what the doctor ordered."

He took her hand and kissed its palm. "My heart is yours, Frankie, no matter who ordered you."

"You know," she said, "if I'd known you were going to be this sweet, I really wouldn't have considered anyone else."

"Considered anyone else for what?" Dewey asked.

"Knock!" Jack said in exasperation, glad he hadn't come in thirty seconds earlier. As it was, he suspected he and Frankie looked a bit too flushed.

Grinning, Dewey knocked on the now-open door and walked to Frankie's chair. Rivera followed more tentatively.

"Hmm," said Frankie. "I think that's my cue to leave."

She kissed him first, soft and lingering on his cheek. "Get better fast, Jack. The diner won't be the same until you're back."

The sweetness in her eyes almost made up for the intrusion.

Per usual, Dewey was full of off-color jokes, none of which—thankfully—had to do with Frankie. Rivera backhanded his arm a couple times in disgust, but Jack imagined she was as grateful as he was for the buffer Dewey provided.

Chances were both his officers had guessed something had been going on before they came in.

Starting to feel tired again, Jack was glad they kept the visit short.

"Take care, boss," Dewey said when it ended, beginning to turn toward the door. "I'm glad we both came out of this all right."

It wasn't entirely surprising that Rivera didn't leave with him. Jack sensed she'd been wanting to say things she couldn't voice in front of her coworker.

She didn't sit down, just stood looking dejected in front of the chair Frankie had been sitting in. "I'm sorry, sir," she said. "About everything."

Jack folded his hands on his stomach, thinking he really shouldn't be obliged to have serious discussions with his employees while wearing a hospital gown. Naturally, there was no avoiding this one.

"I've been thinking," he said, "between visits from nurses. And I've come to the conclusion that you might have been responsible for cracking the case."

Rivera's eyes came up. "But I hid that disc. And would have kept it hidden if you hadn't confronted me."

"Yes," Jack said. "But Ellis thought she'd destroyed her disc because Whittier gave her a copy. I can't help wondering if Whittier held back the original because she didn't trust Ellis, or because your scene was on the other side, and she couldn't stand to part with it."

"I'm not sure I want that idea in my head," Rivera said with a small shudder.

"Think about this then: maybe there's a reason this happened the way it did. Everyone makes mistakes. Put yours behind you, do your best not to repeat them, and stop beating yourself up."

"But, sir—"

"That's the last I want to hear or say about this, Rivera. I mean it."

"Yes, sir," she said and swallowed hard. "Sir? I just want to say . . . good luck with Frankie Smith. She's a nice woman."

"Thank you," Jack said. "I think so, too."

Chapter 18

As far as Frankie knew, Tish Whittier hadn't had any Irish in her. Nonetheless, Frankie's waitress, friend, and self-appointed surrogate mother decided All U Can Eat was the perfect place for a wake.

"People need to say goodbye," Jean said, "and funerals are boring."

The rest of town seemed to agree this was brilliant. Most brought potluck desserts, while Frankie supplied burgers, fountain drinks, and fries.

"Lots of goodwill here," Jean said, patting her arm as the diner filled. "Your business will be good next year."

The toasts began when Officer Dewey of the Six Palms P.D. rolled in an icy keg.

"I know who's drinking what," he called above the packed crowd's noise. "I'm manning the tap, and nobody gets into their car without seeing me."

"We'll walk home," one of Tish's society friends promised.

"Not in those shoes!" Dewey joked back.

Frankie sensed more than one flirtation was in the works tonight. Pete and Dave were, for once, engrossed only in each other, but Troy and Officer Rivera had ended up in a corner, talking in subdued, serious tones. Troy looked sad and lost, and Rivera had the slightly dazzled expression women sometimes got in the presence of the former model's tan and gold beauty.

Frankie wasn't sure their hooking up was a good idea. Jack had mentioned Rivera had a kid, which could be great or awful depending on how well Troy behaved himself. Frankie didn't know how much, or if, all this had changed him. Still, she supposed if it perked up either of their hangdog faces, a little romance wouldn't be altogether bad.

On the whole, the gathering was jovial, mixed, and occasionally choked up. Many examples of Tish's kindness, shyness, and—in two instances—her phenomenal shopping stamina were shared. Sadly but sweetly, Frankie felt as if she was getting to know Tish for the first time. This wasn't the way it should have been, but it would have to do.

Tish's parents were missing out. They were in Monte Carlo and had declined to attend. Frankie expected they'd be skipping Karen Ellis's funeral, too.

The best part of the evening was when Jack hobbled in, in uniform and walking with a single crutch. As soon as everyone saw him, they stood up and applauded. Jack looked embarrassed but also secretly pleased.

The next best part was when he made a beeline straight for her, waved the sour-faced Atkinses out of the back booth, and tugged her in to sit next to him.

"Rank hath its privileges," she observed as his big, warm arm came around her shoulders.

"Yes, it does," he said.

They watched in companionable silence as yet another friend of Tish's stood up on a seat and told a story, this one about Tish loaning her maid her BMW so she could take a driving test.

"None of them knew her secrets," Jack said quietly.

Frankie rubbed her cheek against his shoulder. "I think that's the way she wanted it. She must have gotten comfortable being viewed in a certain way. And her secrets were only part of her. The things she liked having everyone see in her—her sweetness, her generosity, maybe even her need to be taken care of—they were true as well."

Jack made a noise that said he'd think about this. Frankie liked the way that felt. He had his own ideas about the world, but he was willing to consider hers.

She kissed his cheek and didn't care who saw.

"I should go back to the kitchen," she said. "Make sure Mike isn't overwhelmed."

Jack squeezed her knee and gave her a considerably more explicit kiss than she'd given him.

Frankie took a second to catch her breath. "Is that to remind me I'm *your* girlfriend?"

He grinned sheepishly. "Only if that wouldn't seem too high school."

She rolled her eyes at him, let him hold her hand a heartbeat longer than he had to, and then went to check on Mike. He was busy flipping burgers on the grill as she walked in. Evidently, mourning people worked up an appetite.

"You should go out there," she said when he spotted her. "Take a break. Grab a beer before the keg is gone."

"I'm doing all right here," Mike said. "One of Tish's big-bucks charity friends snuck back to ask if I'd help cook for their next fund-raising barbecue."

"She asked if *you'd* help?"

Mike's grin was crookeder than Jack's. "I think she was also making a pass."

"Well, far be it from me to stand between you and such laudable volunteer work!"

"Yeah," Mike said, his smile fading. "I kind of figured that's what you'd say."

There truly wasn't any good way to respond to this. Rather than try, Frankie stepped to the fryer and lifted out the next batch of fries. To her surprise, Mike began talking.

"When I was in Iraq," he said, "seeing what went on, doing what I had to do, I kept thinking, This is it. This is the deep, dark, ugly secret of what life really is, the secret most human beings shut their eyes to."

"And now?"

"Now I think that was only one side of life." He waved his spatula around the fragrant kitchen. "This is life, too. Getting up in the morning. Going to your job and not facing anything more dangerous than hot grease. Thinking about making friends or going on a date." He turned from the grill to her, offering a rueful smile. "Getting your heart broken by a really nice woman. That's as much what life is as anything."

Frankie dumped her now-drained fries into a paper-lined basket and readied another batch for the oil. "You're getting philosophical."

"Maybe. Chief West was talking to me the other day about the police academy, maybe putting my skills to better use. He said they'd probably overlook my record if he sponsored me."

"Well," said Frankie, completely thrown for a loop by this. She hadn't known Jack gave two thoughts to Mike's future. "I'd say that's pretty decent of him if he weren't trying to steal the best cook I've had in years!"

Mike laughed at that, enjoying the compliment. "I'll be here a while, I think. I'm still getting my civilian feet. Anyway, I'm not sure I'm cut out for police work. I was good at following orders, but I'm betting being a good cop takes more than that."

"You could learn it. If you wanted. You do seem like leader material to me."

This compliment surprised him, though she couldn't imagine why. "Thank you. That's . . . good to hear from a person like you."

"Yeah, me big boss lady."

"I wouldn't mind traveling," he went on. "We had a layover in Paris on one of our flights. That city was all right. I could see myself having a little burger place over there."

"A cordon bleu burger place. Of course, you would have to learn French."

"Which might take some time."

Frankie shifted the fries again while Mike flipped his finished burgers onto a platter. A hand—apparently starving—reached through the pass-through to take it and the fries away.

"Good thing you've got a steady job while you're studying," Frankie observed. "Though I should warn you, Jean Li speaks fluent French. She might be willing to help you practice."

"I'd be happy if she'd stop glaring daggers every time she sees me."

Frankie waved her hand. "She'll get over that. She was just worried I was in danger of falling for the wrong guy."

"But you weren't."

Frankie smiled to herself, knowing this was at least half a question. "My momma taught me a real lady never tells."

Epilogue

Frankie and Jack lay in each other's arms beneath her mother's championship oar, slightly sweaty but quite content.

"Your house has no garden," he said, continuing a debate they'd been enjoying between enjoying other things.

"Your house is depressing," she countered, still catching her breath.

"You could hang curtains."

"There isn't a curtain in the world that could fix what's wrong with that stucco box. Besides, my house is an architectural masterpiece."

"Your neighbor might be moving."

Frankie rolled up on one elbow. Jack wore the half-smile she'd been seeing more and more on his face, as if life was too good to keep his pleasure with it inside. "I have a neighbor? I thought that shack next door was abandoned."

"Your neighbor is an elderly shut-in. His daughter wants him to move to her house in Ohio."

"Well, that won't happen. Not to *Ohio*."

"I think it might. I met her when she asked me to check in on her dad now and then. She was very nice, very maternal, and very persuasive." He began playing his fingers up and down Frankie's arm, a habit she'd grown to like. She thought they both liked the reassurance that they were close. "That lot would be a nice piece of land once someone tears down the house and clears the jungle he let grow up."

"You could buy it," she said. "Build your own house. Then *you* could be my neighbor." This seemed like a compromise Jack could handle. In spite of the six happy months they'd spent seeing each other nearly every day, going on actual dates and meeting each other's families, he was still leery of moving in with her. Frankie tried not to bring it up too often. The town, on the other hand, was so convinced Jack already had moved in with her that his mail was beginning to come to her house.

"I thought I'd buy it and plant a garden," he said casually. "Maybe put in a pool. Of course, I'd have to be living somewhere close for that to make sense."

Frankie squinted at him, her brain temporarily unable to fit these pieces together. Then she got it.

"You!" she said, punching his arm. "You've been teasing me, making me worry I was being too pushy. You've been planning to move in with me all along!"

"For a month anyway," he admitted. "I thought you'd like the surprise."

"I do," she said, smiling as she snuggled back against him. His new playful side was one she wanted to encourage.

"If I put in a pool, you could skinny dip," he suggested meaningfully.

"Yeah," she laughed. "And you could handcuff me to the rail!"

He pulled her closer with a happy hum. Frankie closed her eyes at the same time he did. When they drifted into sleep, they both had very pleasant dreams.